The Fulfillment

Return of Mu

Cover © 2002 Jennifer Gordon
First Edition
First Printing 2002
Editor: Gayle Bachicha
Associate Editors: Sue Whitmer and Mardeene Mitchell

Printed in the United States of America
by McNaughton & Gunn

Tickerwick Publications: Light ExPress, An Imprint
P.O. Box 100695
Denver, CO 80250

Library of Congress Cataloging-in-Publication Data

Gustafson, Sandra Elizabeth.
    The fulfillment : return of Mu / Sandra Elizabeth Gustafson.-- 1st ed.
      p. cm.
    ISBN 1-885084-35-8
    1.   Spiritual life--Fiction. I. Title.

PS3607.U75 F8 2002
813'.6--dc21
                                                              2002073286

The Fulfillment

Return of Mu

Sandra Elizabeth Gustafson

Dedication

This book is lovingly dedicated to all of the Lightworkers,
past, present and those to come, guided by Spirit
to resonate and replicate
the simple sound of
One.

Sandra Elizabeth Gustafson
2002

The Fulfillment On Earth

The time has come to remember who you are.
The time has come to release the things that hurt.
The time has come to forgive yourself and the world
    for everything you blame it for.
The time has come to heal completely.

The time has come to remember we are One.
The time has come for noble actions in the world.
The time has come for an end to the illusions.
The time has come for Enlightenment on Earth.
The time has come.

*The Fulfillment is a Spiritual Adventure to help you find Peace
in Earth School and to bless others
along the way.*

Introduction

The Fulfillment takes place on Earth and in a dream state where twelve students study in the realm of Spirit. Their dream adventures powerfully activate a remembrance of sacred truths, remembered from long ago. To paraphrase Victor Hugo in Les Miserables, *During sleep, the soul of the just contemplate a mysterious heaven.* The twelve students contemplate, however, a mysterious heaven on Earth.

In the beginning of the dreams, there is some confusion as to where reality lies. Is the dream real and the life that they are living on Earth an illusion ----- or vice versa? Perhaps they are both dreams, or could they both be illusions? What is reality anyway?

Isn't reality whatever you choose to embrace from wherever it is that you are? As you take this journey with the Mu(s), twelve individuals who have a common thread of previous life on the continent of Mu, or Lemuria, you will know what is real and what is illusion. The test for both is what they resonate in you.

You are about to embark upon an interesting Spiritual adventure! You have been specially chosen because of the person that you are and the commitment you have made to yourself and to the world. Spirit knows of your desire to serve, to become all that you can be and to make the world better because you are dancing through it. Spirit knows that you are aching to be and do *more* than is absolutely necessary.

Enjoy the trip to your remembrance of *Truth* and know, if this book is in your hands right now, that you have truly earned it. Bon voyage!

Table of Contents

Clarification for the Reader

This is the appearance of text when Teachers in Spirit are speaking to characters on Earth.

This is the appearance of text when characters on Earth and in Spirit are thinking. This appearance is also used occasionally for emphasis.

CHAPTER ONE

A New Day!

It had been a dark night but one that seemed brighter than most. Stillness prevailed but all was not as it seemed. Yes indeed, a night like this happened only once in a Blue Moon!

The animal and elemental kingdoms were at peace. The plant kingdoms patiently anticipated the return of Ra and a new day once again filled with warmth. On this particular night, the vegetation had doubled in size in anticipation of the things that were to come, and everything seemed thirstier than usual. The petals of each flower opened slightly to the East, to once again welcome the Light with warm appreciation. Emotion accompanied this process, but it was not understood or perceived by most humans. This would soon be changing.

Inside the house, a couple slept as their brain waves edged from Delta to Theta, then to Alpha and Beta. In sleep, they had aligned with Spirit and with all the kingdoms of the Earth. Birds were chirping and the flowers in the courtyard appeared to be slowly dancing in a gentle breeze as they leaned in, almost imperceptibly, toward the house. The awakening was near.

An alarm went off inside. It was 5:55 A.M. in Alpharetta, Georgia, a sleepy suburb North of Atlanta. Cindy squinted at the clock to verify her whereabouts. Laying her head back down on the pillow, she mused, *That dream was important.*

Placing her hands behind her head, she closed her eyes. For a brief moment, she saw the face of a handsome Asian man and a beautiful bird in flight. *What does this mean?* she mentally questioned, reviewing her dreams. The images slowly disappeared until all that was left was her conscious mind, pondering them analytically. *This will take some serious thinking about,* she mused.

Cindy was a superstar in figuring out most things in her head, usually with analytical intent. She was beginning to consciously understand that she could use this strength to its best advantage when she combined it with the use of her intuition. Even so, sometimes she went overboard with too much analysis of everything. Meditating seemed to round the sharp edges of her mind and allow for other possibilities. Answers could easily change form, like separate ingredients could miraculously make a cake.

Eyeing the clock, she noticed that it was now 6:15 AM and she knew that she had better get going. The traffic on 400 was always heavy at rush hour, and she still had her morning rituals to complete before hitting the road. *Perhaps my meditation will bring me more details about my dreams*, she thought, as she little-stepped her way to the bathroom, still not fully alert.

Pep, an eighteen year old Peek-a-Poo, was also stirring and stretching her hind legs. Cindy noticed her and bent down to say "Good morning Sweetness," as she rubbed her back haunches and kissed her forehead. Cindy let her out the master bedroom door into the courtyard. Continuing to the bathroom, she thought, *I wonder how much longer we'll have her? She's such a sweetheart. Maybe we should consider cataract surgery for her. I wonder if her heart murmur could stand the trauma... Sure wish I could remember more about those dreams.*

She pulled on her baggy T-shirt and warm-ups and went upstairs to do her Yoga stretches and meditate. This centered her and she always looked forward to her morning ritual.

Cindy plugged in the serenity fountain on the wicker table in her study. The sound of running water was comforting to her. Kneeling down, she lit her violet candle as she said, "I light this candle in reverence for The Source of All Good. May I be your blessing in the world today." She then lit a stick of Nag Champa from the candle's flame as her gift to The Source of her being, then placed it in the long and slender incense holder. She sat down on the floor and started her stretching routine, accompanied by deep breathing with eyes closed.

By the time she finished with her shoulder stand, she was ready for her meditation. Slowly, she lowered her legs and torso on a slow exhalation and took a cross-legged lotus position, facing the flame. Morning sun poured through the windows behind the candle and incense, warming her face.

For timeless moments, Cindy dwelled in the silence where all thoughts cease ----- God's Garden, she called it. At the end of this special time, she would often actively elicit help from Spirit for the agenda of her day. She had been gathering information this way for sometime now and she was learning to trust it more. She sometimes saw things with her Spiritual sight. These images were often quite helpful to her in creative problem solving.

Cindy was a marketing genius for a large computer company that offered hardware and software solutions to the business world. Her meditative life often fueled her success in business when she was successful in controlling her analytical mind. Once she pulled back on those reins, the powerful horses of creativity and intuition emerged.

To everyone who knew her, Cindy's thinking was outside-the-box on most issues. While her colleagues gave her the credit for great ideas, she knew quite well that she was only a conduit for something greater than herself. While it was quite unspoken, she also knew that all successful people in the business world relied on their intuition to make judgements about when and how to proceed, even though they tended to justify them analytically. It was a game that was played, with no one owning up to what was really going on. This too would soon be changing, as would many other things.

A cosmic pressure cooker was building and it would soon explode. It would be called Tribulation and it would start the clock on the correction. Individual choice would be the deciding factor. Would humanity on Earth realize their Spiritual potential before 2012? A sound, reminiscent of screeching tires and grinding gears, was being heard throughout the cosmos by everyone who was sensitive enough to hear.

Out of the blue, Cindy suddenly heard a voice: not physically audible, mind you, but audible from within. The vision of the Asian face and the bird in flight again entered her awareness. As the man began to speak, her vision disappeared.

It was interesting to Cindy that she never seemed to *Spiritually* see and hear at the same time. She was either seeing or hearing, but the two did not seem to happen together. She often wondered why this was so, although she had learned to trust them both.

The voice began. **You awakened this morning, questioning if you were really there! Did a Spiritual adventure in your dream state really happen, or was it just a figment of your imagination?**

A flood of visual dream images began to pass through Cindy's awareness. Memories of Sahab, Alcyona, eleven others and important teachings revealed themselves to her in a flash. She pictured herself holding a book entitled *The Fulfillment, Return of Mu* while the pages turned rapidly. The voice returned.

Let me hasten to say that all of it happened and all of it was and is quite Real! In fact, each one of you who is touching this book right now with your hands, your hearts or with your thoughts, know that you were there too! You are back here now, and while it was a wonderful adventure, the real adventure now begins to unfold.

You have completed what we refer to as Basic Training for the New Age of Spirit on Earth. Life will be quite different if you practice the things you have learned. Know that Alcyona and I feel most privileged to have been your teachers in Spirit and we shall continue to stand solidly behind you as you complete your work in the time of The Fulfillment. You will know that we are there for you when you see my face in your mind or as you catch sight of the magnificent Feathered One in the world. All of this will make better sense when you are fully awake.

Although Alcyona and I are One, she is more frequently seen in the physical world. Whenever you see us in your Earthly experience, use this awareness as a reminder to do more, to go further. There is no limit to what you can accomplish if you stay focused on the task.

Cindy sat perfectly still, not wanting to disturb the flow of information. She had lots of work to do but none of it seemed to be more important than what was happening now. Sahab continued.

You know the areas in which you are intent upon making a difference. During your meditations, you may ask of Spirit anything on which you desire guidance and the answers will flow to you through your own intuitional mind. This is how Spirit speaks to you while you are in the Earth's dream. Never discount your imagination as unimportant or unreal. It is the most real thing there is. This is how you Co-Create with your Creator, as long as you remember to dwell in the Present.

Alcyona and I represent the perfect balance of the masculine and feminine in you. This is the place at which you are striving to arrive because it balances the vibration of Love within you and with that, comes Enlightenment.

Cindy took a deep, incredulous breath and slowly exhaled. She had spent many years desiring Enlightenment. She remembered her college days as an undergraduate when, in spite of being raised as a Christian, she had chosen to write a term paper on the Upanishads. How and why had she been attracted to the Holy Books of India? She had often wondered. Were the mysteries now about to be revealed? She could only hope that this was so and she mentally affirmed her receptivity. The voice interrupted her thoughts.

The lessons that we shared with you in Spirit are bound within a manual that will materialize for you. A review of it will be appropriate from time to time. Now that you are back among the many illusions, it is very easy to lose your way. If you do so, try not to be too hard on yourself. Rereading the lessons and realigning yourself with Truth will help you regain your composure, inspire confidence, and give you the resolve to persevere. You have much to accomplish. Think of the review process as course-correction software for a successful flight into the New Age of Spirit on Earth. This is how Alcyona would describe it.

From my own point of view, reviewing these thoughts will continue to take you to deeper levels in your own understanding and this can only help you with your assignments. You will know what they are by where you now stand and what that landscape resonates in you. As a rule of thumb, if you believe that you are responsible for it all, you will accomplish more. So much depends on you!

The transmission ended and Cindy opened her eyes and looked at her watch. It was now 7:31 A.M. "Gadzooks, I've got to get going!" she cried as she rushed downstairs. As she hit the bottom step, she heard a sleepy, familiar voice.

"Cin, Cin, where are you?" called Tom as he awakened a little disoriented. He had stayed up late the night before after having a little too much to drink. This was a problem that was becoming all too frequent. It worried Cindy and she struggled to maintain her composure. This was Tom's third slip off the wagon. True to form, when she thought about his problem, she usually tried to figure out why.

The only thing that allowed her to minimize Tom's problem was the fact that he was able to work and take care of his financial responsibilities. Sometimes this led her to believe that maybe his problem was not as bad as she thought, but then, the wiser part of her always knew better. His personal struggle was immense and she knew it because she knew him, both drunk and sober. At times, the counterpoint of this dilemma was enough to make her scream! A stale liquor smell coming from his direction seemed like dragon breath. "I had the most interesting dream," he said, as he looked at her sweetly.

"You too? I had a dozie myself," she said, rushing into her blue pantsuit. *How in the world did women ever live before these*, she wondered, purposely trying to take her mind off Tom. She didn't have time to deal with the situation that she knew would lead her into a major disharmonic. "I'm running late, Angel," she whispered to Tom. "Let's talk about the dream later." Regardless of what they were dealing with, they had a sweet way of addressing each other. She called him Angel and he called her Angel Girl.

"OK," he said, as he rolled over. Relieved to separate himself from his guilt and remorse for a little longer, he closed his eyes and drifted off. He had burned the midnight oil last night, first on cocaine, and later by bringing himself down with alcohol. It would not be a pleasant thing when his consciousness demanded that he address himself from the waking state. A short respite was indeed welcomed.

Tom was a gentle giant and a successful insurance man. Unknown to those who knew him well, he was filled with self-doubt and a lack of self-love. There were two Toms ----- the one the world knew and the one that he knew who was the antithesis.

Tom had sniffed up a nose full of courage before his insurance presentation last night. It had been extremely successful. He had taken applications for a million-dollar life policy and a large annuity. He stopped at the bar on the way home to celebrate and tipped a few, then had a few more when he got home.

Not wanting to wake Cindy and having energy to spare, he went to his den and changed into what he called his leisure suit. It consisted of an old Hawaiian shirt that Cindy had many times threatened to burn and a pair of comfortable khaki shorts. Tom felt exhilarated about the success of his work this evening. For the moment, it helped to absolve his overwhelming sense of guilt and disappointment that in the morning, he would be starting at ground zero... again! He clinked the ice cubes in the glass as he sat down at his desk and stared off into space.

Tom was grateful for a few more winks this morning. In a moment's time, he was fast asleep and snoring. Cindy certainly knew about his problem but not the specifics or the magnitude. He managed to keep many of the facts hidden from her, allowing his gregarious personality to stand between the devil and the details.

Cindy kissed his forehead and thought, *How sweet he looks when he is sleeping and then... the big lug wakes up!* She sighed and shook her head as she looked around for her knapsack. She always kept a fresh change of exercise clothes packed and ready. Today, after work, was one of her days for the gym. Noticing the black dog hairs on her tan knapsack, she thought, *That girl has been nesting in here again.* She dashed out, thinking about her business agenda and the traffic. *I hope 400 is not too backed up.* Grabbing a protein bar, she ate her way to the car with a to-go mug of coffee.

As she got into her white PT Cruiser, she noticed a book sitting on the front passenger seat. She picked it up and looked at the title. There, in bold print, it read *The Fulfillment, Return of Mu.* "Mind blowing!" she said, looking again with concentrated intent to make certain her eyes were not playing tricks on her. Backing out of the garage, she somehow lost the time it took to reach the ramp that led her onto

7

400. Deep in thought, she sailed to work on automatic pilot, with her right hand gently resting on the book. Every now and then she looked at it again, as if to verify that it was real.

Before she realized it, she was coming to the tollbooth. Reaching in the coin stash, she pulled out two quarters. "Easy Does It, Forward Motion," she said out loud. Without knowing why she said those words, she tossed the coins into the basket with the minimum of effort, moving forward and smiling.

It was the end of summer in Atlanta and the pink and purple crepe myrtles were displaying their last stages of color for the season. She associated them with bittersweet memories of her childhood. Every time she saw a flowering crepe myrtle, it reminded her of her mother. They were her mother's favorite. *I'm going for the scenic route this morning.* She took the first exit toward Lenox and the Buckhead section of Atlanta.

While she was driving on Peachtree, a bird swooped down and almost collided into her windshield, screeching a loud birdcall that sounded like "*One!*" The noise seemed to pull it upward at the very last minute. With an adrenaline rush, Cindy reflected on the meaning of One and the power of One without exactly knowing why. A series of dream thoughts and images flashed into her awareness. Pulling into her parking space, Alcyona's words floated through her mind. Again, she heard her voice.

For each of you who hold this book in your heart or hands, there is no doubt that you too, are a child of Mu. If this were not so, you would have wakened from the dream before the teachings finished. You see, only those who were willing to complete the entire course are permitted to have the manual you now hold. Do you remember the number for which you have the greatest affinity?

The number 9, then 12, popped into Cindy's awareness. She also saw the number 5. She remembered that, according to numerology, she was supposed to be a number 5. She wondered if there was any significance to this, in addition to being a Virgo with 12 screws loose in her head. Alcyona's voice then commanded her attention.

While you are predominantly aligned with one of them, you also resonate to other numbers to lesser degrees. For each individual, the exact number of degrees is captured within your star design which, as you remember, you yourself created.

Innately you do know who you are and what you came to do, even though you may not always remember it consciously. Everyone has a personal mission and is also a part of a greater plan as well. You have personal challenges to overcome and world work to complete, and this is why you are sometimes restless. You see, you came to make a difference. Such is true for every child of Mu. Never forget that you came to make things better. Act as though everything depends on you! Do your work from this perspective and you will accomplish many great things, said Alcyona.

Cindy thought about Tom and his most recent slip off his 12 Step Program *the third time!* It had been a month now that she had noticed empty vodka bottles in practically every plastic bag of trash. *Who does he think he's fooling? For him, 12 Steps is more like a spiral staircase to nowhere! His sobriety does not depend on me! Is he a child of Mu? Who exactly, I wonder, are the children of Mu?*

Most of you are children of Mu, to a greater or lesser degree. Some are pure strain, some are half-breeds and the remaining ones are pure strain Lagitard.

In pre-ancient times, that is, more than 500 million years ago on the continent of Lemuria in the Pacific Ocean, the Mu flourished and lived in peace and harmony as a loving and quite advanced civilization. They thrived and prospered for many years. Technologically, they were more advanced than anything you know in the world today. Their Internet not only reached throughout this world but throughout the other galaxies.

In fact, there was a cosmic incident that they learned about through their Internet. It informed them of the dire circumstances of those known as Lagitards. They were on the brink of destruction unless they could find another home in the universe. The Lagitards were going to be burned and re-constituted into a lower life form. It was the time of their planet's revelation and the Lagitards had failed in evolving their consciousness into a Love form. They were the most base and dark of anyone in the cosmos. They were to be zeroed out to begin again through a lower life form. Their clock was five seconds from being cleaned!

The Mu had always been a compassionate people and they took pity on them and brought the Lagitards to Earth. The Mu empathized with them and agreed to receive, nurture and mentor them on Lemuria, to try to teach them the ways of Love. It was shortly after they arrived that trouble began. Since the Lagitards had no frame of reference for the lessons of Love, it took many years of failure before the Tribulation began.

Here lay the crux of the problem. The Lagitards brought fear with them and the Mu experienced it for the very first time. This was quite disturbing to their sensitive and loving nature and they could never understand why it was so difficult for the Lagitards to change their war-like ways. It was the first time on the Earth when both fear and love co-existed and it was terribly confusing to the Mu.

When fear and war began to thrive, prejudice was born and "this" became better than "that." From that moment on, the civilization of Mu was on the decline. This continued until a critical mass was reached and the continent itself was finally ripped apart by Tribulation in the landmass. When Lemuria broke apart, a portion of it drifted south and would later become known as Australia. Another part submerged, and the tips of the higher elevations became islands in the Pacific.

While the Tribulation was taking place, the people dispersed to other continents and both the Mu(s) and the Lagitards' influence has continued throughout all civilizations from that time onward. Both Love and Fear have continued from that time forward.

What is important to understand is that prior to the dispersion, many Lagitards married Mu men and women and mutated strains resulted. This was actually a good thing as it accomplished a softening of the war-like nature in many of the Lagitards. Even though it was at the expense of the Mu's loving nature, it was the only way to accomplish the task. It is important for you to realize that every Mu who sacrificed their nature did so willingly.

So now, we have the situation where approximately 25% of the world population is still pure strain Lagitard. They are cruel and advance the cause of war upon the Earth. Some of them still prefer to live in caves. The mental process of their *thinking is quite unreasonable and strange. Only another Lagitard can understand the mental process that justifies cruelty in the name of God. It is impossible for a pure strain Mu to understand such thinking.*

While pure strain Lagitards are found in all religions and all walks of life, they still seek to learn the ways of Love even though they do not consciously realize this. It is up to every child of Mu to teach them Love, for they accepted this as their responsibility long ago when they welcomed the Lagitards to planet Earth. But I emphasize ----- the 25% who are pure Lagitard are very dangerous.

Then there is that 50% of the population that is part Mu and part Lagitard. They are the Mulags and they are quite teachable because, at a cellular level, they have known Love. It is already a part of them and it can be easily awakened. The pure strains of both Mu and Lagitard now work to gain inroads with the Mulags who are quite impressionable and easily swayed in either direction. Time is speeding up and moving toward another time of critical mass.

You see, your own planet now dawns upon its own revelation, so one side must win and the clock is ticking. Fifty-one percent of either population will constitute a critical mass in that direction. Your civilization has until 2012 to accomplish this. As you know, Tribulation in the landmass has already begun.

So we could say that the beginning of an ending is now at hand and it is up to the 25% of pure strain Mu to make the difference by first purifying themselves through personal healing. They shall then be able to lead the way in teaching the Mulags to find their way back to Love. The clock runs out in 2012. Prerequisite to the Mu(s) accomplishing their goal of global transformation in the name of Love is their own personal healing.

Yes my child, Tom is a Mu and sobriety will lead him to his personal healing. You are also a Mu and you too will find your way. Bless you, child of Mu.

CHAPTER TWO

On the Roof

Holding on to her book, Cindy entered her office building and took the elevator to the top floor where she could be alone with her thoughts. Too much was happening. She needed time alone to think about the implications of all of this.

The mid-rise office building had a fenced outside patio area on top, often used for lunch breaks and smokers. At this time of morning, Cindy welcomed the total privacy that she found. She sat down and closed her eyes to concentrate.

Mu(s) and Lagitards, this would take some thinking about, and yet there is indeed a ring of truth about it all. And it all stemmed from a co-existence of Love and Fear. It's plausible and it makes perfectly good sense to me, she thought. Again she heard the voice as she sat down on a bench.

Remember ----- where you must begin is with yourself. By healing yourself and by finding Peace within, you then become capable of experiencing it in the world. It is the only way that Peace is found, and Peace and Love are One, said the feathered Alcyona. As her avian image faded, the face of an Asian man named Sahab became more prominent.

The key words for you to remember are Easy Going and Forward Motion. When this is not your experience, your wheels are off the track. Creativity with Intention will give you the correction that you seek.

Remember that whatever you see is what you are. You must experience your inside self as your outside world. That is how you heal it. You must see it first. Should anyone see arrogance in the world, it's because they, themselves, are arrogant. If they see fear in the world, it is because fear is within them. It is the only possible explanation. You may discover the things you have allowed in yourself by looking outward at the world. This is the purpose for what you see out there.

Cindy was grateful to be alone on the roof. There were so many profound ideas that were flowing freely and resonating Truth within her. Psychically, she was aware that this communication was also being shared with others.

She stood up and looked down at the people on the street going on their way and wondered who was pure-strain Mu. Which were Lagitards and could she tell the Mulags by how they looked? Did they have distinguishing facial characteristics or mannerisms that were recognizable? She wondered...

Cindy also wondered how many Mu's already had their manual and how many more would soon complete their "Basic Training." *How many were hearing the same teachings and having the same dreams?* Of one thing she was absolutely sure, the fruit of the Motherland was ripening.

Around the power grid of this sweet Earth, the voices of Alcyona and Sahab were being heard. Everyone willing to experience *Fulfillment* would be hearing it soon. Some, like Cindy, were already in possession of the manual. As others were ready to hear the call, their manuals would magically appear. The main purpose of the initial group of students was to heal and then to help others find their manual and replicate the process. The growth that would take place would indeed become exponential!

I hope that Tom is ready for this, she thought. *If only he would conquer himself! I know he wants to heal and God knows, he tries!* Cindy remembered the many wonderful things about their relationship and the challenges they had experienced. She wondered if she had made the right decision about not having children when she began to notice his addiction problems. *It was fear that influenced that decision. I'll have to think about that one. Was it the right decision?*

Cindy's mind drifted to her circle of friends. Who among them was ready to profit from *The Fulfillment?* She thought about Alice and Kim. *Could they be Mu(s) or were they Mulags? Alice is too self-centered to be a pure-strain Mu and Kim is as vain as they come? She's certainly not a Lagitard but she's probably not a Mu.*

She heard the voice again as Sahab continued: **Do not waste your time chastising or judging others. Treat your neighbor as yourself. In other words, practice** *the Golden Rule because it will help you end Separation and find Oneness with everyone and everything. This is the purpose of it. The Golden Rule was the modus operandi on Lemuria prior to the arrival of the Lagitards. It is the only rule that's necessary to find the way back to Love.*

So, for heaven's sake (no pun intended), stop worrying about others whom you believe fall short of the mark. Seeing their failure only points to the shortage in you. They are simply helping you to see it. Work to correct it in yourself ----- for everything that you think you see in others really belongs to you.

Cindy's face flushed with the embarrassment of a Mulag remembering the stronger portion of her lineage. *How could I think such thoughts?* She still was not 100% sure of what this Mu-thing meant. She had heard about Atlantis and knew that Lemuria or Mu was an advanced civilization that preceded it. *Did being a child of Mu mean that she had once lived there? If so, what did all this mean?* She was about to fall through the analytical trap door of her mind when she again heard the voice of Sahab.

You are a child of Mu and yes, you did live there, but what's important about it is that you have experienced Love and life from that prospective. More is required of those who know more. Once you accomplish your personal healing ---watch out world!

Cindy thought about "the big lug" who was probably still sleeping it off. *I do love him, in spite of everything! I wonder if we were together on Lemuria?* In spite of the ambivalence of her thoughts about him, Tom was certainly the one who made her heart sing.

Work then, only on yourself. When you are perfect, you will see perfection in others, for you must see in the world the things that you are. When you see only beautiful things, my child, you will know that you have allowed your own beauty to find its fullest expression.

Now that's a good one. I become perfect and Tom heals! No, no, no, I'm getting the picture here; I need to work on myself and let Tom work on Tom! If I allowed that, I wonder what the outcome would be? No telling!

Cindy's thoughts then moved to her nemesis, Mommy Dearest, and she

15

wondered, *What could the meaning of this trip with her be all about?* Cindy always called her Mother but referred to her by her given name of Clarice, sometimes pretending that Anthony Hopkins was uttering the word with great feeling.

You think that she has limited you. Make no mistake about it; the only limitations that you have are the ones you have placed upon yourself. Nothing else has ever limited you. So, stop blaming those who gave you life. You chose them and they have sacrificed their own personal expression at times to be what you needed them to be. They have also given you great opportunities for Spiritual growth.

Know this my child, all that life seems to have given you are but seeds you Co-Created for planting long before this time began. Your Life-Givers have merely played the part you needed them to play. They allowed the curtain to rise and you should honor them for volunteering for such a mission. They afforded you entrance that you might heal some of the pain and fear created in so many other times when you were lost in the circular maze. This is why there are no exceptions to the commandment to honor your mother and father. However, it is quite all right to disagree with them, for you are here to find your own truth, not theirs.

Cindy felt a sense of guilt about her disharmony with Clarice. How could she honor her when the woman set her teeth on edge? *Quieting a five-alarm fire is not as easy as he makes it out to be! I lied! How about an earthquake that's 9.3 on the Richter Scale? That's more like it!*

Cindy's pain was immense. From gestation on, it had always seemed like the wrong womb. She could remember moments before she was born when she kicked to keep from entering Clarice's world! From the first moment, there was trouble. Cindy was a square peg that never seemed to fit into Clarice's round, flowing world. It wasn't that Clarice was physically abusive; it was that Cindy never was the person that her mother wanted her to be. Clarice had visions of Cindy becoming an artist, molded in her image. Although Cindy had an artistic side, she was basically a personality that was grounded in logic. Cindy emerged from the womb full-grown and her mother never quite adjusted to this reality.

Clarice had trained as a modern dancer, big on discipline and perseverance. She had trained with Martha Graham and Hanya Holm; Isadora Duncan was her inspiration. A coffee table book on Isadora was a constant reminder of their differences. Cindy, her change of life baby, was more of a scientist than an artist. On occasion, she had imagined violent uses for Isadora's scarf!

Cindy remembered the first time that she took Tom home to meet her. After he left, Clarice had the gall to say, "Cynthia, I think you could do better!" *How am I to make peace with the pure, unadulterated uppity bitch in Clarice?* Sahab voice again gained her attention.

Whenever you experience pain from your life experience, sit down and review your manual for you are certainly stuck somewhere in the Red Zone of the Past. When you experience fear, you are dwelling inappropriately in the Blue Zone of the Future. Your soul has already discovered that these are not your most productive zones.

You could choose to dwell in the Present with your Creator where you can work with ease as a Co-Creator. This is clearly your goal, for here you will experience joy from pure creative fire, and pleasure from sweet delight with your creations. Here, you can accomplish great things; the choice is always up to you. You can tack from left to right if you desire. It will simply take you longer to finally arrive at your destination. You can do whatever you like, but you will find your way back to the importance of living in the Present and experiencing the ways of Love.

Cindy took a deep breath as she gazed Southward from the midtown skyline of Atlanta. "Clarice, I know you are out there somewhere. I want you to know that because I cannot quite forgive you yet, I shall forgive *myself* for being different from your heart's desire for me. Thank you for the opportunity to find and celebrate the freedom that this creates in me." *Fake it til you make it!* Cindy took another deep breath and as she exhaled slowly, her mind was alive with possibilities. She felt a surge of love and compassion for Clarice move through her as tears from the many years of personal pain rolled down her cheeks. She was making progress.

Here are the only real important choices that you make: you can live in the Past; you can live in the Future, or you can Co-Create with your Creator in the Present.

These are the pure and simple choices that every Mu must make on a daily basis.

You can measure your progress by the number of times you choose to Co-Create those things that help you overcome your personal challenges and bring Oneness to your personal situation and then, to the Earth's experience through your actions in the world. Healing yourself is prerequisite to overcoming the world but, in a way, they are also synonymous. Overcoming the world is nothing more than using your ability to heal yourself because you are Divine and you recognize it!

This is blowing my mind, thought Cindy. *I hope Tom is hearing this right now with me.* Tom was still asleep and dreaming but he was also experiencing the same messages through the dream state. A loud bird call abruptly awakened him. He lay there thinking about his dreams.

Cindy again began hearing Sahab's voice in her head. *Once you get the drift, your actions will consciously align with Spirit. In other words, your will becomes God's will and vice versa. That's when serving the needs of the Whole will become more important to you than only serving yourself.*

You see, all that you can give to the world must come through your actions in it. Thinking is simply not enough. Many great ones have disappointed themselves by failing to take action on some truly great ideas. Thinking is only the first step in Co-Creation. You must take action!

Clarice, who had left the physical plane this year, surveyed her daughter's dilemma with great interest. She could now more fully appreciate the role she had played in her daughter's life. Clarice had had her own misgivings about their relationship while she was in the physical body. There was no mistaking now that she had been the perfect catalyst in her daughter's life. Clarice smiled broadly as she sent both Cynthia and Tom her message of Peace and Love.

Cindy listened intently to the inner voice. *This drama, dear Mu, is all your own. Do not fail to take responsibility for it by blaming your Life-Givers and hasten to make peace with them now. This, more than most things, will release you from the roots of your pain. Once you have killed the roots, the rest of it can dissipate.*

As you have already learned, there is always a different way of looking at things. Isn't there? Your challenge is to create a way to transmute your emotional pain into something higher. This requires some amount of creativity on your part. It is always helpful to paint with a full pallet in the Time Zone of the Present, since it is the only place where creativity and change are possible.

Yeah, Right! Cindy shook her head as if she were clearing water in her ears.

So, dear Mu, there is much work to be done and many lives to bless. May you go forward in life to exemplify the Truth that sets you free, that blesses others and that recognizes we are One. When the majority of us find this understanding and begin to live from this perspective, The Fulfillment will soar over the horizon like a beautiful bird with powerful wings, changing everything in its shadow to pure and perfect Peace. Yes, the return of Mu assures The Fulfillment and makes whole the prophecies of long ago.

You, dear Mu, are one of its sentinels. You recognize these words as Truth because of what they resonate in you. Yes, you must always do more because you know more. Rejoice in knowing that your work on Earth will unfold as the quiet spaces of your heart find form and are given freely. Bless you, child of Mu.

Looking at her watch, Cindy rushed to the elevator to make her 8:45 AM meeting with the *Big Wheels*. On her ride down to the fifth floor, she dried her eyes and powder-patted her cheeks to conceal her revealed emotion. As she entered the front office door, she saw a flurry of activity with office workers rushing toward the break room area. As she moved down the hall, she heard an escalation of excitement in their voices.

What's going on? Cindy put down her briefcase at her office door and ran the rest of the way to see what was going on. It clearly was something distressing!

John, the President and CEO, stuck his head out of the break room and yelled, "Cindy, come here quick! Look at this!" Cindy could now see that some employees were crying, some were hugging each other and others shook their heads in apparent disbelief at the happenings on TV. John excitedly pointed toward the screen and said, "A plane has just hit the World Trade Center!"

"My God!" Cindy screamed as her wide eyes fixated on the CNN replay. Other employees continued running in to see the unbelievable. Everyone was in shock.

The last 12 hours have been positively unreal! As Cindy thought about the catastrophic, senseless act, she wondered if Tom was awake yet. *I've got to call him,* she thought. She was reaching for her cell phone in her purse when she heard everyone scream, "Oh No!"

Janie shouted, "Look, Look! I don't believe it!" as a second plane flew into the second tower. "My God, my God, it's unimaginable! Think of all the children who are going to be without a parent tonight!" Janie worked on special projects for the company and supervised the mailroom.

A tremendous explosion erupted and the fire ripped through the structure like a well placed missile. How could this be happening? Like the hot molten lava of an erupting volcano, Tribulation trembled in the Trade Center Towers on September 11.

It was 10:11 A.M. when Cindy finally sat down in her office chair and dialed home. "Tom, you won't believe what has happened! Are you up?"

"Yes, Angel Girl, I'm stumbling around for a cup of coffee now."

"Turn on CNN. Two planes have just flown into the World Trade Center towers! You won't believe it until you see it! Turn it on and take a look. I'll call you back later."

Cindy hung up, leaned her elbows on her desk, closed her eyes and held her head for a few moments. *Is this real or am I caught up in a nightmare?* Her thoughts moved from the reality of her world to the reality of her dreams and back again. *Unbelievable! Unbelievable!*

John was back in his corner office. He stood looking out the glass windows at mid-town Atlanta thinking about how surreal the happenings of the morning seemed. He also wondered about the effects that this event would have on the business world. He went to his desk, sat down and turned to his computer to see what the stock market was doing.

Janie had gone back to the mailroom and senselessly by rote, began sorting and thinking about the children who would soon be learning that they had lost a parent today. *How do you tell a child such a thing?* She began thinking about her own son Adam who was three years old and in daycare. How she longed to be able to stay home with him! It just wasn't possible now. They needed her income.

The replay on CNN, the coffee and the night before were all too much for Tom. Running to the bathroom, he barely made it. Falling to his knees, he grabbed the seat and held on tight as he vomited with a vengeance. *God help me!* He rinsed out his mouth, put a wet wash cloth on his forehead and sat down on the commode to steady himself.

Once the wave appeared to have passed, he went into his den, sat down at his desk and leaned back. Something told him to open the door to the compartment where his computer tower stood upright. One of his favorite booze hiding places was immediately behind it. It was the perfect height to conceal a fifth. For some reason, the bottle was standing higher than the tower. *This is weird!*

He reached back there to check it out and found that the liquor bottle was sitting on top of a book that was standing vertically and slightly opened. It created a perfect triangular base on which the bottle rested. He reached from behind the opened compartment and lifted up the bottle and the book. He then put the bottle back, once again safely hidden, and sat down.

Tom frowned at the front of the manual. *"The Fulfillment, Return of Mu,"* he read. He wondered if Cindy had left it for him. *It probably has some inspirational stop-using message! Then again, maybe it's a message from Clarice. The old girl always threatened to zap me from the grave!*

From Spirit, Clarice observed her son-in-law with great interest and smiled. Even though she had been a little hard on him when she was on the physical plane, she had grown to love him and to appreciate the love he had for Cindy. Time had shown her that his drinking was the only thing that riled her. In later years, they had even developed a nice way of kidding and making each other smile. Clarice remembered how very kind he was to her in those last days at the nursing home before she passed.

21

Those dreams...seems like there were a lot of them last night. Maybe all of this is somehow related. He closed his eyes and saw flashes of Light, as bits and pieces began coming back to him. He saw the number 6 and a group of people who hugged him and supported him. He never felt such love! It was like the moments he had heard described from a near-death experience by a friend of his who had once been in a car wreck. Tom was now in the Light and he didn't want to come back. He visualized the face of his Spiritual Teacher. It was wonderful to remember his teachings!

CHAPTER THREE

Transcending the World

The time of *The Fulfillment* was at hand. In the realm of Spirit, Sahab made his final preparations to teach the course. A stored memory from another time shot to the forefront of his mind. It stopped him in his tracks as he remembered a time when he looked outward through a small Temple window and gazed at a vast expanse of sky. *Now* felt so very much like then. He had been a high priest contemplating matters of Spirit. In fact, in many past lives he had aligned with what he considered to be his *real* purpose ----- making Spiritual Truths manifest in the physical world.

His goal now was quite the same, even though his role was that of Teacher on the Spiritual plane. The many healing crises that were now a transitional part of this time on Earth made success with the next class all the more important. Sahab's Spiritual energy mass constantly changed shape and color as he contemplated these thoughts.

In Spirit, the full record of his many Earthly experiences was available to him. He thought about the many lives he had lived in service to Spirit and dedicated himself anew to becoming a clear and perfect channel for Divine Truth. By comparison, all the other lifetimes had merely been the warm-up. *This* was clearly the main event ----- the goal and purpose of all those other times rolled up and tied together as One. Mentally, he approached his teaching with great anticipation and humility. He moved toward the Garden of Goodness for one final alignment before meeting the class that would be waiting for him.

At precisely this *"Now Moment"* on Earth, Cindy stared at her computer, totally unable to focus on her work. Confusion was at the helm as her mental attention bounced from her dreams to the attack and back again. She struggled to make sense of life, its events and the juxtaposed meanings. All of it seemed like a dream. Cindy felt grateful that her little family of Tom and Pep were alive and well. She also felt a bit guilty that it took an event of this magnitude to bring forth from within the gratitude that she truly felt for the things she sometimes took for granted.

On Earth, it was indeed a dark night, while in Spirit, the peace of crystalline clarity reigned. Sahab mused about the differences. *In Spirit, the natural choice was always to renew itself through integration with The Source. On Earth, the choice too often was to maintain Separation.* This was the membrane through which osmosis of The Fulfillment would penetrate to bring change. Sahab was aware of the importance of his mission.

The Garden of Goodness was a sphere of space approximately five hundred feet in diameter and lined by a ring of mature oak trees. A stepped pyramid stood in its center, some seventy feet high. Glistening at the top was an amethyst altar. There were many beautiful things in this Garden, all treated by the brilliance of the indigo light cast by the stone facets of the altar. Perfection grew in this circle of Light. There were succulent fruits, vegetables and flowers which were ten times their normal size. Everything seemed to grow perfectly here, and with accelerated growth.

The Garden itself required no care. There were no weeds to be found anywhere; the soil around the base of the plants was always loose, as if it had just been tilled. Whenever plant growth reached completion, the plants simply de-materialized in the light of the moon. By the next mid-day sun, there was a perfect replacement, lush and beautiful.

A large lion freely roamed the Garden. Devoid of all will to attack, his nature was loving and peaceful. Gently, he purred and played with the produce. While he was free to go beyond the oak trees, he chose to stay within.

An assortment of orchids asserted themselves in elegance, like ballet dancers in white leotards with violet feathers in their hair. The delicate botanical scent pleasurably permeated the environment and the orchids had a depth of color that made them seem real to the infinite power. In the front of the pyramid lay a circular pool of water contained within a form of dark green marble and measuring some thirty-three feet in diameter. A blanket of gigantic pure white lotus blossoms adorned the blue-green water as they opened to their Creator with love and willingness to achieve their full potential. Everything in this place dwelled in harmony and the beauty was inordinately complete. Sahab always returned here to align his Spiritual essence with the work to be done.

As the Spiritual energy that was Sahab moved into the Garden, his good friend, Leo, came to meet him as usual. Sahab always showed himself to Leo in a slightly different form. Today he took the form of a ragged, malnourished beggar, barely an appetizer for the massive Leo. It was a little game that Sahab enjoyed playing with him to test his recognition. Leo was never fooled by his many different appearances and was always delighted to see his old friend.

Purring peacefully, Leo rolled over on his back encouraging Sahab's affectionate pats on his tummy. He had come to know and love Sahab and he always enjoyed the love energy exchange they shared. He followed as Sahab slowly made his way past the lotus blossoms, becoming One with the beauty of the Garden and taking back his colorful energy form. This was as far as Leo allowed himself to go.

Sahab glided up the stepped pyramid to the top, as Leo sat on his haunches, watching him ascend. Sahab then fashioned his energy field into a ball of Light and rested itself on the amethyst altar in The Garden of Goodness, as peaceful as a sleeping child in a cradle.

The altar had a solid triangular base, equilateral in appearance. At the apex sat a perfectly formed and hollowed out half circle. The entire structure was one piece of pure multifaceted amethyst gemstone.

Sahab's energy field rested inside the half circle. He allowed his energy to expand above it to complete its other half. When the sphere was made complete, a shaft of white light infused the entire circle allowing the round sphere to cast healing Light throughout all facets of the gemstone. The brilliance of this laser-like experience infused the entire Garden of Goodness with Divine Light. It had the ability to heal, to equalize and to accelerate the growth of everything in its presence. From below, Sahab could hear the guttural sounds of Leo purring with delight.

The Teacher's energy field and his mission were now aligned and made One with the will of the Creator. All dross had been transmuted. From below, Leo looked upward, pawing the air playfully toward Sahab, as his energy field continued to rest upon the altar. These alignments affected him deeply and he always chose to enjoy the perfect peace that they produced within him.

The energy pattern of Sahab's Spirit was magnificent. It was a large mass of swirling color, uniquely integrated to give complete expression to the entire color spectrum. It was like a work of art in progress, yet purely perfect in each evolving moment. Like a liquid ocean of predominantly cool colors, it ebbed and flowed while always maintaining a Divine sense of itself. Ever deepening as a sea of Spirit, it revealed more and less of itself through its integrative patterns of changing color.

In a honeycomb pattern, a thin gold band contained most of this magnetic field of energy. Its edges of color danced through the twelve open spaces of the band. They created interesting designs of wholeness in transition, moving toward a greater Whole.

Regardless of how the content of the space changed, the elements of style and balance were completely satisfied. Dissonance, harmony and rest seemed to fit together perfectly, evoking the experience of artistic pleasure at every angle from which the twelve evolving forms were experienced.

The band itself represented the level of Master Teacher on the Spiritual plane. It was through this gold band that Sahab performed alchemy of thought purification with his students of Truth. Successful students were able to bring an end to errant and erroneous perceptions which better prepared them to succeed in overcoming the illusions of the physical world. A teacher's teacher, Sahab had mentored many great masters on the path.

He had the ability to divine the appearance in the classroom that best suited the lesson to be taught. When not in the teaching mode, Sahab was simply an androgynous energy field of great beauty, thus making it difficult to assign the male or female gender. In a manner of total integration, Sahab was both beautiful and handsome, a perfectly unified energy field exuding love, compassion and great wisdom of the Spirit.

The core of Sahab's teaching was to reveal the Inner Light in the individual. He did so by acting as a catalyst for Truth with his students. Every thought, word and example had the purpose of allowing students to find their own Light from within. The outer happenings were for the purpose of allowing inner transformation to occur.

As Sahab's energy field continued to rest upon the altar, thoughts about Enlightenment on Earth began to flow. In a vertical direction, Sahab's Spiritual energy elongated itself, extending straight up, forming a wide funnel. The base became a single point for a cylinder of violet light. The entire mass of energy began to rotate clockwise as shafts of Light danced around it. Each one was prismatic, emphasizing the colors of green, blue and purple which melted into a soft violet ray. As the movement continued, Sahab's powerful thought forms found mental expression.

Source of All Good, in gratitude, I come once again as a humble vessel to reflect your Light and Truth into the world. Of all the classes which have been mine to teach, I know that this is the most important one, and I dedicate myself completely to this next group of students. Strengthen my sensitivity to their needs as I lead them to the necessary tools for the achievement of Enlightenment on Earth. Guide me in helping them to overcome the illusions of the world in this, the time of The Fulfillment, as I help them to refine the focus of their Light. Source of All Good, help me to always be your catalyst for Truth, Love and Compassion in the world. To this, I dedicate my being.

No sooner were these thoughts completed when a violet flame spontaneously ignited on the altar, quickly enveloping Sahab's energy field. Building to a crescendo and then dissipating, the Teacher's energy body emerged much larger and more luminous than before. The band of gold was glistening. Slowly softened into liquid by Divine fire, the band began to revolve slowly clockwise, the edges dripping downward as it melted into the colors of Sahab's vibrant energy field. Once the mix occurred, Sahab's energy completely vaporized and reconstituted itself in the Garden of Atunement where the students were eagerly waiting.

There were twelve students. While their physical bodies slept on Earth, they were now here in Spirit to continue their studies. They came by choice to make the most of their sojourn in the times of transition that were at hand. It was agreed upon long ago by each individual present.

This Garden was perfectly attuned for the vibration of teaching. There were twelve gemstone pedestals for the students and for the teacher, a clear quartz crystal chair and round table facing the students. The symbol for this Garden was that of a large tuning fork which stood as a majestic sculpture of pure gold, slightly back and to the right of the Teacher's chair. A garden of perfect yellow roses took the shape of a vertical Crescent Moon and stood to the left. Their fragrance was sweet and mentally intoxicating. The Teacher's chair was centered in the space to the right of the Crescent Moon. The Garden itself was exactly fifty-five feet square.

Sahab entered the Garden of Atunement. With purpose, he moved to the Teacher's chair. Standing to the right of it, he collected his thoughts. He appeared to his students in human form, choosing to appear as masculine. He wore white silk trousers, a white silk shirt with a Nehru collar and an opened purple vest trimmed in gold. His body type was Asian and his skin was bronze and soft. Sahab had a thick shock of shining black hair and dark eyes that sparkled with Spritual intention. He was quite handsome and striking in appearance.

Sahab began to walk among them, pausing now and then to look at the twelve energy fields of his students. Their energies were twitching like a closing baseball pitcher in a one-up game. He noticed that each was wearing the nametag he had prepared for them in the center of their round field of spiking energy. Sahab knew they did not realize the significance of the name or number that they wore. In due time, they would come to understand more about this. For now, it was merely important for him to verify that all of them, Mu(s) 1-12, were present. He made note of this as he thought: *Yes, this is good. I see a lot of willingness here.*

"Enlightenment Potentiates, welcome to the Advanced Course in Transitional Earth Energy 2000+, otherwise known as Ra to the eighth power. I am your Spiritual Mentor for this journey and I am called Sahab," he said, with a slow and purposeful bow. The students noticed that he pronounced his name with soft a(s). "Let us begin by honoring each others' Holiness through the recognition of our Oneness with The Source."

All twelve energies drifted to the front of their gemstone pedestals. Extending arm-like projections of their energy field toward each other, they joined together to create one large field of circular design. Then while creating fingers of energy projections upward and outward in red and yellow, they created a symbolic representation of the sun's rays as their symbol of The Source. It was a ritual that was known and understood by all. The sound of a single flute filled the air as they completed the form. This ritual seemed to have a balancing effect upon them. As they reclaimed peace, the energy spikes dissipated.

They separated and floated back to their individual gemstone pedestals in the Garden of Atunement. Each began reflecting that somehow, they seemed automatically drawn to a specific gemstone and no two of them gravitated to the same one. They were not aware of why this was so, nor that their natural gravitation to a particular gemstone had the purpose of intensifying the learning experience for them. Touching down, the twelve energy fields began to slowly open and pulsate like the petals of a fragrant flower in the wind, preparing for pollination and exponential growth.

As Sahab stood before them in human form, he glowed with magnetic radiance and the students studied him carefully. Sahab was clearly an example of the Spiritual Growth that they were seeking. They yearned to know more about him and to experience him more fully.

"Class, we prepare for a deeper experience in the magical, beautiful place called Earth. It is one of many places that we go to prepare for the deepening of our lives in Spirit. All of our experience everywhere is for that very purpose. And why, you might ask, is this Earth experience even necessary?

Well, it is part of what we willingly experience to more deeply appreciate our Divinity. Some fare better than others with this. Some become trapped on the wheel of Karma or the working through of illusionary cause and effect. It is pure choice and it is always out of Love that we go back, to experience our Light in the darkness. Earth is one of my favorite places and the most magnificently beautiful of all our waking dreams."

Sahab seemed to be experiencing something deeply internal as he gazed upward and then appeared to look through them, apparently delighting in his memories of some far off place.

The students immediately began to form some mental questions. *Dream? What is he talking about?* No one seemed to quite understand and this became evident through the stilted and jagged movements of their energy fields. The fluidity of their movements gave way to starts and stops.

"Yes," Sahab said, "It is only a dream but it always seems quite real because of the vibrancy of our emotional reactions to energy while we are in the physical form. Emotions make it seem real; it is however, an illusion. We choose to experience this colorful dream to strengthen our knowledge of Oneness while we are in a physical form of self-expression."

Checking out the tuning fork and the bed of yellow roses, Mu 10 thought, *Maybe this is Racetrack Heaven. We're the horses and he's the announcer. Sooner or later, this is going to go somewhere. Someone is going to win the race and wear the roses.*

Mu 10's creative thoughts did not go unnoticed by Sahab who chose to ignore them and continued on. "Here in Spirit, as Energy Thought Forms or, as Mind and Spirit devoid of a physical body, we are quite naturally One with The Mother-Father Source and with each other. You see, without the body, we know the Truth of Oneness for there is nothing to impede that understanding. We can merge or separate without a loss of that knowledge.

Earth, on the other hand, is essentially an illusionary experience of Separation that we are to overcome. The illusion seems quite real but the purpose of it is to find that it is not real and to embrace and rediscover the ultimate reality of Oneness. To a neophyte in Spirit, it looks easy, but each of you can attest that this is not the case at all. And so, we continue our Spiritual study "here" so that we may put it into practice "there"." Sahab paused, looking around at his students, as he became aware of the energy thought formation emanating from Mu 5.

Here, there, where in the world are we anyway? Where am I now? I asked for a Spiritual adventure but what kind of "Do-Wa-Ditty" is this? thought Mu 5. *And yet, it's interesting... it seems real.*

There were many of the Mu 5 vibration now on Earth. This particular one happened to be a businessman in Decatur, Georgia who was now fast asleep and dreaming. His name was James A. McCall: a tall, slender, good-looking guy in his early forties. He had a thick shock of blond wavy hair and deep blue eyes that focused intently on the person, object or issue at hand. Everyone loved Jim who was a great listener, always full of empathy and reassurance. He was generous and well liked by all of his friends, especially his best friend, Tom.

In business, Jim was sharp and unyielding. Nothing escaped him. His attention to detail and his wise decisions had enabled him to amass quite a fortune. However, he did have a problem. While it never consumed him, it did claim his attention at odd times. It was a secret that he wrestled with.

Sahab picked up on his thoughts but did not address them. He began to walk among his students as he continued speaking. "A large part of the problem is the vehicle or body in which our thought form travels while we are caught up in the dream on Earth. It creates the first level of cause in this whole idea of Separation. The body itself sets up the appearance of duality because there appears to be space between one body and another. This too is an illusion but Separation results from this. Seeing the body as density and definition fools us. Yes, it seems *real*, right up until the moment that the Spirit departs from it.

I knew it! We're in Woo Woo Land for sure, thought Mu 1.

The students would learn that there are many Mu 1 vibrations on Earth now. Generally, these individuals have natural, innate leadership skills. They are both men and women who generally rise to the #1 leadership positions in all fields. This particular Mu 1 is now a General in the military with a stern facade, a dry sense of humor and a soft side he rarely displays. Mu 1 individuals are also owners, presidents and CEOs. While there is much diversity in their personality characteristics, they have one thing in common, the Pied Piper Syndrome. They march and others fall in step behind them. Mu 1(s) have a special mission to join as a group to lead in creating a better world.

Sahab picked up on Mu 1's Woo Woo thought. *And I thought I had heard it all before. I wonder how long it will take for them to figure out that they are not thinking these thoughts privately?* He paused at the pedestal of Mu 1, placed his hand upon the gemstone, as if he were checking its temperature and then addressed the group and continued.

"With exception of the Soul anchor, the Spirit goes and comes as it pleases for the duration of the Earth dream. Of course the Soul anchor is no more than the manifest intention to remain with that particular body for the duration of the sojourn. It is a loosely planned event by the individual for the purpose of Spiritual growth and for the opportunity to be of service to others. It is precisely, however, this belief in Separation that keeps individuals unaware of their unity with each other and with The Mother-Father Source. A good example of this is that they pray to The Source as if it were something completely separate from who and where they are, usually up in the air somewhere," he said, as he pointed upward. "Big Daddy in the sky is simply not correct, nor is Big Momma." Sahab then looked around at the group and smiled.

You can say that again! thought Mu 4. Janie was primarily of the Mu 4 vibration; however, she has moderating influences of other numbers as well. This was the reality for most individuals, regardless of their main number. Rarely were they purely any one number on Earth. Balance resulted from a mix; insanity was often the result of too strong a concentration of any one number.

The class began to buzz with energy, acknowledging a vague remembrance that was characterized with fluidity of movement followed by many question marks. These appeared as energy spikes. The students were aware that Sahab's words stimulated recognition of Truth within them but they were not quite sure why this was so.

Sahab surveyed the sea of energy before him with a pleasant smile. Taking a sip of water and placing the glass upon the table, he looked directly at them and said, "Enlightenment Potentiates, you are here in this class because you have volunteered for an important mission on Earth and because you are Advanced Spiritual Energy Forms.

One definition of this might be, in previous lives, you have tried and tried and tried... *and failed* many times before," he said as he smiled at them. Hummm..." said Sahab, as he smiled again and raised his eyebrows while slowly gazing around the room at each of them. Sounds of nervous laughter quickly erupted from the twelve Spiritual bodies. The emanating energy forms had the appearance of baby rollercoasters in joyous motion. The Mu(s) enjoyed Sahab's injection of humor into a serious Spiritual matter and they reciprocated in jest.

The Mu(s) playfully moved to create a circle, which revolved around Sahab's energy body for three fast revolutions of red and yellow jagged Superman streaks of Light. Sahab then released his human form, drifting up above the chair and, for a few moments, became pure energy with them, allowing them to merge with him. The Teacher then formed a long arm with the extension of his energy field and gently deposited each one of them back upon their gemstone pedestals as he again assumed his human form in a standing position and continued, "It is good to see that you still have your sense of humor. It will come in handy on this trip. As a matter of fact, it can make the Earth experience quite enjoyable. Now, let's get back to Do-Wa-Ditty in Woo Woo Land at Race Track Heaven."

Mu 1, 5 and 10's energy fields contracted, turning an embarrassing shade of red. Sahab and the rest of the Mu(s) enjoyed a good laugh at their expense. Along with this came a powerful recognition that thought was not just individually experienced. It was part of a Collective Whole. This was a brand new awareness for each of them.

Sahab continued, while addressing the group from front and center, "Notice, for instance, that now I am appearing to you as male. I may also appear to you as female." Sahab then changed into the form of a beautiful woman with long blond

33

hair and the tail of a fish, and just as quickly released this form, reappearing to them again as pure energy.

Through amplified Thought Form he projected, "In Spirit, as we are now, there is no real significance to gender, for we are both. Each of us is quite complete in our positive and negative energy charges.

On Earth, however, we must select one specific gender. We choose the expression that complements our learning goals; it is totally our choice. We still have a unified energy field inclusive of both charges, but we give predominant and visual expression to one charge. There is usually a corresponding body type but there are also variations on this theme. None of this really means anything. It all corresponds to the lessons you are trying to learn. Every selection has a purpose," he said, while he assumed his human form.

Mu 10 thought, *How perfect and effective are his gestures. I wonder if he choreographed them or if they are being spontaneously improvised.* Mu 10 had the mind of an artist, always attentive to line and design.

Sahab continued, "You have already selected your gender for this time but do not forget that you are a unified energy field encompassing both positive and negative charges. Practice the separation of your charges now, in order to remember that you are both. Getting stuck in gender problems is part of what you are to overcome. It is the second level of cause in the Separation issue. Let us practice together the separation of our charges to gain better perspective on this."

Sahab again released his physical form and his energy form and slowly began to alternate movements between soft and contracting to firm and advancing. The Mu(s), 1-12, began to join the party with the separating expression of their own positive and negative charges. They undulated into softness and soared into firmness as they explored the full range of their nature.

"Very good class," projected Sahab. "We shall call this dance, the, *sometimes very limiting*, shehe shuffle."

An energy chuckle moved throughout the group as they continued this alternation of energy expression with Sahab. He moved about, observing each one of them. Once he experienced the success of all twelve Mu(s) with this exercise, Sahab soared upward, then powerfully expressed as a unified field in climactic delight reminiscent of the sexual experience that all of them so well understood. He then drifted down to their level, let out a very long sigh as the twelve Mu(s) followed suit. A joyous round of energy banter filled the garden.

Mu 8 thought, *Now, this is the ticket to ride!* He turned to his friends for approval. Cindy's boss, John, was predominantly a Mu 8. His fiery nature presented many personal challenges yet, there was no doubt about it ----- John was here to make a difference.

Sahab chuckled to himself as he then soared into the air overhead, in clear visibility, commanding their full attention.

The twelve Mu(s) did not fail to notice the increased intensity and vibrancy of color displayed by Sahab's energy field. It seemed so much more expansive, radiant and beautiful. The students then looked around at each other and noticed exactly the same thing in each one of them. They were beginning to remember many sacred truths.

CHAPTER FOUR

The Gospel According To John

Taking on his human appearance, Sahab began to speak. "Class, in the Earth experience, we forget that we are a unified energy field. We seek to find on the outside of us that which is already present within. This is because our visual expression and our own perceived gender identification appear to be one-sided. If it is negative, we look for a positive charge and vice versa. We seek what we think will make us complete because we lose the remembrance of our Oneness and forget we are already Whole. This can lead us into many adventures and sometimes misadventures with others, I might add. Mu 8 could tell us some stories about this, couldn't you?"

Mu 8's energy field moved forward and back questioningly and then began to spin wildly as everyone laughed. There was no doubt that John had a wonderful sense of humor about his sexcapades in his outer world. It somehow helped to mask his inner sense of remorse. He searched for that something missing in his life over and over again through extramarital sex.

John never found what he was looking for because he sought outside himself for the thing that lay within. He, therefore, only accomplished periodic suspension of the search which he would replicate unsuccessfully over and over again.

"You see, we think that we are capturing *Oneness* through another," said the Teacher. "However, we are really revisiting it all by ourselves. As we have just now experienced, each of us has everything we need to function as a unified energy field, regardless of appearances. It is the very nature of how we operate in Spirit. On Earth however, we experience great pleasure in sharing our energy with others, thinking all the while that we are separate. That's entirely another matter. Mu 8 happens to have more experience in this arena than the rest of us," he said, as he looked at Mu 8 and smiled. Mu 8 began to spin out of control as the energy of laughter erupted uncontrollably.

John had indeed shared his energy with countless members of the female gender. This part of his life he somehow separated in his mind from Lynn and the kids. He loved his family but they were not enough. This had nothing to do with them and everything to do with restlessness in him that he could not explain or understand. The business world was his refuge. His friends called him a workaholic. This was not entirely true. It was also a way to succeed while escaping his dark side, or was it? One thing was certain. His vocation and his avocation had one thing in common ----- winning!

Think of the time I've spent searching for my perfect mate, thought Mu 10. The rest of the Mu(s) turned to their classmate and bobbled their energy, acknowledging agreement, as Sahab continued.

"Now, there are many areas where Separation appears to be the rule. This issue of gender is just one of the many which may cause you to forget your Oneness. You certainly could say that it increases the difficulty of the experience."

The students continued to practice the separation of their positive and negative charges. Sahab observed the changes in color, ranging from the red to the blue portions of the color spectrum, with varying amounts of yellow used by different Mu(s). Every now and then they expressed as a unified energy field, which appeared as white light with gold flecks.

Sahab thought to himself: *This is indeed an interesting group with so many mental-emotional combinations, all seeking self-love. Yes, when this group breaks through, Earth will need time to recover.* Sitting down in his chair, he continued.

"The problem is basically one of recognition. Here in Spirit, we are able to see ourselves clearly and to recognize our Holiness. Knowing Oneness allows us to express our Divine nature through love and compassion. This is exactly what we are trying to achieve in the Earth dream experience. To know Oneness on Earth is to live there compassionately, because what I do to you, I do to myself. Acting on this knowledge is what removes Separation and the many barriers to love."

In seriousness, the Mu(s) acknowledged their understanding by sending a violet extension of color upward. Sahab nodded his approval and continued.

"While the lesson appears simple to us in Spirit, it is quite difficult when all the illusionary evidence seems to be showing up as Separation. When we come from the core of Oneness, the concept of *ours* describes our point of view. When we come from Separation, *yours* and *mine* go on endlessly."

Oh yes, I know all about that! thought Mu 8. This Mu had experienced many struggles with the issue of *mine*, not only with sex but with money, power and material things in general ----- the birthright of successful business men in the world, according to Mu 8. In ways that were not completely understood, this teaching resonated Truth within this student.

On Earth now, John continued checking the markets and contemplating the business ramifications of the terrorist attack. He mentally prioritized the first businesses to be adversely affected and those likely to be stimulated by this event. He would implement this data in his company's marketing strategies to beat the competition.

John closed his eyes for a moment and the face of an Asian man moved in and out of his awareness. He then began to hear a voice.

Students of Truth, one of the most baffling things you will face while you are lost among the illusions of the Earth dream has to do with your medium of exchange, or the amount that you give in order to receive. It is quite confusing. Many try to give as little as they can for the things that they receive. Actually, the opposite should prevail because the more you give, the more room you create for receiving. It never fails to be true, like cleaning out your closet and giving things away. Giving always creates more space to receive. Learn to be charitable with others and Spirit will never fail to bless you.

John had a moment of guilt through his remembrance about yesterday's events. Sarah had asked for an increase in pay. She was an excellent employee who fully deserved a raise. Sarah had been with the company for seven years and had been working two jobs to make ends meet. John had declined to give the raise, citing his usual "expense excuse."

In an instant, Spirit revealed to him a vision of the consequences had he chosen to fairly reward Sarah. The vision showed Sarah quitting the other job and freeing up energy for even greater productivity for John. His realization of what he had lost was immediate and profound.

Remember too, that there is always more than enough for everyone to have all that he or she desires, so be fair in your business dealings with others. Find the point of balance at which both parties are well served and happy with the outcome. Every business transaction should create the mood of celebration for both parties.

John thought about the business deal he was trying to put together. He had a real talent for presenting things in their best light. He was working on a deal with a company in Lawrenceville, Georgia, a start-up that would sell products to the construction industry. Their needs included computer hardware, software, a web site and e-marketing strategies and set-up. These were the kind of deals that John loved. He referred to start-ups as pigeons.

John had padded the price in a few of the categories, not easy to verify, to come up with an overall price that was double the amount that was fair to the client. He counted on his sales ability to pitch the benefits of using his company for the whole job and the client's desire to get the job done fast.

John was skillful at this and the success of his company had rested upon this kind of sales and marketing expertise, or so he thought. Cindy was the brains behind the presentation, the graphics and the text; John handled the pricing and the pitch. It was a great arrangement, as long as Cindy didn't know about the dark financial cards that John held close to his vest. He felt a pang of guilt as he thought about that one sentence that stuck out in mental neon. *Every business transaction should create the mood of celebration for both parties.* With full disclosure, this would clearly not be the case. He would need to think more about this.

And whatever you do, try not to mistake money with self worth. If you have more money, this does not mean you are worth more, and if you have less, it does not mean you are worthless. Money is not real, you know. If it were, you would be able to take it with you. It is the greatest of all illusions to be found within the Earth dream.

40

This does not mean that it is unimportant. It is what turns the wheels on giving and receiving, you see. Money makes the process mandatory. Through the experience of working with money, you are to gain an understanding that giving and receiving are One.

John considered this for a moment in relation to his business deals. He could see no way to incorporate the teaching and to get what he wanted. First of all, he had a need for self-approval that was tied to money. Having it made him feel like King of the Hill. He would have felt worthless without money. *And what does he mean, it's not real?* John loved all the symbols for money: accounts receivable, P & L statements, his Porsche, his expensive three piece suits, the upscale gated community where he, Lynn and the last one of their kids lived. Alfred, the reluctant adult, is what he called his twenty-nine year old hippie son, who had not yet left the nest.

John would indeed have to think about Spirit's idea on money. It certainly didn't jive with his get-ahead philosophy nor to his belief in the Vince Lombardy School of thought where "Winning is Everything!" John's consciousness was still camping out in the eighties when greed was good. The voice continued and John listened intently.

While it is by giving that you receive, do not confuse money with love. Money and love are not interchangeable. In other words, do not think that you can get love by giving money or things that money can buy. Whatever it is that you give, that's what you get more of. Giving more love allows you to receive more love and giving more money opens the door for you to receive more money. That's the way it works. It is a simple process. So, whatever it is, dear Mu, that you want more of, give more of it!

Whatever it is I want more of... Well, that's easy! But it looks like I'm setting things up for my business clients to screw me if I accept this premise. John thought about the Muller account in Gainesville. It was another start-up where he struck up one heck of a deal, only to find out he was written off in a bankruptcy before he was paid for his services.

Think then about all of the things you need and want, and then, simply give those things away. Give food so that you are never hungry. Give clothes that you may always be warm. Give Love that you may experience the joy of being loved and give money so that you will always have more than you need. Give as much as you can. You see, there is only one reason for having either more or less than you need of anything. It is for allowing you to learn the meaning of the blessing that giving is receiving.

John held his head between his hands for some moments of deep reflection. *This makes my modus operandi completely antithetical to his Truth. I don't know about this.*

Those who have less money are blessed with an opportunity to heal their self worth issues without confusing money as a necessary part of the process. It is simply impossible to ever use anything on the outside of you to heal what lies within. Money is no exception, but it is the thing that is most confused with this idea.

So that's what I'm doing, trying to feel better about myself? John reflected on the way he projected himself to others ----- like he knew it all! He also thought about the fact that he projected this at his best when his Porsche or the Mercedes was in the coveted parking spot and he was in an expensive suit. John did not like what he was starting to see about himself.

And why have we exalted gold coins and green paper to the status of Heaven on Earth in the first place? The only reason to create money beyond the level of our need and desire is to be able to do something useful with it in the world, wouldn't you say? To hoard it makes no sense at all.

John thought about the social times that he and Lynn had spent with Cindy and Tom. They had dinner together every month or two. Cindy often voiced her opinion on what their skills and the company itself could do to make this a better world. She wanted them to hire disabled workers whenever possible as long as their competency matched the job. Her motto was "Let's help those first who need the most help."

Cindy also had some strange ideas about giving things away. "Let's donate our services to some worthy charitable organizations," he often heard her say. She was fond of animal rights and environmental organizations. She was a person filled with loving-kindness. Every Thanksgiving, Cindy cooked for the homeless.

John admired her, even gave lip service to living compassionately in the world, but in reality, his silent business practices spoke otherwise. When Cindy was on her "let's give it away" kick, his usual response was, "I'll get back to you on that." Many a night while driving home from dinner at Cindy and Tom's, John had expressed to Lynn, "She'd give away the whole damn company if I'd let her!"

He clearly felt he had to rein her in on "giving" but the Truth just might be that Cindy's consciousness, from Spirit's perspective, might be the greater reason behind the company's financial success. *So that would mean that Cindy's consciousness of giving, and not my business practices and silver-tongued sales ability, is the thing responsible for my success. I don't know about that!*

Sahab mentally sent Mu 8 a message of peace and love.

John sat at his computer. Closing his eyes for a moment, he thought *Compassion in, Compassion out.* He took a deep breath, exhaled slowly and felt a remarkable level of relaxation.

CHAPTER FIVE

The Sound of One Note Singing

Cindy sat at her desk digesting what she thought she knew. Several persons in her circle of friends and acquaintances seemed to be a part of the dreams and the Spiritual teachings. She knew that she was primarily Mu 9 with some other numbers of moderating influence. Her beloved Tom was definitely Mu 6 and John was certainly Mu 8. Then there was Janie who was a Mu 4 and Jim, Tom's very best friend, who was identified as a Mu 5. *So what does it mean that we are all in this together?* It was not abundantly clear, except for the fact that none of them were perfect and all had personal healing to accomplish.

Sahab continued. "Class, the goal is Oneness and there are group unifying moments in the Earth experience when we feel this quite naturally. The performing arts and sporting events are such examples. We could consider these the Yin and Yang of group oneness. Such activities allow the group to momentarily unify in feeling and expression. It is a wonderful experience. It's unfortunate that the Earth's dream evidence too often shows up as Separation.

Your mission is to see through the facade and to recapture your Remembrance of Oneness in every experience, to live in the world from this perspective and to help others to do so. It is your Divine nature. Are you following me?" Sahab asked, as he began to move effortlessly as an energy field through the Garden.

The twelve Mu(s) flowed into a line and floated along behind him in a snake-like follow-the-leader fashion. Sahab played along and took them on a small adventure in energy maneuvers. They twittered in laughter, especially enjoying the Sunfire, Starburst, and the Bluemoon. These were galactic design studies in red, white and blue energy expression, accompanied by marching band music. Sahab knew this would be effective in allowing them to feel unified. He then led them back to their places, as he assumed his physical form and continued to address the group.

"Yes, Earth is quite different. It is pure illusion, which appears to be reality. The more you conquer the illusion of Separation, the more you allow yourself to experience who you really are. "

The philosophical Mu 12 asked, "Could you say that the Earth experience is like a circular maze around a core of Light and that while we are trying to reach the Light, we seem to go in the wrong directions?"

"Yes," said Sahab, "You could say that, as opposed to a sea of Oneness with no barriers and a vertical path to Light. By getting lost in the circular maze, we use the Earth experience without really gaining from it."

Boy, do I know about that, thought Mu 6. *I have been going around in circles for ages!* The other Mu(s) quickly sent Mu 6 the energy of Love and Compassion.

Sahab moved among the Mu(s), pausing for emphasis here and there, allowing each Mu to feel that the communication was individually directed at them as he continued.

"We could say that the Earth dream is a training camp for Spirit knowing itself as One, even in the most difficult of situations. We have many experiences there because these lessons are not easy to master. The goal is always Oneness. Some of you have found the Light at least once, others many times and some not yet. So, Mu Energies 1-12, the mission this time is for all of you to get there together."

"Are we able to use our creativity in any way we choose," asked Mu 5?

"Yes," said Sahab, "as long as you do not hurt anyone or anything." Walking to the front, he turned to face the group.

"Class, in Earth terms, it is like looking into a distorted mirror. What appears to be true is but illusion. All of the distortions, and there are many, serve the purpose of strengthening the perception of Separation. Your goal is to see through them and to help others to do so. That's all you are trying to do. That's what Enlightenment is, seeing through illusions.

Now, let's look at this through a specific example," said Sahab, as he motioned Mu 7 to come forward. Sahab divined a large mirror made from Spirit. It looked like floating white smoke, almost surreal. He placed it in front of Mu 7. "What do you see?"

Mu 7 took a long and lingering look and finally began to speak. "I see Oneness with The Source of All Good. I see my Divinity. I see Beauty, Peace and Love."

"Very good!" said Sahab. "There is no distortion to this mirror and you are seeing clearly. Your challenge is to always see this clearly, regardless of appearances. Thank you, Mu 7."

Floating back to the gemstone pedestal, Mu 7 noticed the increased intensity of white light displayed by the other Mu(s). Having a knack for seeing Spiritual Truth, Mu 7 was happy to have participated in this example of its revelation to others.

"Now, for the sake of comparison", Sahab divined a distorted Earth mirror. It was a vertical rectangle, solid and framed in gold. The Teacher asked Mu 2 to come forward as he created a large, dense, Earth, female body around Mu 2's energy field, allowing everyone to view both, the earth body and the energy field simultaneously. "Look into the mirror, Mu 2, and tell me what you see." Mu 2's energy began spinning counterclockwise with jerks and starts. She appeared horrified as she looked into the mirror. After a long and tenuous pause, Mu 2 blurted out, "I see a fat body and an ugly face!"

As Sahab looked at the class, he saw their energy forms also spinning counterclockwise in jerks and starts. Then Mu 12 seemed to somehow get it and began spinning clockwise in a free and easy motion. One by one, they joined the intuitive Mu 12. "That's right, class, easy does it. You are getting the idea; *Easy Does It* and *Forward Motion*. Excellent, C+!" chuckled Sahab. "The lesson here is to pay attention to what is going on with your energy field *before* the wheels fall off the cart," he laughed.

Sahab walked toward the tuning fork, head bowed, as if he were thinking. He stopped, faced the group and began to share his thoughts, punctuating them sparingly, with gesture. "The secret of success is not to get bogged down in the density of the vehicle, or body as it is called on Earth. You are not it. You are only riding in it for the duration of the dream. Keep your focus on the Light of Love within. This will also help to keep the body in tip-top shape. Negating the Spiritual Light within will break down the physical body. At a cellular level, Spirit's Light is very nourishing."

Tom walked into the kitchen for another cup of coffee, thinking about the Spirituality of the 12-step program. *This is how it worked, Spirit's Light nourished me. Why did it stop working for me, like three times now? What happens inside of me to allow me to slip? Why do I keep losing Spirit in the bottle?* Tom wanted to face his problem but he did not know exactly what it was. He stood at the sink sipping his coffee and looking out the window.

"Keep that energy spinning in an easy-going clockwise fashion and you will shine Light on your Divinity wherever you go and in whatever you do. In other words, just be who you are. You are Spirit! This is the secret to a healthy ride on an unpredictable rollercoaster. It is also your most important tool for accomplishing your goal of helpfulness to others. Remember, they are Spirit too!"

Tom recalled the many derelicts he had helped, by sharing who he was and where his alcoholic self had been. On several occasions, individuals had made it a point to thank him after the AA meeting for the inspiration that he had been to them. Tom felt remorseful today that the tail of the tiger had slipped through his fingers one more time!

Walking to the center, Sahab motioned: "Come back, Mu 2, and let's try this once again." Mu 2 quickly complied. "Begin to spin your energy clockwise in an easy manner while maintaining *your* tempo. See how it captures and supports the essence of what you are. Now, as you look at the mirror, actually create the feeling that you are looking through it to the Truth of who you are and not at that "Hummer" in which you appear to be riding. Now, what is it that you see?"

The outline of the body-vehicle then began to fade and to appear as a dim outline of a larger reality of Light. "Oh yes, I see," said Mu 2. "I Am radiantly Beautiful. I Am Divine."

As Sahab projected his awareness toward the class, he noticed that the other Mu(s) were practicing their clockwise revolutions in an easygoing and peaceful rhythm as they looked toward the distorted mirror. "Remember to look *through* the mirror to the essence of what you are." They were mesmerized by the experience of seeing clearly.

That's it! thought Tom. *For a moment, I helped them to see through a distorted mirror. They saw their Divinity through me and it gave them hope!*

Sahab walked closer to them and softened his voice for emphasis. "Yes, Enlightenment Potentiates, we are preparing once again, for the experience of Enlightenment on Earth. Those of you who have achieved this before will go to deeper levels. Those who have not yet achieved it will seek to arrive, for the first time in the Earth dream, at what is our natural state of being in Spirit. Realizing that we are One with The Source of All Good, and with each other, helps everyone else on the path to Light."

Tom thought for a moment about some of his most embarrassing episodes. The time when he passed out in the lobby of the Penn Hotel was at the top of his list. He was drinking vodka martinis, barely eating and becoming the death of the party. They were at a birthday party for one of Cindy's friends. When they got up to leave, he got as far as the lobby and passed out. Cindy didn't speak to him for two weeks!

In Spirit, Mu 6 pondered the many bad examples he had experienced in his many lives on Earth. This was not his first sojourn as an alcoholic but he was hoping that it would be his last. His energy slowed in fits and jerks and his colors became muted and merky. The other Mu(s) quickly rushed to him and bathed this tortured Soul in the field of Compassion while Sahab continued.

"In more scientific terms, Enlightenment is the transmutation of the dense Earth energy into Light, the Light that it always was! We experience life on Earth to figure out this puzzle. This revelation must first take place within you. Then it can become a light ignition experience for others who need assistance with finding it, because now, they can experience an example of what they are looking for."

That's what happened, thought Tom. *For a moment, they saw the Light in me!*

It's like riding a bicycle," Sahab said, as he divined one, mounted and began to ride around. "Seeing someone ride is more helpful than talking about it. Becoming an example of what you know to be true is what teaches it." He then dismounted and de-materialized the bike, holding the Mu(s) wrapped in complete attention as he continued.

"You see, the Truth is there all the time but you cannot see it without Light. It is like using a flashlight in the dark to be able to see where you are going. You must first decide to turn the sucker on, as Mu 6 would say, and let there be Light! Yes, dear souls, we could say that, in a sense, you have volunteered to become flashlights in the world! Hummmmm ..." said the Teacher as he raised his eyebrows, smiled and looked around at his superstars.

Laughter erupted among the Mu(s) as they jolted ten feet upward, merging with each other in dive-bomber style. They then quickly circled Sahab three times and merged with his energy.

"Whew, that felt good," said Sahab, as he took on his physical form again and staggered around like a blind man.

The Mu(s) began to dissonantly move their energy in various directions mimicking him.

"Oh, you are a wise bunch, aren't you? Well, if you are to become the flashlights of the world, we'd better get to work!"

With that, the Mu(s) began expanding and contracting their energy fields, increasing the radiance of their Light.

Sahab bowed in acknowledgment. "Yes, *you* control it all. The recipe for success with Earth experience is to remember who you are, that you are Holy, and that you are a part of everything that is. This is what Oneness means."

The truth of the matter is so simple, so very, very simple, thought Mu 11. "Why do we make it so difficult?" All of the Mu(s) pondered this thought for a moment as Sahab strolled back to his chair.

Turning to face them, he said, "Stop trying! There is also something else to consider here and it has to do with our Creator. The Source is called by many names on Earth. It depends upon where we choose to actualize our Truth. One of the most common names for The Mother-Father Source is God. Notice that this name evokes only the male gender. Do you see a problem here?"

The Mu(s) all bobbled their energy together.

Cindy thought about the glass ceiling for women in the business world. *This has more to do with how we think about God than anything else. If God were contemplated in the female gender, women would hold the power!* She pondered these thoughts for a moment.

"Now, there are many belief systems about God," the Teacher said. "Most have some similarity to our understanding in Spirit, except for the connotation of one-sided gender, and most have far too much complexity of meat around the bones. While we *know* that we are a part of the mind of The Source, some religious belief systems think that they *know* what is *in the mind* of The Source," he said, pointing to his head. "Everything, even their one-sided God, is seen through the distorted Earth mirror that so easily creates Separation."

Maybe all that needs to change is the way that we see God, to bring equality to the system of power in the world, thought Mu 9.

"While we are in Spirit, we have no divergence of opinion on The Source. On Earth however, there are many different opinions on the subject. Each group sees the Creator differently and herein lies the reason for disharmonies. The Taliban is a prime example of this.

If everyone related to The Source of All Good in a manner of simple convergence that aligns with good, and not with right or wrong, there would be no prejudice or war. Just imagine what a difference this would make. Your goal is to make a difference because the time of *The Fulfillment* is at hand."

The Mu(s) buzzed among each other with conversational mental energy boldly arcing among them, but Mu 11 was clearly doing the neutron dance.

"Yes, Mu 11, what is your question?"

"Master, what exactly do you mean by *The Fulfillment*?"

Looking intently at Mu 11, Sahab began, "It is the ending of Separation in the Earth dream through the Remembrance of Oneness. While some of you have experienced this before, *The Fulfillment* will be the time when we accomplish this together. It will usher in a time of Peace and Love that has not been known on Earth since the beginning of Creation. There will be no prejudice or war when Separation ends, not even Holy ones," he whispered.

"Peace and Love will become the mode of interaction with each other, with the Earth, with all creatures of the Earth and with all things. *The Fulfillment* is the time when Spiritual Truth will manifest as the predominant Earth reality. Every one of you has a part to play in this drama." Sahab and Mu 11 bowed to each other in unison and greater understanding.

On Earth, the physical manifestation of a Mu 11 jolted to attention. It resided in a male Taliban body, expressing the extreme of masculine polarity. He was praying in a Mosque and, for a moment, there was a transfixing moment of clarity and understanding. The energy of every Mu 11 had the potential of a Christ or an Anti-Christ, depending upon how integrated and exponential the energy became.

For instance, in Boulder, Colorado, there was another Mu 11 who was a Buddhist. He ran an ashram dedicated to the expression of Compassion in the world.

The same was true for all the other Mu vibrations. An integrated expression created Goodness while an overboard positive or negative charge could create an *Oh my goodness!* response. Sometimes the extreme end of the masculine polarity was found in the pulpit. This potential could include the same degree of male Taliban energy, masquerading without a turban."

In the foothills of the Blue Ridge Mountains, there was one who had fallen well into the extreme of such polarity. His struggle to try and fail to integrate his loving and compassionate potential would again be known by his comments following the terrorist attacks in New York City and Washington, D.C. Publicly, he cried that abortionists, feminists, gays and lesbians were responsible for the September 11 terrorist attacks. *Oh, my goodness!* The potential for his personal healing was there, even though it still lay hidden from him, darkly covered, unfulfilled.

CHAPTER SIX

Illusions in the Light

Cindy was on the analytical track thinking about the religious right. She wondered about the Lagitard influence in any group that was based in fear. From it came judgement which could lead to irrational thought and action. She thought about the bombing of abortion clinics and the death of doctors who worked there. Such thought and action clearly seemed Lagitard in nature.

Sahab continued with his explanation. "While most Earth entities know The Source as Good, they feel quite separated from it, and therefore, from each other. From this situation comes confrontation. The narrower the view of the group, the more in need of Spiritual healing they are.

You see, individuals attach to the belief system that helps them to amplify the areas within self that need healing. Unfortunately, they do not see this need as their own. They project their need for healing onto others. The illusionary Earth mirrors trick them into thinking that their problems really belong to someone else. If the problems they see were not their own, they would not be able to see them in the world or to be affected by them."

The entire class of Mu(s) acknowledged their understanding by sending yellow streaks of color upward while Sahab continued.

"Their mirrors distort everything viewed through their physical sight. And yet, it is easy for anyone with undistorted Spiritual Sight to see that the hatred or fear of others is but a hatred or fear of self, projected outward because to hold it within becomes too painful."

Sahab's attention jokingly turned toward the Mu who semed to go around in circles. "Mu 6, I am getting your drift and no, it would not be easier if we reglazed all of the distorted mirrors on Earth!" The energy of laughter worked its way around the group as Sahab bowed to Mu 6.

Moving closer to the students, Sahab continued: "There is no substitute for remembering who we are. By remaining in touch with our Divinity, our energy becomes brighter and bolder. It makes us stand out although it often takes others quite some time to understand why. They know that there is something different going on and they have been known to have various reactions to it before they recognize the Truth in it. A fear response is often quite common in these circumstances, which can cause them to lash out, attack, and even kill the body." He whispered for emphasis, "As if this would kill the Spirit."

The Mu(s) leaned in and doubled their attention. They remembered living many lives of persecution in times and situations where the Lagitard expression had prevailed. One remembered the burning of Solomon's Temple and several remembered the most horrific of times during the Crusades when they violently transitioned back to Spirit.

"Intolerance and death have happened many times to those who's Light has shone too brightly. Brightness is frightening because it challenges the dark illusions. The Master Jesus is a good example; some of the rituals of those who honor Him are interesting. There are some Lagitards who celebrate his death even though they killed him. Some revere his teachings, yet they do not practice them. These are just some of the problems that fear and Separation cause." Sahab walked to the table, took another sip of water and turned to face the group.

"If, instead of feeling Separate from the teachings of Jesus, Moses, Mohammed or Buddha, they felt Oneness, they would be more inclined to practice the teachings of Goodness and the Golden Rule. More importantly, they would celebrate his Life, not his death. There would be no 'This is better than that,' and all prejudice would die."

"Even the prejudice against religious intolerance, against Jews, against people of color, against women and abortion?" asked Mu 9. "And what about homosexuality? These prejudices seem to have always existed in some form! Will they ever end?"

"These prejudices did not exist before the arrival of the Lagitards and they will end. It will come to be when *This* is not better than *That*. Then, there simply could not be a war on anyone or anything. Imagine the difference this would make," said Sahab, opening his arms to the universe.

"And we can make a difference?" asked Mu 5.

"Yes, you and all the other Mu vibrations on Earth now. This is the time of your *Fulfillment*! There are so many misperceptions on Earth. We study now to pierce the illusions and to remember what Spirit never forgets. We must remember our Oneness, even in the most difficult of situations."

"Isn't this dangerous," asked Mu 11. "Isn't there a chance of being killed on such a mission? Are we to be martyrs for the Light?" This Mu had experienced Enlightenment many times before, the hard way.

"Yes and no," said Sahab. "Remember, this is a dream state we are talking about. A dream always seems very real, yet when we awaken, we recognize that it was not real because we continue in a different form. You are living proof of that right now, aren't you?"

The class reverberated with a questioning energy buzz. Sahab paused for a moment, allowing them more time for assimilation before continuing.

"In the Earth dream, you are all going to die because it is necessary to wake up. Rest assured that you *always will* wake up. It does not matter how the body dies. The reason and the method are unimportant. The larger issue is this. While you were moving in the Earth dream, did you stay in the Light and did your actions bring the Light to the remembrance of others? Regardless of how that dream-life ends, this is what's important! Just know that you *will* wake up and you will surely give yourself a grade on your performance."

Sahab's body began to slowly rise about seven feet higher than the Mu(s). He appeared to be suspended in the air. A golden light shone on him as he continued to speak.

"We are half way there and this, dear class of 2002, is what our mission is all about. We are to help others by helping ourselves to find freedom, by ending the part

55

of the dream that speaks of Separation. *The Fulfillment* is at hand. It is time to transmute the Lagitard experience into something higher.

When everyone catches a glimpse of this, it will change the way they see things and, DOMINOES! It will change the world! We must help to bring remembrance to the fact that we are Spiritual beings living in a Spiritual universe, governed by Spiritual laws.

The energy field of Mu 6 started easing backwards, not escaping Sahab's awareness. The Teacher cupped his hands to either side of his mouth, allowing his words to reverberate with echo as he said, "Mu 6, if you are going for refreshments, bring me back a beer!"

An energy laugh rumbled through the other Mu(s).

In several Earth experiences, Mu 6 had been a hopeless alcoholic, his foot caught in the spoke of the wheel for countless revolutions. Mu 6 was having second thoughts about doing this again, just as Tom was having second thoughts about another try at sobriety.

Realizing his doubts, the other Mu(s) quickly soared over his head and merged into a ball of Light, brilliant and magnetic, and drew Mu 6 up into the Light for healing. Instantly, Mu 6 was at peace. The 12 Energies then separated and returned to their gemstone pedestals as Sahab gently lowered his body to center stage and continued.

"Class, see how healing Love is? Mu 6, for a moment, you got caught up in the illusions as you listened to me speak about them. You have a high level of suggestibility and you need to be aware of this. To help you, I shall inscribe a Divine point of focus or mantra within your Thought Form. You will be able to activate this any time you choose by touching any two parts of your energy form together; thumb and forefinger work well. The mantra is One-One-One-One, etc.

Always remember ----- whenever you are in your Earth body and you experience fear, for any reason, this is certain proof that you have bought into the illusions of the Earth experience and the Lagitard influence. You have forgotten your Oneness with The Source and with your own Divinity. When you experience fear, implement your mantra and it will immediately trigger this remembrance. Try it now for practice," he said, as he sat down in the Teacher's chair.

"We need this too!" chimed the others.

"Of course! I am glad to know that you can see the value in constantly reclaiming your Divine point of focus."

"One-One-One-One-One..." they all chanted.

"Excellent, class. Remember to use it whenever you are trapped in illusion, and how do you know when this is so?"

"We experience fear!" projected the Mu(s).

"Excellent! C+!" said Sahab, as the energy laughs reverberated once again.

Standing to face them, Sahab continued: "Class, this was meant to be an overview of the course and we have already veered off into several directions. It is important however, to establish as many simple and practical ways for you to remember that you are Spirit.

Once we reenter the dense earthly vessel, it is easy to get caught up in the illusions. We can easily lose our way. Be vigilant and apply yourselves. It is the time of *The Fulfillment* and you were hand picked because you volunteered to implement the healing of a particular illusion gone awry in the Earth experience," he said, as he walked closer to them.

"Each of you will serve as a healing catalyst for all those trapped on a different part of the wheel of Karma. The solution for each group is a simple one. Ending Separation and experiencing Oneness is everyone's path to freedom. You have been chosen to lead your group because of your special affinity for, and prior failure in, your particular area. Guess which contingent Mu 6 is heading up?"

The energy laughter equal to that of a Fourth of July fireworks display exploded as the group did countless bouts of merging and separating with Mu 6. "I've never felt so loved, so healed; I'm ready now", said Mu 6, with energy extensions resembling a thumbs-up.

Sahab bowed reverently to Mu 6 and said, "Because you have tried and failed, you have gained great compassion and this is what you needed. Your compassion can become the necessary catalyst for the healing of your group on Earth. As you heal, they heal. Your example shows them *The Way*.

If you had not been there before, you could not be there now. Bless you, Mu 6, as you go forward to heal your lack of self-love. Hanging in the balance is the healing of the world. We have great faith in you, Mu 6; we know that you will do well. However, remember this ----- when you are looking into that mirror over the bar, touching two parts of your energy form together and you see your mantra looking back at you, repeat it: 'One-One-One...' please do not interpret that to mean 'One More'!" The class once again went wild with laughter.

On Earth, Tom had taken his manual and moved outside to his favorite chair in the courtyard. The sun felt warm and healing on his flaccid face, as he sat silently, with eyes closed, seriously contemplating sobriety. Pep was by his side, licking his hand every now and then, and sending Tom her messages of Peace and unconditional Love.

Addressing the class again as a group, Sahab continued, "In all seriousness, you must not get lost in the Separation that the rest of your group is thinking, seeing, feeling and experiencing. Have compassion for it, but do not get lost in it. We're depending on you, but more importantly *they* are depending on you."

Tom patted Pep on the head and then held her ears back, making her look like a baby seal. *Pep, would you believe it? Every drunk in the world depends on me!* Pep looked lovingly at him and yawned.

"You cannot teach by just intellectually knowing the truth of Oneness, for we all know that truth at some level of our being, even when we are lost. The way that we teach Oneness is by becoming that truth, by living the truth that we know. That's what the teachings of the Great Ones are about. In the final analysis of every dream on Earth, living Oneness is all that really matters for it is the way we live by the Golden Rule.

You see, the Earth experience is not meant to be an intellectual exercise without Spiritual awareness. The only way to overcome the illusions of the world is to focus on our Spiritual nature. It is the only thing that's real!" Sahab walked to his chair, allowing them the space to think about these things.

The Mu(s) were mesmerized in thought, contemplating many different facets of Sahab's teachings and how they personally applied to them. When Sahab began to see a slowing of the synapses, he began to speak, "Class, we have had enough for now. Suspend your thought and rest for awhile. You have a lot to assimilate. Your next dream will take place in the Garden of Remembrance where the Angel Alcyona will be your guide. Listen and learn from her. We shall meet again later."

Sahab had thrown a lot at them. He had challenged much of the Truth that their physical manifestation held sacred. He knew that osmosis and remembrance would purge these illusions in the Light. Sahab's energy dissipated and slowly disappeared, while the Mu(s) fell into a deep sleep.

CHAPTER SEVEN

The Garden of Remembrance

"Wake up, my darlings. We have work, work, work to be done," chirped the Angel, Alcyona. The expression of her energy assumed a form, appearing as part human in body with a disproportionally smaller bird-like head. Her wings were downy soft, appearing to be delicately translucent as the light shown through them. She was quite colorful: an interesting mix of Mayan magic and Egyptian elegance. She divined this form and appearance for her own teaching purposes.

Mu 6 stirred. *Where am I? This sounds amazingly like rehab.* "Good grief!" *Maybe I'm in a hospital and I'm delusional!*

"Wake up, wake up and open your energy to what I have to share with you."

With his vision still a blur, Mu 6 thought, *Clarice, is that you?* It obviously was not.

Alcyona's manner of expression was feminine yet with a flair for assertiveness. Her face was delicately thin, with wide, slanted, yellow eyes rimmed in black that seemed to look right through you. Each Mu was certain that she was looking directly at them, but the truth of the matter was that she was seeing far more than appeared to be there. She had a large, dark beak that curved downward slightly at its end: impressive yet clearly not her most attractive feature. Her feathers were pure white around her eyes and beak, giving way to subtle gradations from blue to indigo. Her feathers wrapped around her small head, sweeping upward and ending in a lavender, arched pouf upon her crown.

Even though they were not fully alert, Alcyona continued, "Do not think this little head has no brains at all. This tiny tufted beauty," pointing to it with the extension of her wings, "has radar like you wouldn't believe, and you are going to learn to use your own. You could say that you're going to try to get the hang of it, or… if you should miss… the bang of it," she cooed and chortled.

The Mu(s) felt groggy as they emerged from a very deep sleep. A closer look unveiled the appearance of an outdoor bird carnival. Birds were chirping everywhere they looked. A large silk-like banner stretched across the back of the platform where Alcyona stood. Capital letters spelled out BIRDLAND in bold letters of green on gold.

Colorful birds of many different species were flying to and fro, randomly lighting here and perching there. On both sides of the platform stood two large blue spruce trees. In the trees to the left, a bird band sat perched upon the branches, holding tiny instruments and playing jazz. On the right, another flock sang delightful melodic lines of birdcalls softly in the background. Spread throughout the trees, the musical members looked like colorful Christmas tree ornaments, playing well-rehearsed melodies.

Cindy alerted herself with a jolt. She had allowed herself to space out. It was indeed difficult to concentrate on work. She remembered the birdcall that had claimed her full attention on the way to work this morning. She looked at her manual and opened it slowly. She felt compelled to begin reading.

Alcyona then fashioned her energy form into a flowing mass, which undulated into a downward and outward motion with wings out-stretched to honor her students. "I am the Angel, Alcyona. I am named for the great Central Sun of the Pleiades; I greet you in the remembrance of your wisdom. Fashion a button right here," she said, pointing to the middle of her energy field, "And push it now!"

Even though they were not sure they had the ability to do so, all twelve Mu(s) promptly divined their buttons and followed her directions. Deviant rainbows of radiant color began shooting off in twelve different directions. They pushed their buttons again and again, with the idea of exerting directional control over their out-of-control energy fields.

The harder they tried, the more jagged streaks of yellow were made visible. To no avail, they continued shooting off, erratically, in various directions. Observing this fiasco Alcyona thought, *This certainly reminds me of a Moliere play on stage before rehearsal.* While control seemed to be out of reach, they were all in amazement that none of them collided with each other.

"Are we having fun yet?" she asked.

The Mu(s) felt a little bewildered, resting a bit while Alcyona continued to speak.

"As long as you think of yourselves as separate, you remain separated ----- *your mind* controls it all. Sahab began your preparation with some interesting and quite truthful comments on Separation and Oneness. Unfortunately, you were thinking more about the former than the later before you did the exercise. Whatever you think about, my darlings, becomes reality and produces evidence of itself. You see this happen over and over again in the Earth experience. Change your thought and the evidence will change. Now think of yourselves as One and again push your buttons."

The Mu(s) began pushing their starters once again and their energy fields again began shooting off in all directions, but an interesting thing began to happen. Each time two of them crossed paths, they merged into one, becoming one field, more powerful than before.

These more powerful fields then pushed their buttons until they crossed paths with another energy field and merged again. This continued until all twelve fields were *One* ----- one button and one energy field. They came to rest as a huge ball of energy, then separated into twelve fields, taking their places on the lawn in front of Alcyona's platform.

"Very Good, my darlings ----- there is a great deal to be said about practicing what you know. This is just another lesson in Separation and Oneness for you to remember. Every lesson that you remember and practice makes the journey easier. I shall assume that you are thoroughly awake now and ready to continue."

The Mu(s) began to spin in an easy-going clockwise motion. Alcyona understood and started to continue when an energy display caught her attention. Mu 9's energy field had created a long, slender extension upward and, frantically, began to wave.

"Yes, Mu 9, what is your question?"

"Well, I am a little confused. In the Earth experience, birds seem to fly swiftly just as we have and yet they always seem to avoid collision. They appear to remain separate. Why is it that birds seem to choose Separation in the Earth experience?"

Alcyona smiled, looked intently at Mu 9, and said: "Remember this, things are not always as they appear to the analytical mind. Your use of it has brought you to this conclusion. You have over developed that part of you, Mu 9, and you must be careful for overanalysis can often lead you to the wrong conclusion." She walked closer to Mu 9 and stretched her wings to full extension.

"In the Earth experience, birds never choose Separation. They *always choose* Oneness. It is because they welcome the sky merging with them in Oneness that they are even able to fly. How else do you think those tiny wings would be able to get the job done?"

Mu 9 thought about Alcyona's response with great interest. In spite of the fact that it did not seem logical, at the same time, it seemed reasonable. This was exactly how Cindy's deductive mind worked and it sometimes led her to the wrong conclusions.

Allowing her wings to relax, she continued, "Birds are your teachers while you are within the Earth dream, if you will only allow them to be. The lesson they are trying to teach you is the importance of Oneness. They present to you a visual demonstration that, by choosing Oneness, miracles appear to happen. Watching them fly displays the miracle, doesn't it?" she asked, looking around the group.

Mu 9 was digesting this while thinking, *A miracle does appear to be happening. Something else must be going on here.* Why things were as they were was a problem that Cindy often tripped over. For years now, she had applied this rationale to Tom's problem and had gotten nowhere.

"Oneness is the thought form behind the symbolic meaning of flight," said the Angel. "Actually, it is not a miracle at all, but simply the natural course of events resulting from consistently choosing Oneness. There are similar lessons to be learned from everything that you experience through the five senses. There is always a different way of looking at things," she said, as she began to address the group as a whole. Clearly, she knew that this lesson belonged to everyone.

"To all seemingly complicated questions, there is always a simple answer of Oneness. Finding how it fits is what separates the Spiritually sighted from the Spiritually blind. Earth experiences test your Spiritual knowledge and help others to test themselves, so that all of you advance in the remembrance of Spirit. Analytical mind will often steal the miracle if you allow it to do so. This is because appearances can be deceiving.

This has been happening for quite some time on Earth. It is one reason for so much depression there now. Far too many miracles have been stolen, creating hopelessness. Be very careful with analytical mind. It can be a slippery slope," she said, as she quickly levitated up to sit upon a branch of a large pin oak tree, in front and to the right of the platform. Adjusting her wings, she listened closely.

"Are you saying that we are not to use our analytical mind?" asked Mu 9. "How, pray tell, are we ever to arrive at the Truth?"

Alcyona smiled; she looked down at the class and said, "Any takers?" Dangling her dainty feet, she surveyed the group.

Mu 10, who often had a very artistic flair in energy communication, projected, "No, stupid, I think that Alcyona is merely cautioning us not to over-use it. I think she is saying that we must find balance in the use of both analytical and intuitional mind."

"I agree with you, Mu 10, about everything except the 'no, stupid' part," said the Angel. The class twittered and the energy laughs rumbled.

"Just a figure of speech," said Mu 10.

"Yes, and a poor figure of speech at that," said Alcyona, as the class laughed with satisfaction.

Mu 10 and Mu 9 then turned to face each other and began projecting beautiful energy thought forms toward each other. This act totally filled the space between them until they merged completely. After their experience of Oneness, they drifted, effortlessly, back to their places as Alcyona lowered herself and began to speak.

"Beautiful! When you are back in the trenches on Earth, remember this moment", she said, stretching her wings expansively. "No matter what kind of disagreement you may be experiencing, Oneness can always be the end result if you will choose it over Separation. This is sometimes called Forgiveness."

"But why does this always seem more difficult while we are caught up in the Earth experience?" asked Mu 7.

"Because you forget that after projecting the thought form of Oneness, you must then communicate. It's about this space between your mind and your mouth," she said, pointing to each while crossing her large yellow eyes. The Mu(s) began to giggle. She had an interesting way of catching them off guard.

"You need to think it first and then talk about it," she said, as she moved each thumb to meet her fingers in rapid motion, mimicking mouths talking. "In density, you need to elaborate more on the thought that is being projected. It's as simple as that," she said. "Failing to do so can create another miracle lost."

A warm pink mist of love enveloped the Mu(s) as Alcyona wrapped them in her healing energy and said, "Whenever we choose Oneness, we allow the natural course of miracles to flow into our lives. Whenever analytical mind allows Separation to appear as the right course of action or conclusion, look again with intuitional mind to verify your conclusions. Is this perfectly clear?" she asked, as she crossed her eyes again while subtly bobbing her head from side to side. The Mu(s) were thoroughly tickled by this and by the pouf on her head that jiggled as she moved.

She paused for a moment in thought as she looked upward, and then directly back at them and said, "And if you should ever feel yourself stuck, and you surely will from time to time, just look to the sky," as she pointed upward. "Sooner or later you are bound to see a bird flying and this will help you to realign with the miracle that you're missing."

As if on cue, the Christmas ornaments flew to the other side, landing in the other Blue Spruce trees to the left and the band members flew to the trees on the right. Alcyona smiled at them.

"Birds flying effortlessly will trigger your Remembrance of this teaching. Moving closer and fixing her gaze directly upon them, she said, "If you really want to cultivate this reality, try putting up a bird feeder to nurture us. Remember that whatever you take care of is always taking care of you."

Mu 9 nodded while thinking about Pep, the wonderful little doggie who was part of her energy field. Pep was in the yard now with Tom, basking in the sun.

Alcyona nodded toward Mu 9 and divined a bird feeder in the pin oak tree to the right. The birds immediately flew over to it, chirping on the way and keeping their distance until it was their turn. Most of them were courteous but a few were a little too over-zealous about what they thought belonged to them.

Mu 9 thought, *Interesting... By feeding them, we get to see the miracle more often as well as the worst side of ourselves! Talk about a mirror!*

Walking among them, Alcyona continued, "Because human eyes are nowhere near as powerful as the eyes of a bird, you might try getting yourself a pair of binoculars."

The Mu(s) continued watching the birds changing their positions from different directions, then flying in to take their turn at the feeder. They delighted in the songs the birds were singing.

"Every chirp that you hear is the word 'One' voiced in a different bird language dialect. It is the only word in their vocabulary."

"I've heard bird calls that seemed to be a sound of warning," said Mu 3, "As if there's danger ahead."

"Those are your own thoughts, fears and emotions, my child. 'One' is the only word they need. Yes darlings, it is the simplest things that bring us into alignment with the Truth and the Truth *is always* Oneness. Are we ready to continue?" she asked, as she moved to the front of the group.

All Mu(s) began slowly spinning their energy fields in a clockwise direction allowing the vibrancy of their rich colors to display the answer.

"Good," she said as she began to fashion a beautiful garden of lilies. They

67

appeared to be extending from her as they established themselves in circular motion around her feet. She motioned the Mu(s) to come closer. They did so, while remaining a reverent distance just beyond the lilies.

"Dear ones, we are in the Garden of Remembrance. It is important for you to know that the lily is the symbol of remembering who you are, who you have been and the importance of all of your journeys on the Earth. The details are unimportant ----- but the current status of the Soul evolvement is very important. Getting in touch with this will be of great benefit to you. In a moment, you will be asked to select a lily from this garden and merge your energy form with it to recapture your Remembrance. Go ahead now, look them over carefully and select the one that seems to call out to you."

Each Mu surveyed the situation closely, circled around their selection and merged their energy field with their chosen lily. A myriad of thought forms from many lives colorfully revealed themselves. Their life experiences rapidly progressed and Alcyona closely observed the arcing of the energy surges taking place. As she read them, she took her mental notes. *Yes*, she thought, *It is always a journey to self-love. Only the paths to freedom change*, she thought, as she paused to allow her own awareness of these truths to deepen within her.

Mu 6 remembered many lives but seemed to focus more strongly on a life that he had lived on Atlantis. He held a position called Keeper of the Crystals in the last stages of that civilization. An association with a Lagitard named Isha had led him down the path of inebriation and he had almost lost the Crystals in the sea.

Tom found it interesting that he was now living in the Atlanta area. He wondered what, if anything, it had to do with that life in Atlantis. The similarity of the names intrigued him. His guilt about his lack of control regarding alcohol and his inability to forgive himself for almost letting down an entire civilization had created for him many lives of turmoil that must now be undone.

"Notice," she said, "that one aspect of your Remembrance stands out stronger than the rest. You could say that it is the current status of your Soul evolvement or the "thorn in your side," if you would like a rough Earthly equivalent."

She chuckled as she gently poked her finger into the energy of Mu 9. "It is the place where you are choosing to work now to experience your miracles. Once you have arrived at your "thorn," detach from your lily and experience it.

Mu 9 felt a strong amplification of the energy field along with a sensation of tingling in the core, which rippled out to the periphery in waves that felt electrical. She was experiencing the energy of the Crystals. *Were these from Atlantis? No, they were from Lemuria! And why was she experiencing them?* A visual experience revealed her protecting the Lemuria Crystals in those last days of Tribulation. She and the Crystals were on the landmass that had broken off and drifted away to later become known as the continent of Australia. She saw herself protecting them until they were safely placed within the stone monolith. Those Crystals were the Love power source regenerators for the Mu(s). They were instrumental in preserving the wisdom of The Source for implementation on the Earth.

Cindy had been instrumental in saving the Crystals from the Lagitards who were trying to destroy them. She wondered about the significance of that life to this one. *What did this have to do with Tom and his Crystals on Atlantis?* She wondered. And what about the rest of the group in the dream, the ones that she knew now on Earth? *Why were they a part of the dreams and the teachings? Were they with her on Lemuria? Did they all have some common denominator? Did the Crystals have something to do with The Fulfillment? Were they all part of some special mission that no one seemed to remember?*

CHAPTER EIGHT

Digging In and Getting Real

With a broad sweep of her right hand, Alcyona instantly divined a cloudbox. A mental formation made visible, it was divided into twelve sections which stood as both a vertical and horizontal field beyond the Mu(s) and about eleven feet away. The cloudbox sections were stacked two-by-two for a total of twelve boxes, each box having its own number. Clouds appeared to be floating and changing shape in each box against a vast expanse of sky. The numbers, 1-12, remained visible at all times in the upper right hand corner of each box.

"Record your experiences in the section of the cloudbox with your number on it. Then rest quietly and thoughtfully until all of us are ready to continue."

As the Mu(s) participated in the Remembrance activity, Alcyona enjoyed watching the *Light Show* while observing the Lily-Mu(s) glowing with energy and luminosity. Some lingered longer than others. One by one, each energy field separated from his Remembrance, slowly and peacefully, and floated to his section of the cloudbox to complete the assignment.

They began to pour out their thoughts by using their minds to project those images in bold black letters. It looked like a strange arrangement of hieroglyphics, which collectively formed a symbol. The writing seemed to somehow affect the shape of the clouds. The borders of the sky began to expand as needed, to allow adequate space for capturing the personal expressions in their entirety.

The Mu(s) took varying amounts of time and space for this expression while Alcyona waited patiently and lovingly. When they had finished, what appeared to everyone was an interesting design with evocative power. Each Mu understood the meaning of his own personal rendering while the Angel Alcyona understood them all.

After the last Mu had returned to his place, the Angel said, "Did you enjoy your experience, my darlings? Was it Enlightening?"

"Yes," projected Mu 12, "It was like experiencing a drama of myself revealed."

"What was revealed to you?"

"Alpha and Omega," said Mu 12.

Alcyona nodded, acknowledging her comprehension and continued. "Now you understand why lilies are often given to those who are waking up from the Earth's dream. The catalytic properties of lilies in memory retrieval are quite strong. While some call the waking-up process death, it is really the remembrance of life, *real* life." The Mu(s) seemed to be quite taken with this idea and contemplated it with great interest.

"Well, let's see what we have here," Alcyona said, as she moved to the cloudbox to view the results. "Well now, isn't this interesting! All of you seem to be in a juxtaposition of one kind or another to the energy of Love. Yes darlings, no matter how many Earth experiences we have, there is always more to learn about Love, isn't there?"

The Mu(s) thoughtfully acknowledged their agreement with a slow energy spin in a clockwise direction, displaying a pink energy expression as they contemplated Love.

Cindy stopped reading and thought for a moment about Love from her own personal perspective. Tom was certainly the love of her life. She thought about the beginning of their relationship. How magical it was! It was as though they were meeting again after a long time. They were totally comfortable with each other. She loved his humor and his gentle way of expressing himself. His total acceptance of everyone, just the way they were, was indeed a lesson she was trying to learn. There were no drugs and few drinks in the beginning. How had things gotten so out of control?

Alcyona continued: "For some, it is learning more about self-love; for some, it is more about love of others which might mean specific individuals or groups. Some may be learning more about love of the Earth and many are learning about love in relation to money and power. The goal is simply to remove all barriers to love and to find Oneness.

You see, the barriers are not naturally there. We construct them from improper use of the analytical mind or by accepting another's improper use of it. This brings to mind one group who went to Lily-land drinking Koolade," she said, thinking about the Jim Jones group, as she fluffed her wings and shook her head.

The Mu(s) laughed even though they were not entirely certain why this seemed funny.

Alcyona continued, "Every Holy war, including the ones going on now in Afghanistan and Israel, is an improper use of analytical mind in relation to Spiritual beliefs. One wrong assumption can lead you down the road to Hell-in-a-hand-basket, as they say on Earth. The truth is that the Koolade group discovered that Hell is nothing more than a state-of-mind within each individual," she said, as she stretched her wings. "The Christians started a mess during the Crusades and the Muslims are trying to finish it. The Jews came before and after these things and have also played their part in the drama of life. Cause and effect goes on and on, but all of this will be resolved once and for all, and the world shall know peace.

Removing the barriers to Love created by erroneous assumptions allows Love to flow freely to everyone and everything. This is Oneness in action. This is what we are looking for." Moving closer to them, she said, "Be very observant of the areas in life where you disallow the energy of Love to flow freely."

Is this what happened, thought Cindy. *Did I not love him enough? Did I channel too much of myself into my work? What part do I play in Tom's alcoholism?*

"Identifying and removing those barriers is what will end Separation on Earth. There is no other way to Oneness." The Mu(s) thought seriously about this as their rainbow of colors took on a kaleidoscopic appearance.

"Why do we have those barriers in the first place and how do we go about removing them?" asked Mu 5.

Alcyona noticed that the energy of this Mu spun a little faster than the others. Mu 5 had a wonderful mind and was a risk-taker: always concerned with integrating ideas and conquering challenges. In physical form, Mu 5 often appeared to be

73

jumping off a cliff of one kind or another. "More was better" as far as change was concerned to Mu 5; it added stimulation and interest to life.

Tom's phone was ringing. He had taken the cordless with him to the patio. "Hello, this is Tom Gorman."

"Hey Buddy, how are you doing? Have you heard what's happening in the world?"

"Yeah, Cindy called, yelling, "Turn on the TV!" Unbelievable, isn't it?"

"Yep and you know, I am already looking at things differently!"

"What do you mean?"

"For one thing, life's too damn short to stay chained to the cash cow!"

Jim had a business that evaluated workman's compensation disability claims. It made money hand over fist.

"Tom, I've had an excellent offer to sell the business and this morning's events have made up my mind. There's more to life than making money! I've been ready for a new adventure for a long time now and I'm going for it! I plan to strongly consider the offer and I'm getting my ducks in a row."

"What do you mean? Where are you going?"

"As soon as the deal is done and planes are flying again, I'm heading down to Costa Rica. I'm kicking back for awhile and I'm gonna do it! I'm going to buy that boat and start the charter fishing business; life is too short. I don't intend to go HOME chained to the cash cow!"

"Jim, that sounds great! But can you handle not being on the fast track?"

"Just watch me! And Buddy, I've got a present for you. How would you like to have my two Tech season tickets?"

"Alright!"

"I want you to have them. You'll just have to find another Techie to go with you. Think you can manage that?"

"Yep, I can do that but I sure will miss not going with you!"

Tom and Jim had been yellow jacket roommates at Georgia Tech and forever faithful to every football game that they could manage. They had only missed two

74

home games together since graduating: once when Jim was in the hospital having his appendix removed and once when Tom was at Ridgeview drying out.

"Buddy, the events of this morning have set the stage. I'm on my way, as soon as I have everything in order. By the way, did you leave a book in my mailbox?"

"No, what kind of a book?"

"A strange one called *The Fulfillment, Return of Mu*, like what the hell is Mu?"

"Did you have some dreams last night that you remember?" asked Tom.

"Well no, well yes, I think so, but I don't remember them. What do dreams have to do with the book?"

"Well, let me tell you Jim, there's something going on here around this book that I don't fully understand yet. I found a copy of the same book behind my computer tower. For a brief hung-over moment, I thought it was the hand of Clarice, reaching out from beyond the grave! I'm sitting in the back yard right now reading mine with Pep. So far, I would describe it as being on the weird side of interesting. Have you started reading yours yet?"

"Hell no, like I have time! The cash cow needs me! Maybe this weekend. Gotta run now Buddy. Wanted you to know what's happening. I'll catch you later."

Tom hung up the phone and looked out across the yard, as if the flowers, trees and shrubs would help him make sense of this book deal. *How could both of them have the very same book? Who was responsible for this and what did it mean?* His eyes came to rest on the lavender crepe myrtle that Cindy had planted in remembrance of Clarice, along with some of her cremated ashes. Tom had named it Crepe Clarice. "OK CC, what do you know about this?" he asked. True to form, CC never answered, but the tree's namesake observed her son-in-law and the whole drama with great interest, on both sides of the veil. She recognized Alcyona as the lovely Angel who had helped her across.

Alcyona paused for a moment and continued, "Let's go back to something that you heard Sahab say in your first session. The purpose of our experience in the Earth dream is for the strengthening or deepening of our lives in Spirit. You see, it's

75

not about fast cars or money." She placed her hands on both her hips as she flapped her wings and opened her eyes as wide as possible, surprising them.

"It's about work ----- Spiritual work. Each of you knows the areas where your Spiritual life needs strengthening. That's what our recent exercise in Remembrance was all about ----- identifying the major Spiritual issue on which you are determined to make a difference. There may also be tangential issues where you are concerned with making progress. All of your barriers to love have a direct relationship to these specific goals. We might say that the barriers become synonymous with all of the prejudices you find so easy to hold while living the Earth experience: those areas, which easily keep you in Separation.

So, darlings, here it is in a nutshell. You establish your prejudices and the barriers to love so that you may overcome them. You choose the life situation that will nurture your predisposition to those prejudices because they are what you seek to overcome. You *have* them but you do not want to keep them. Otherwise, there will be no progress made in the life experience and the Spiritual life will not be strengthened or deepened when you wake up.

The purpose of life on Earth is to break through these prejudices and your barriers to love because they are the things that keep you in Separation. As you have heard many times already, the goal is to end it and to find Oneness with all things ----- if not in this lifetime, then the next, the next or the next. It's all up to you. Is this starting to make sense?" she asked, as she stood up and paced to the left, looking down.

The Mu(s) continued spinning in clockwise direction, as Alcyona turned to view the full pallet of their energies.

"There is a Spiritual process sometimes referred to as the Dark Night of the Soul." Those who make the choice to experience the darkness are intent on experiencing the Light *before* they wake up, or while they are still in the dream. This is called Enlightenment.

By doing so, they kick-start the process and help to advance everyone else on the path. This continues for as long as they remain a part of the historical record of

Earth. Ah, and that's another matter in itself ----- how the Earth's historical record has been altered to serve the egos of those in power.

Sahab once had to sacrifice his thumbs in one lifetime. He was a scribe who was intent on recording the Truth. He inscribed a code in his writings which, when deciphered, told the real story. He was found out and his thumbs were severed so that he could never write again. He can tell you more about that horrible story sometime," she said, while shaking her head in apparent disbelief.

"Of course, Jesus, the Buddha and many others are examples of those who took on tremendous challenges for the greater good of others. Yes darlings, this quest for Love and Compassion is quite a team effort and, unless everyone plays at their best, the game cannot be won. So, periodically, the Creator sends a different team captain to try another approach. The goal is always the same, to live the Truth of One." Alcyona once again levitated to her perch in the pin oak tree. As she did so, the leaves turned a more vibrant green.

"Yes, dear Mu(s), we are always yearning in one way or another to become a Christ or a Buddha because it is the ultimate possibility and we are all achievers at heart. Earth is little more than a training ground for this development. In your early lives on the ancient continent of Mu, you began to yearn for this metamorphosis. Those thoughts are what paved the way for much progress then and for the many Spiritual Masters who followed." Enraptured, they looked up at her as she moved closer.

"You were also their students. You continue to choose to go back again and again to refine their vibrations in you and to help others to do so. It is part of the healing that must take place to align with the will of the Creator. *The Fulfillment* is all about the living of this Truth by the majority of those present in the Earth experience. Everyone has a part to play in this process. It is all about waking up, in one place or another. Some will leave to assist the process and some will stay to fulfill it. Each individual chooses his destiny. Nothing is accidental even though it sometimes appears to be."

"Do you mean that everyone on the planes that crashed in the World Trade Center Towers, the Pentagon and in the field in Pennsylvania all agreed to be there?" asked Mu 5.

"At a Soul level, they chose to play this part in the Tribulation and the transition that it brings for achieving The Fulfillment on Earth."

"And what about the people who perished in the buildings?" asked Mu 4.

"This was the role that they agreed to play," said the Angel. "This is true, even for the perpetrators. They all contributed in their own way to bring us closer to the Fulfillment."

Looking intently at Alcyona, they began to think about these things. They huddled closer together to feel each other's support and a Spirit of Oneness.

Dark Nighting

John was sitting at his desk preparing a memo for his department heads to address with their staffs. "A downturn is expected in the fourth quarter. Profit projections will most likely not be achieved. All managers should run a tight ship to control expenses..." John looked out the window for a moment and began to think about the personal fiasco he needed to control. Her name was Bunny and she was an Easter basket he should have let pass.

A few months back, he had gone to the Gold Club in Buckhead for some action. There he was, a well-dressed, 55-year-old man with hair a little too brown and a little too perfectly combed-over. A rug was definitely out of the question; he thought about how ridiculous Bob looked in his.

John was good at rationalizing his behavior. He worked hard, made a lot of money and never failed to take care of his family's financial needs. A little fun was not too much to ask. He was due some down time for working so hard!

Bunny sized up the situation and closed in for the kill. Bleached blond, bound and determined to bag this bounty, Bunny bounced on over. Her cleavage had sunk a thousand ships and John was not going to be an exception. Bunny knew just how to work it and yes, he got lucky all right! She made him feel young again. Now he was lucky enough to pay through the nose for her condo in Buckhead, not to mention the credit cards she loved exercising at Phipps Plaza.

John was beginning to tire of the situation. She wasn't someone who could move in his world, nor did he want her to. Lynn was beginning to suspect something and the whole deal was about to hit the fan!

John would let his secretary, Evelyn, handle the details. He knew he could depend on her loyalty. She had helped him out with closure on more of these situations than he wanted to remember. He would be generous with Bunny's severance package as he always was with these escapades. He reached for the phone. "Evelyn, come in for a moment please." John turned back to his computer and began checking the markets again.

The Mu(s) observed this from the Spiritual realm while the energy of Mu 8 contracted in an "Oh, ouch" manner. Yes, Mu 8 was owning the John that he was and it was painful. The other Mu(s) immediately sent him pink rays of empathy and love.

Alcyona swooped down and cradled him with her wings and whispered to him, "You are brave and strong and you have not chosen to make things easy on yourself this time. Know that the ways of alchemy are difficult but the rewards are great."

The Angel continued on with her teaching. "Choosing the Dark Night of the Soul is a commitment to alchemy, my darlings, the alchemy of the Soul, the Spiritual process that turns, even the basest of metals into gold. It is like an oyster manifesting an exquisite pearl, where many irritations finally culminate in the creation of a thing of great beauty. "

Alcyona moved even closer to them, softening her voice as she continued. The very thought of what she was saying touched her deeply. "When you have led most of your dark places to the Light, it will create that magical experience of Enlightenment.

The mysteries of life are revealed, Yes! thought Mu 9. Understanding the esoteric meanings of life was important to the Mu 9's of the world and especially to the one called Cindy Gorman.

"While I call it magical, what it really does is simply change your focus. It is a time when the remembrance of the Truth brings so much Light that you are in this world but not of it. You become both a participant and an observer of your life and you cease taking it too seriously."

The Mu(s) began to expand their energy fields while increasing the presence of the violet ray. They were intrigued by the Teacher's words, whose information they accepted without reservation because of what it resonated in them. They took in a deep breath which allowed their energy fields to increase. They followed with a long exhalation, slowly assuming their normal size as they released their tensions.

John was thinking about Lynn and wondering just how much she knew. How Lynn had put up with him was hard to grasp. She was an intelligent and beautiful woman. The kids were definitely his buffer. He was a wonderful dad and a not-so-terrible husband, except for the secret life he lived. He never could seem to get enough of extramarital sex. This had nothing to do with Lynn. It had everything to do with his own misperceptions about power and money and his lack of self-love.

Alcyona continued, "With Enlightenment, the focus changes from you and the idea that there may not be enough, to others and the knowledge that there is always more than enough!

And this can be applied to everything: *more than enough* money, love, success, sex, alcohol and so forth. It is the very concept that 'More is better', which brings about the Dark Night. Spirit helps you to make a correction in your thinking by bringing it on. When it is done, Enlightenment follows. "She paused to look for evidence of their understanding and slowly repeated: "Not *thinking* that there is, mind you, but *knowing it*, with every fiber of your being. The faith that you've placed in the things of the world is then transferred to The Mother-Father Source of All Good.

Ownership of your own Christ self or Buddha nature is the only real ownership that claims your devotion. The rest of the things of the world merely claim your attention from time to time. Yes dear Mu(s)," she said as she gestured in the distance, "Your boat is afloat in the sea of Spirit and you are heading into the wind trusting The Source as your navigator. You are positioned at the rudder as directions for your course are softly whispered to you." She pretended to whisper to Mu 11 as the energy field fashioned itself into a large ear, appearing pink and flesh toned in color. This tickled the rest of the group.

The Mu(s) listened intently to what she had to say about the Dark Night and the Enlightenment that would follow it, as if they were listening to instructions for disaster preparedness. Directing her attention back to the entire group, she continued, "You are having a conversation with Spirit and what often seems mystifying to others is that you are totally willing to act upon this information. Yes, you have moved to the other side of distorted mental perception into yourself as the Light of the world and your joy is, for the first time, *complete*."

Cindy sat at her desk transfixed, devouring her manual when, all of a sudden, a gut feeling told her to call home. She picked up the phone and dialed; it rang and rang. *Where is he?* Cindy thought about some personal healing issues relevant to the Dark Night. Tom's was obviously drugs and alcohol and hers probably had something to do with Clarice, *or was it self-love for both of them?*

The Mu(s) were beginning to feel overwhelmed by these grand possibilities. Mu 2 interrupted, "But what does this feel like? Will we have magical powers?"

"Yes, the most magical powers of all. When you pass through the Dark Night of the Soul into Enlightenment, Peace will be your experience, my child, and your manner in the world will be soft. It does not matter if you are rich or poor. You recognize that your needs are always met. You have then made the journey from Spirit rising to Spirit walking and that is about as magical as you can get, wouldn't you say?"

The Mu(s) leaned their energy fields toward Alcyona, giving her their full attention as the Angel continued. Their vibrant fields of color were turning clockwise, relaxed yet attentive.

"Seekers on the path are drawn to you. They are not quite sure why your energy is healing to them but they seek it out anyway. Those who are trying to hide out and avoid their own work will always become uncomfortable in your presence, without knowing quite why it is so. You should not take this personally. And, here comes the part that you shouldn't take too seriously," she said, as she continued using her hands and arms to punctuate while her wings fanned outward.

"They may sometimes look for reasons to malign and persecute you since they must project upon you all those things about themselves they are unwilling to see and to heal. If you truly understand what is going on, these things are not that difficult to dismiss. You understand that you are presenting an opportunity for these dear souls to learn from your example. At the same time, they are also strengthening love and compassion in you.

Blessing them with your softness, you pass through their lives. You have become the butterfly and you are expressing the very freedom that they seek as the Light of the world. You are showing them The Way as you, yourself, understand it more deeply." A tear was visibly forming in the corner of her right eye, as she turned, taking a couple of steps back to gain her composure. She looked at them and smiled radiantly.

This is my desire, thought the Mu(s) simultaneously. The longing within them was wonderful to behold.

"I know, my darlings. This is why you are preparing for the time of *The Fulfillment*. Making it through your own Dark Night is part of it. The importance of this was created in your own mind long ago. As we learned in our first exercise, the goal is always first created in the mind, isn't it?

Now, let's move on to the other issue of importance ----- removing our prejudices or barriers to love. We cannot be enlightened without removing them and we cannot remove them without first identifying them."

"And how do we do that?" asked Mu 5. "How do we even know when we have them? I can see them in others easier than I can see them in myself."

"Yes, I know it seems difficult but it is really quite easy. Remember when you were reading your book of life during your Remembrance? There were many instances of anger and fear, weren't there?"

The Mu(s) began to spin forward, displaying muted red and murky blue in their energy fields as they remembered.

"Anger and fear point the way to your prejudices or barriers to Love," said the Angel, Alcyona. "These emotions create Separation energies. Think for a moment, who do you push away? Doesn't this say it all? Use these recognitions as fodder for the analytical mind. You can figure this out."

Oh good, thought Mu 9, *I'm glad I'm finally going to get to use it!*

Alcyona smiled, indicating her awareness of the thought as she continued. "If we would use our analytical mind in those irrational moments of anger and fear, we could quickly release all of our prejudices, our barriers to love and our separation energies. In the act of doing so, we would find Oneness. Isn't it more wholesome to experience love than to stand alone as separate from others and from our Creator? We must learn to use analytical mind where it truly matters, where it can dispel myths rather than create them."

Hummmm... thought Mu 9, *I have used it to separate rather than to unite and more than once, it has led me to make judgements that were not valid.*

"At the very first sign of anger or fear, a good dose of analytical mind, properly used, will often neutralize those negative emotions. It can quickly defuse prejudice which created the Separation energy in the first place."

"I see," said Mu 9. "I need to start using analytical mind in areas where I have never thought of using it before?"

To this, Alcyona responded, "Yes, and you need to lighten up on using it in the areas where you have overemphasized its use. If scientists used intuitional mind a little more often, they might have a great deal more to verify with analytical mind." She chuckled at this, using her wings as laughter accompaniment. "The miracles are there, whether or not they are seen. Intuitional mind can bring them to Light just like that," she said, snapping her fingers. "And then analytical mind can prove their existence!" She laughed, as she waddled in a circle, poking fun at Earth's pollution of the process with her restricted movement.

Mu 9's energy field was becoming more vibrant in its colors of blue, green and yellow as it contemplated the far reaches of these ideas. The scientific method was taking on a whole new meaning. She pondered the use of it to identify and eliminate her own prejudices.

"One thing is for sure," said Alcyona. "Anger, fear and its judgment, *hatred*, are indicators of work needing to be done. Whenever *you feel* these emotions, remember to acknowledge that they say far more about *you* than they do about *them*. If you are the one experiencing the anger, fear or hatred, then the prejudice or barrier to love belongs to you, doesn't it? Who else could it belong to? Analytical mind will allow you to see it!"

Mu 9's colors began to undulate, changing shape and brilliance in creative contemplation while emphasizing the color yellow and integrating it in different ways within the spectrum of color that defined Mu 9. *The analysis should be in relation to myself instead of in relation to the other person or group. Then intuition can help me apply it.* Alcyona realized that Mu 9 was on to something and she graciously bowed, acknowledging the dedication to go within oneself to get beyond it.

The Angel then addressed the group and energetically said, "It's test time! I want to know what you have absorbed from this discourse. I shall give you an opportunity now to work together and to later present to me a demonstration of the knowledge that you think is important to remember and carry forward from The Garden of Remembrance. Be as creative as you dare to be. Anything goes. I'll be back shortly." With a sweep of her right hand, Alpha then divined a sun rising in the distance and, spreading her beautiful wings, she took flight.

With a brightening of his colors to the edge of psychedelic, Mu 6 blurted out, "Bird lady gone!"

"Yes, and Bird-Brain on the loose," replied Mu 9, turning backwards in fits and starts above Mu 6's energy field!

Facing the rest of the group, Mu 6 expressed, "It is situations like this that have driven me to drink!"

Everyone had a wonderful laughter release as Mu 6 and Mu 9 made bubbles of energy, emanating upward in every color, resembling champagne, complete with the sound of a cork popping. They then merged their energy fields into a hug that was filled with Spirit. This was followed by a joyous and energetic pile-on by the rest.

Yes, Cindy and Tom related in Spirit the way they interacted on Earth. It was a good relationship even though they were good at vexing each other. *Where in the world is he?*

"Hello, this is Tom Gorman."

"Where have you been? It's been ringing forever! I was beginning to get concerned. Where were you?"

"I was in the yard basking in the sun with Pep, thinking some serious thoughts. What's up Angel Girl? Is something wrong?"

"No, I just wanted to let you know how much I love you!"

"I love you too, Angel Girl."

"Tom, this day has really blown my circuits! I can't believe what happened this morning in New York and Washington! Last night I had these powerful dreams and I don't know how to tell you the next part. Tom, I'm reading the most fantastic book!"

"It wouldn't be *The Fulfillment*, would it"

"How did you know?"

"You left me a copy in a strategic place."

"But I didn't."

"Really? Interesting! Well, listen to this. Jim just called me and said he found a copy of it in his mailbox this morning."

This is heavy stuff! "I found my manual on the car seat this morning. I know this must have something to do with my dreams last night. Something very unusual is going on here. I haven't quite figured it out yet. Let's talk about this at dinner tonight. Are you cooking?" she asked.

"Yep. It's your workout day, isn't it?"

"Yes, but I may skip it today."

"I'll either cook or pick up Chinese. Are you up for that?" he asked.

"Sure, that's fine, remember no MSG or my ankles will look like your neck!"

"Well, thanks!"

"Love you!"

"Love you too! See you later."

As Mu(s) 6 and 9 separated, Mu 1 took charge by spinning out to project thoughts to the group from a comfortable distance. Mu 1 had many natural qualities of leadership. With emphasis, this Mu said: "All right group, let's get to work."

All the other Mu(s) bowed profusely and projected in unison, "Yes, your Mu-ness!"

Mu 7 projected softly to Mu 8, "Bet if it's a she this time around, she's a

86

princess!"

"Yes, probably from Belgrade," expressed Mu 8. The two of them could hardly contain themselves.

Her Mu-ness began to suggest: "Why don't each of us identify the major ideas we think are important and then come together as a group to decide on how we want to present them?" The Mu(s) acknowledged their agreement. As she finished her instructions, she quickly created some jagged edges of her energy field and pointed them toward Mu 7 and 8.

Mu 7 and 8 buzzed Mu 1 with a little playful tweak and all of the Mu(s) then separated and began to think.

Far beyond the horizon, Alcyona could hear the melodic sounds of twelve flutes, pensively playing.

Allowing them sufficient time to complete the assignment, Alcyona swooped in for an efficient landing. Stopping on a dime directly in front of Mu 6, and spreading her wings slowly and with elegance, she joyously exclaimed with a little more volume than usual, "Bird lady back!"

Wonderful moments of laughter enveloped them all as the entire group of Mu(s) then became one large energy field, which merged with Alcyona in the expression of love and joy.

They separated and she eyed each of them carefully and smiled. She was quite pleased with the intensity and balance of the spectrum of colors displayed by the group. She was careful to notice that all colors were present in each field, even though each field was quite unique. "Are you ready to present the demonstration of what you have learned from this session?" With great seriousness she said, "The hope of the world depends on you."

All of the Mu(s) were spinning clockwise at different speeds. They looked and sounded like an orchestra tuning up. Alcyona moved through them and divined a large and elegant director's chair upon a pedestal, which slowly revolved for one complete revolution. On the back of it was written: Alcyona B. De Mille. She took her place front and center and smiled. The Mu(s) delighted in her sense of humor and her complete comfort in allowing herself all forms of self-expression.

Mu 8 nodded to the Mu(s) and moved to the side as the rest of the Mu(s) formed a group in the center. This Mu divined the physical form of a male dressed in formal attire consisting of a tux, high hat and cane. It was John at his best!

Alcyona thought, *Wonder if he's going to tap? He might even pull Ginger Rogers out of his hat!* Before she knew it, she was humming a thought or thinking a hum, *La da da da da, the Continental, la da da ....* Alcyona prided herself on her knowledge of theatre, especially the part of it that was recorded on film. When she was between classes, she was often in the screening room watching while playing every part.

Mu 8 began, "In our dramatic presentation, the group will express itself through action and movement and I shall serve as our moderator."

"This sounds fascinating," said Alcyona. "I am pleased that you have used your creativity. Exercise it often, my darlings. The creative process can often be a method for bringing Light to Truth. Do we have a name for this little ditty?" she asked.

"The title is *The Blanket of Love*," responded Mu 8, as he bowed grandly to Alcyona.

The group energy began to swirl and to move into a rectangular form displaying a pallet of the entire spectrum of color within its borders. It formed a large blanket of moving color.

"In the beginning, *The Blanket of Love* began as a thought in the mind of The Source of All Good. It was created as a visual representation of the greatest potential for the Earth experience, with everyone and all things united in the warmth of love, compassion and Oneness. This blanket was indeed very large, soft, warm and comforting. It was known that when individuals separated from it, as they could do at will, they were only able to take a small portion of the Blanket with them, as well as only a small portion of the warmth and love. Instead of Oneness, they then experienced Separation."

The Mu(s) then separated into 11 smaller individual Blankets of Love.

"Individual mind and free will control the experience of Oneness and Separation," Mu 8 continued.

The Mu(s) merged into one large rectangle and separated again, as Alcyona experienced this dance of design and color with delight.

"Analytical mind sometimes convinces us that Separation is in our best interest," continued the Moderator.

All of the colors within each blanket then became separate and distinct, appearing as horizontal stripes of rainbow colors.

"Intuitional mind allows us to use our power of thought to arrive at new conclusions," said Mu 8 with the wave of his cane as a wand.

The colors in each individual blanket then began to lose their distinction, flowing and merging into each other Impressionistically. Then, each individual Blanket of Love began to alternate, separating their color bands. Using sound, suction seemed to organize each band of color to suggest analytical mind at work, while the sound of flowing water allowed the colors to integrate with each other to suggest the use of intuitional mind. Analytical mind was the inhalation and intuitional mind, the exhalation.

On Earth, John, the Mu 8 vibration, found himself thinking about Lynn and his family. He was experiencing the manual on a super conscious level and was consciously surprised that he was thinking these thoughts. He picked up the phone and dialed home. No one answered. He called Lynn's cell phone and went to voice mail. He hung up without leaving a message.

Alcyona found the visual display quite interesting. She thought to herself, *Not only have they learned their lessons well, they are very adept at expressing their ideas. This should help them with their communication skills when they return to physical form.*

"Using the full complement of our mental expression can lead us to Oneness," said Mu 8, looking like a flying Peter Pan, levitating himself to become part of the group. Golden stars radiated outward as the process of Oneness completed itself.

The Mu(s) then again merged into one large Blanket, expressing more of their warmer colors. "One large *Blanket of Love* is warmer and more comforting."

All the colors in the One large *Blanket of Love* began to move, forming a pattern, appearing as a field of lilies in a garden.

Mu 8 rose upward to walk among the lilies as he continued, "Remembrance of the Light of Love is the answer to all questions. It is the path to the release of Separation in the world."

The Blanket of Love then began to move away from Alcyona. "Fly over us, Alcyona, that we may be reminded to always reflect upon Oneness as the answer," he said, as the entire pattern then began to move.

Alcyona then divined the pure white body of a bird as all traces of her human form disappeared. Immediately thereafter, Mu 8 released his human appearance. He became the pure energy of a radiant rainbow and merged with the *Blanket of Love*.

Alcyona began to fly over it like a weightless pilot, safely guiding them to the Truth of One. Together, they flew through an understanding that the Dark Night of the Soul allowed them to align with the Truth. The Angel Alcyona looked down at them and felt endless love and compassion. She wept as she continued making her way toward the horizon. Catching her breath, she began projecting her thoughts to her students. "You have done well; you have done very, very well! Just remember to always live in the world as if you are still in The Garden of Remembrance." The *Blanket of Love* then merged with her as she continued her flight into the Central Sun.

On the other side, they separated once again, reflecting upon their journey with Alcyona. Mu 6 blurted out, "Fantastic!"

"Talk about a trip!" said Mu 8.

Mu 9 whispered, "Very interesting…"

As they looked around at each other, they noticed a beautiful golden glow to their energy fields. Alcyona had turned back into her familiar form of half woman, half bird and was arranging her pouf. She then continued.

"Whew, what a class! I am so thoroughly pleased with your progress and the depth of your understanding."

All twelve of them sent her a silent message of gratitude..

Mu 6 said, "I promise that I am going to try to remember everything this time."

Mu 1 exclaimed, "I'm going to do my best to lead the way."

"Thank you for your wisdom as I try to remember mine," said Mu 9.

Alcyona bowed once again to all of them. Catching a glimpse of her tears, the Mu(s) felt deeply touched and blessed.

Sahab's energy then began to be felt by everyone and Alcyona said, "Well, darlings, I guess it is time for you to go now. We shall meet again in heart and mind every time you see a bird flying. If you're lucky, you might just see one with a lavender pouf," she said as she patted it and preened. "Of course, we are very rare."

The Mu(s) giggled.

"Yes, darlings, a special part of us shall always recall this wonderful time we've shared together," she said, extending her arms out to the fullest while stretching her wings. Allowing them to relax, she smiled at her students.

The Angel looked at Mu 6 for what seemed like the longest period of time and then said quite dramatically while expanding her wings in a haughty manner, "Bird lady never gone!"

One last round of energy laughter expressed itself as a joyous end to a wonderful experience and a new beginning.

"I shall become the Light for you now," she said, as she again completely released her human form, taking back her avian body. Flapping her wings efficiently, lifting up and pausing to display the miracle in humming bird fashion, she said, "Follow me."

With her flock in tow, they flew to the West in perfect "A" formation.

CHAPTER TEN

Classroom #22

Tom felt a strong urge for a drink. He was even somewhat ready to accept that his problem was once more out of control. One more drying out period just might do the trick. Tom usually allowed himself a period of time when he worked up to facing the problem, and then Bam! He was on the way to giving it his best. It was always a mystery to him, as to exactly how that moment arrived.

Today he was craving alcohol but instead of giving in to it, he decided to use it as an exercise to learn more about himself. *What is it that happens inside of me to precipitate the urge?* he thought, for the first time in his life. He longed for understanding.

Tom found himself standing at the kitchen sink without remembering his trip there. Briefly, he thought about the bottle that was hidden behind the trash can. He then poured himself a glass of iced tea, went back outside, picked up his manual and continued reading.

Sahab took the form of a large, handsome, black male with dark hair, curly and soft. His skin was light brown and his nose was thin and sculptured. His dark eyes danced with mischief, yielding in importance only to his broad and generous smile. He was over six feet tall, with the chest of a football player. His golf bag by his side, he was casually dressed in a white and black polo shirt, black trousers and black, designer, leather shoes. He appeared as an interesting combination of darkness and light. Visually, everything was black and white. Sahab would use recent Earth realities to more strongly evoke awareness among his students.

The Master Teacher then began preparing his materials and teaching aids for the continuation of the course. There was a large lightboard up front. He prepared to use it by affixing the laser extension writer to his right index finger. He then connected the color pallet, which rested flat on the back of his right hand, and secured it around his wrist. This method allowed those more accustomed to physical reality to see how things were happening. The whole concept of control was more important while the Soul was in the physical world because one was less aware of the mind's involvement as Spirit.

He could also use this apparatus exclusively in mental mode by projecting thought to the colors on the pallet. This was a much easier method when operating from Spiritual awareness. He tried out the manual method for a moment or two, making certain that it was operating properly. He then put a snug dark glove on his right hand and a white golf glove on his left.

The lightboard would now give color definition to the projection of his thoughts however he desired. The students would be able to better see how things were happening. While the students would need to begin making peace with analytical mind, he knew Mu 9 would especially enjoy this vestige of visual proof. Mu 9 always sought to understand "how" and "why" things were so.

Sahab chuckled to himself as he contemplated this. He knew that from a Spiritual perspective, _how_ was none of our business but the conventions of the Earth dream experience demanded treatment of the visual-proof idea. He must teach with awareness that his students had one foot in both worlds, without the realization that this was so. If the students were to succeed, making use of the proper conventions would help to facilitate the learning process.

Sahab then projected Spiritual energy through his eyes to each of the twelve gemstone pedestals. As he focused intently on each gemstone, his dark eyes emitted violet rays, as a dance of energy crackled around the half-circle of gemstones. They were arranged in the pattern of a half moon, with the indented section facing the front of the class where the lightboard was now clearly visible.

The gemstones glowed with vivid radiant energy. Sahab was tuning them to serve as a catalyst in the learning process. The tuning process was slightly different for each of the Mu(s), and was determined with prior consideration of Alcyona's report on their individual Soul evolvement status.

Facing the gemstone pedestals in the front of the room, from left to right, they were numbered 1-12. The gemstones were as follows: 1. Ruby 2. Diamond 3. Garnet 4. Turquoise 5. Quartz Crystal 6. Pyrite 7. Rose Quartz 8. Jade 9. Sapphire 10. Malachite 11. Lapis Lazuli and 12. Amethyst. Once the gemstone pedestals were energized and properly tuned, Sahab was ready for his students.

The Mu(s) floated in on the energy of joy and laughter. They anticipated their reunion with their beloved Master Teacher. They noticed the black man standing there, smiling at them. They thought they were to meet Sahab but this man looked nothing like him. They couldn't quite figure it out. The familiarity of this man seemed to somehow create a strange kind of unrest and uneasiness that they couldn't quite understand. They also did not understand the significance of why he was here. Their thought processes searched the room for Sahab.

Failing to find him, they tentatively moved to their gemstone pedestals where they fully intended to think things over while they waited for Sahab. As they touched down, the increased energy surprisingly sent each one catapulting straight up into the air like a hot potato. Sahab chuckled as he eyed this event. Their forward motion was anything but easy going. Slowly and tenuously touching down, separating quickly and then touching down again, they began acclimating to the increased energy emanating from their gemstone. The Mu(s) began to communicate with each other on the meaning of this strange man.

Mu 1 flashed thoughts to Mu 7, *What do you make of this situation? Where's Sahab? Do you recognize this man?*

Mu 7 responded, *I'm as much in the dark as you are. Maybe Mu 9 knows what's happening here.*

Beats me! expressed Mu 9.

Sahab absorbed everything but did not reveal this to them.

The Mu(s) concluded that perhaps he might be there to deliver a message from Sahab. They bowed to him, hoping that he might offer some explanation. He bowed back to them and smiled.

After an uncomfortable silence, Mu 3 projected, "Are we in Classroom #22?" The dark man nodded yes, and continued looking at each one of them in scrutinizing manner.

Mu 5 expressed concern, "Sir, we're just a little confused. We thought we were to be meeting with our teacher, Sahab. May we ask who you are?"

"I am Sahab. Do you not recognize me?" he said, gesturing with both hands.

The twelve energy fields began to circle him, pausing here and there for a closer look. Returning to their pedestals, they twitched as they turned to face each other. There was a long silent pause filled with many unasked questions.

Then Mu 5 expressed, "Why do you look so different? Are you trying to tell us something?"

"Bingo! What do you think that I am trying to say?" he asked, looking around.

Once again, the Mu(s) began to buzz around him in scrutiny, pausing here and there for a closer look.

"Are you trying to say something regarding darkness and Light?" asked Mu 4.

"Yes, they are One," said Sahab. "Darkness is like the back side of the moon. What else am I trying to say?" asked Sahab as he took a putter and a golf ball from his golf bag and began to practice.

"Perhaps it's something about tapping the golf ball," projected Mu 5. "Maybe it's a symbol of the Earth?"

"Watch this," said Sahab, as he took off the dark glove from his right hand. Activating the manual control with his left hand, he projected color onto the lightboard creating a well manicured golf green complete with flag in cup. Like virtual reality, Sahab sank the ball into the cup with one stroke of the ball and said, "Oneness is always the goal and this happens to be called a hole in one. What else am I trying to tell you? What do you think Mu 6?"

Giving him the slow once-over from head to toe, Mu 6 said, "Those shoes are ugly enough to drive a person to drink," as the group reverberated with the energy of laughter.

"Just remember that the group you are guiding will use absolutely *any reason* for that purpose," Sahab chuckled. "Class, we may have a case here of the blind leading the blind!"

The class circled noisily around Mu 6 and then merged with his energy field, as they exuded feelings of love and compassion. They truly loved this Soul even though, at times, Mu 6 was often not quite certain of it.

It was exactly the same problem for Tom. He was well liked by everyone. The man clearly never met a stranger. Unless he was tanked, he was never offensive. One of his problems was that he could never see or accept how much he was loved. It had to do with the vast amount of guilt that he carried for being weak. *If they only knew, they could not possibly love me!* The only deviation from this formula was Cindy. Without reservation, he knew without a doubt that she loved him, in spite of himself. And of course, there was Pep.

Tom sat in his favorite chaise on the patio. He read voraciously and seemed energized by the process. Pep absorbed Tom's thoughts through his hand, as he petted her gently. Whenever he paused for too long, she licked his hand to start the process again. He stopped for a minute and looked at her. Leaning down to rub her ears, he said, "With you and Cindy, what more do I need? You're my girls!"

Sahab looked around at the group and questioned, "What else, what else?"

The Mu(s) huddled together to confer for a moment. Then Mu 9 turned to address Sahab. "I've got it; I've got it. Your shirt is light and everything else is dark. Your golf bag is mostly light with just a little bit of dark on the trim. One glove is dark and the other one is light. Each has the goal and potential of Oneness and one and one are two. Are we to discuss the concept of duality?" asked the analytical Mu 9.

This Mu had clearly been around the block before and would carry forth much intellectual knowledge gained through many previous Earth experiences. Mu 9 intended to hit the beach running, using the intellect to make sense of the world.

On Earth, Cindy was very much the Mu 9 that she was in Spirit. She was sharp as a tack. She could figure out how to do anything that she wanted to accomplish. Right now, she was intent on making some sense of this manual. She placed a "Do Not Disturb" sign on her office door and continued reading.

Sahab smiled and said to the group, "See where analytical mind can take you? That and about three dollars these days will buy you a nice Cappuccino on Earth. That is, if you buy it before the markets do strange things."

"What?" exclaimed Mu 8, excitedly, "What about the markets?" Sahab ignored him and continued.

"What I am trying to say to you, my dear students, is that you may not always recognize your teacher. When you came into the room, you began looking around for me even though I was standing right here all of the time. You had expectations of how I should appear and this created the problem of your not being able to recognize me.

What I am going to say to you is one of the most important things you will ever hear me say. While you are on Earth, everyone, *absolutely everyone and everything* is there to be your teacher, but the lessons you learn are always up to you. If you do not recognize the teacher, you will judge the lesson and, in doing so, you will fail to gain from the experience."

"Oh yes," said Mu 12 slowly and thoughtfully, "I think I know who you are impersonating." This Mu was extremely comfortable using intuitional mind and remembered a criminal trial where violence seemed to be the victor.

Sahab continued, "It is usually easier to embrace those who follow a path of Light and to reject those who follow a path of darkness. It is also easy to forget that those who follow a path of darkness are trying to find the Light, just like you are. They have simply made a choice that has made it more difficult for them to get there. Anger and fear are driving the car and it usually leads to a loss of control.

To the far extreme, this becomes hatred. What you must understand is that it is hatred of self, projected outward. It will always get them lost in the circular maze where they may continue to make poor choices and go in directions that make the trip more difficult. That's what happened to this man that you think you recognize. That's what's happening now on Earth with the Terrorists.

Nevertheless, they are trying to get to the Light even though that's not how it looks. It is your judgment of their choices that can steal your lesson because it keeps you from recognizing them as your teacher. The lesson to learn here is where fear, hatred and anger might lead a person. It is an important lesson to be learned. "

The Mu(s) buzzed with contemplation energy as the intensity of their colors randomly brightened and diminished. *This color choreography appears to be moving in the right direction*, thought Sahab. *This is so important!*

"You see, my students, we can only write the outline here. It is there that we develop the term paper, and we do so by the choices we make. Once we make a difficult choice, the only way to clear it is by affirming the Truth to ourselves and to others. It is only through forgiveness that we can clear the slate.

The tendency, however, is to misperceive, to lie and to avoid taking responsibility for our actions. We must find the truth, tell it and accept the consequences. In the end, there is no faster way to peace. We cannot forgive ourselves until we do so nor can we be forgiven. We can choose to lie to everyone else but it is impossible to ever really lie to ourselves. It is *that* lie that will consume us and *that* Truth that sets us free."

Tom thought about how he had lied to himself, to Cindy and everyone else in his world about his addictions. *Why do I continue lying to myself*, he thought? If he but knew the answer to this question, he could accept responsibility for those lies right now, forgive himself and things might be different.

Sahab thought, *Mother-Father Source, use me now as a catalyst to complete their understanding. Speak through me now as I step aside.*

"Do not fail to recognize a teacher in everyone you meet. Those who live in the Light will show us The Way. Those who take a path of darkness will show us what happens when we lose our way and choose Separation from the Light. And those who choose Separation and call it Light, well, that's quite another matter. That's what Holy Wars are made of."

Sahab used the manual control on the lightboard to illustrate a choice gone awry in the circular maze. It looked like modern dance choreography by Martha Graham, filled with contractions and dissonant staccato movements. A young man went around in circles as his frustration escalated. Colors danced, moving from yellow to red and then to black.

"Choosing Separation, regardless of the name we give it, is the only poor choice that we ever really make. We can learn from everything and everyone if we will turn our judgment into compassion, not approval mind you, but compassion."

"Sahab, when we are in the physical body, why do we seem to lose our mind? How can we know we are choosing Separation instead of Oneness?" questioned Mu 4.

Sahab looked thoughtfully at Mu 4 and said, "The answer lies in the feeling that accompanies the thought." He once again worked the lightboard and on one side he wrote in the warm color of pink ----- "Oneness always feels good and Love is associated with it. This is Mu." On the other side, he wrote in the cool color of midnight blue ----- Fear and Separation go together and they never feel good. This is Lagitard.

"There is also another important way to know. When our choices create pain for us or for others, we know that we have chosen to separate. In other words, listen to the things that cause you pain and make a different choice. If it should bring you peace and joy, then you will know that you have chosen a path of Light."

"Sahab, is there a way that we can know the choice is going to be a difficult one *before* we act on it?" asked Mu 4.

"One of the most important functions that our feelings serve while we are on the Earth is to alert us that we may need to choose again. If anger and fear are a part of the feelings that either dictate or accompany the choice, for heaven's sake (no pun intended), choose again!"

The group gave way to laughter, which seemed to lighten up their energies as Sahab continued. They began spinning clockwise, slowly and easily.

"There is far greater good to be achieved by making many choices which finally result in peace and joy, than by making a few choices that never seem to get us there. Forgiveness is the thing we can employ to avoid staying stuck with a *difficult choice* that only serves to amplify our pain. Rationalizing why it was necessary for us to make that choice only fuels the fire of our internal pain. In other words, stop trying to be right! Forgiving ourselves and receiving the correction that it provides is the best way to relieve ourselves of pain."

Mu 6 imploringly asked, "How in the world do we forgive ourselves? We just can't ignore what happened? How can we change history?"

Sahab looked at Mu 6, asking Spirit to direct the symphony of understanding. "Forgiveness is a matter of release," he said. "Let's suppose that you are in the physical body and you have a large boil on your back.

The infection and inflammation around this boil is what makes it painful. Once that hurtful part has been released, you feel better, even though there may always be a scar to serve as a remembrance of the fact that it was there.

So, it is not a matter of changing the historical event. It's about changing the way you think and feel about it. Here's the secret of how to forgive yourself and others. Release your judgment of the event and you will be able to see it differently. Think of judgment as being synonymous with inflammation. That is what causes the pain; release it and you will be able to forgive."

Thoughtfully, Mu 6, said: "Like, I've messed up and I've fallen off the wagon. Instead of making myself into an idiot and feeling guilty about it, I simply say, The Devil made me do it?"

"Not exactly." said Sahab, "You must accept the responsibility for your actions. Judging yourself to be a bad person and feeling guilty about it only sets you up to fail again. By avoiding judgment, you can release the pain accompanying the event. While it will not change the historical fact, it will change the way you feel about it."

Mu 6's energy field began spinning forward in an easy going manner, changing in color from yellow to pale blue and then to soothing pink. Sahab surveyed the energy closely and thought to himself, *We're moving in the proper direction, thank you, Source!*

Tom continued to read his manual and to operate the petting machine. For no apparent reason, his breathing suddenly became slow and deep. He stopped reading the book and petting Pep and looked up at the clouds. Both his inhalation and exhalation became measured and equal in duration. He felt totally at peace. He watched a bank of clouds drift by and thought, *There goes the past.* He felt Pep's nudge and he began to give her what she wanted as he again resumed his reading.

Addressing the group, Sahab continued, "To be able to release our pain, we sometimes also need the forgiveness of others, but it is always secondary to our need for self-forgiveness."

The Mu(s) pondered these thoughts with varying amounts of energy. Some seemed wiser than others but the truth lay in the fact that each one was perfect and complete in his wisdom. It was a matter of slowly finding the parts of it that had been overlooked. Mu 11 and 12 had a fairly complete understanding of the intellectual part of this process but needed more work in its implementation. Mu 5 and 9 sometimes got stuck in placing blame. Mu 1 often found it difficult to get beyond the fact that it was the fault of others, but Mu 6 was beginning to put two and two together.

It was the same way on Earth. While everyone was primarily of one Mu vibration or another, each had different challenges and hang-ups. Even within any one numerical vibration, there were many variations on the theme of lessons to be learned. Everyone was striving toward the same end ----- to find their way to Love. They were all in the same play but they were coming onstage from different positions, with different obstacles in their paths.

Sahab was on a roll and he continued, "So, here's your gauge for determining your progress on the way to realizing Oneness, Mu 4. If the thoughts you have and the actions you take bring you peace and joy, you have chosen wisely. If they cause you pain, then choose again.

Your choices will lead you to your plan of correction which always involves forgiving yourself and others for any misdeed. Your perception of this has little to do with it, even though it usually looks that way. It has everything to do with you, with the thoughts you think and the pain you feel. The whole drama can *only* be about you as you contemplate it," he said, while gradually moving closer to the Mu(s).

Sahab then used the mental mode to reestablish the golf green on the lightboard. He then addressed the ball. With an easy motion, he took just enough of a back swing and followed through to make a hole in one.

Easy does it, forward motion thought the Mu(s). They began displaying this through the clockwise movement of their energy fields. Sahab bowed to them with his approval and then he disappeared.

CHAPTER ELEVEN

The Other Side of the Moon

Moments later, Sahab reappeared standing at the left side of the room in Classroom #22 dressed as a Magician. He appeared in the physical form they recognized as Sahab. The hat and cape were purple, with the sun, moon and stars aesthetically placed in silver and gold: woven into the fabric, strengthening it. The tall hat extended upward to a point and matched his cape perfectly. With a flourish, Sahab extended his wand, waved it in a circular motion around the half moon of students and divined a human body for each of them.

Mu 6 was given the body of a male. He was casually dressed in tan slacks and a colorful Hawaiian short sleeved shirt.

The body of a woman was given to Mu 9. Her blond hair was in a bun on top of her head, giving new meaning to the term "uptight." She wore a tailored light blue oxford blouse with a buttoned down collar, navy blue slacks and sensible shoes.

Mu 8 was divined into a male body, wearing a three-piece blue pinstriped business suit.

Given a female body, Mu 10 was quite a sight ----- a gorgeous black woman with short, nappy hair covered by a multi-colored headscarf. She wore an elegant and boldly colorful kafgan. In her own description, this was considered all-purpose wear which she loved to uniquely accessorize.

An interesting thing began to happen as they looked around at each other. They began to form judgments about what they saw. It was somewhat disturbing.

Mu 9 took one look at Mu 10 and thought, *That's about as gaudy as you can get!* Mu 10 looked at Mu 9 and thought, *Plainest Jane I've ever seen!* Mu 8 looked at the ladies while smiling broadly and thought, *Bunny and Lynn everywhere!*

Sahab then used the wand to point in the direction of the lightboard. Using the mental mode, he raised it while lowering the apparatus for the Potential Projector Image Reflector. It looked like magic.

Emanating from it was a three-dimensional well-dressed man who stood behind a podium in a political arena. He appeared to be in his fifth decade. His hair was gray and coarse, and his face appeared boyish and sincere. His expensive blue suitcoat accented the color of his eyes, which danced with intelligence. He was handsome and this man was clearly one step ahead of the pack.

Mu 8 studied him with great interest.

The man began to speak in a voice that seemed very familiar to them. In a Southern drawl, he said, "Look deep into my heart and tell me what you see."

While closing his eyes and placing both hands on his forehead to conjure intuitive insight, Mu 1 began, "It was that first lie so many, many moons ago that never was undone, that never was owned up to, that never came to Light, that never was forgiven."

"I see," said Mu 6, "He never forgave himself. He never cleared the slate."

"Very good," said Sahab, "Now let's continue with the process. Mu 2?"

"The lies had to repeat themselves so they could come to Light," expressed Mu 3. Sahab's gaze then rested on Mu 4.

"Because he never accepted responsibility for the first lie, he was likely to make difficult choices which would then lead to more lies, over and over again." Sahab nodded to the next one.

Mu 5 continued, "Righteous or difficult behavior only begets more of itself. The lies tied themselves to sexual energies and great risk. All of it was but a call for healing, which could not happen until the lies came to Light."

Mu 6 then compassionately expressed, "What does it profit a man if he gains the whole world and loses his own Soul?"

"There is a greater lesson here," expressed Mu 7. "This is not drama on a high school stage ----- this is World Theater! If this reality is large enough for everyone in the world to experience, what is this saying to us about our own lies? In a profound way, does this not speak to the entire world about the tremendous amount of lying that all of us need to heal? If it were not in us, we could not see it in him."

Sahab nodded his approval and pointed to Mu 8.

The man in the business suit responded. "Each of us has the choice to use this man and his difficult choices as either a lightening rod and a wake-up call or as a rush to judgment. If we lose ourselves in judging him, we miss another miracle." Across a stream of consciousness, John swallowed hard, as he faced his own wake-up call.

Mu 9 began as Cindy joined her in thinking the same thoughts at the same time. "A wake up call allows us to learn ----- judgement denies us growth. We think that all of this has something to do with him and it does so, only as he contemplates his own behavior. As we contemplate his behavior, we can only face our own reality. *The Way* can be shown to us by many different methods and reverse analogy is but one of them," said the analytical one. *I need to remember this one*, thought Mu 9.

Sahab was nodding in agreement and said, "Students, you are doing very well with this. Let me ask you, why do you think that you are able to view this fairly recent part of Earth's memory, with such objectivity? Mu 10, what do you think?"

Mu 10 pondered a moment and said, "Could it be because we are looking at the situation through our Divinity?"

"Yes, and just what does that mean, Mu 11?"

"Through our Oneness?"

"Yes! When we join with him, we are able to look into his heart with love and compassion. We are then able to learn the lessons that are there for each of us. When we separate from him, we judge his actions and learn nothing that we can put to any good use in our own lives."

Mu 12 quickly interjected, "And when we judge him harshly, we are looking into our own hearts, not liking what we see ----- therefore, choosing Separation from him and from the Light within us."

"Yes, yes, yes," said Sahab. "This is the kind of vision that is so needed now. We can only punish ourselves with our lies, whether or not they come to light in the moment. His own lies are punishing him and that is quite enough. That's what we should see. That is the lesson."

They looked again at the man and noticed that he was weeping. The students projected their thoughts of peace and love as they looked at him with great compassion. It felt wonderful to complete their own correction.

Sahab said, "Love and compassion, big lessons in life, now let's use the Potential Projector Image Reflector to get in touch with other probabilities. Suppose a plan of correction had been put into place after the first lie?"

For a moment, the screen went dark. Pure colors then began to swirl amid dissonant sounds. They formed the image of a young man named Will, playing saxophone in a joint on Beale Street in Memphis, Tennessee. The melodious rendition of "Ain't Misbehaving" got everyone's toe tapping. The Mu(s) began to move and sway as they enjoyed listening to the joyful sounds. There was great freedom and joy in this man and his music. Sahab timed the descent of the Image Reflector with the end of the piece. The Mu(s) thought to themselves, *Cool man, Cool!*

"Is this what you meant when you said we write the outline before we are born and the term paper by the choices that we make in life?" asked Mu 12.

"Yes and no," said Sahab. "Yes, he had many choices, each one with different outcomes. He took on the more difficult ones to make Spiritual progress for himself, fulfilling Karma while also providing us with a vehicle for releasing our own judgment, finding our own forgiveness and *waking up*. It is the timing of the choice that you do not understand. This is because you are in two worlds now, each having its own set of rules. You don't know which to apply. It is easy to mix your metaphors and lose your way. Don't worry about it. Everything is for the purpose of creating good, either now or later.

Have you not already started to wonder how it is that you seem to know who this man is? How is it possible that you know everything about his dramas and the evolution of his lies? There is only one simple explanation. It is because you are there now."

There was a long and thoughtful pause. Mu 5 was the first to speak, "You mean we aren't here now?"

"No, you are also here."

"How can that be?" asked Mu 3.

Sahab began. "You are in physical form on Earth. When you go to sleep at night, you come here to enrich your Spiritual knowledge so that you may put it into practice there when you wake up. You don't remember being on Earth when you are here and vice versa. In other words, it allows you to focus with greater intensity and clarity on the issue at hand. It is easier this way.

While you know the story regarding the physical facts about this man, you are growing in your Spiritual knowledge about the facts involved. You will also grow in your knowledge of the Taliban and the things that are to come. You see, your goal is to be able to live in the physical world from a Spiritual perspective. We are not talking about dogma so please do not confuse this with religion. When dogma and judgment join, as is often the case, they have nothing to do with Spiritual Truth."

"So, what you are saying is that we are there right now and here as well?" asked Mu 7.

"Yes, your Soul anchor is in a physical body on Earth which is now sleeping. As a matter of fact, your Mu vibration is in more than one body and representing both genders in different times, which also appear to be separate. Dealing with all of that will really blow your circuits unless you alter your beliefs about time, so let's not even go there. Let's just accept that you are in a physical body there now and the energy of your mind and Spirit is also here now with me."

He then began to use the Potential Projector to illustrate his thoughts as he continued. "Students, you are very old Souls. Your Spiritual essence goes back even beyond the historical record presently known on Earth. Almost 500,000 years ago, you were present in the ancient civilization of Mu on the continent called Lemuria," as a large landmass in the Pacific appeared through the Potential Projector. He continued.

109

"She was the Mother to the early civilizations of India, Babylonia, Persia, Egypt and Yucatan. Mu was more advanced than any civilizations which presently exist on the Earth today. She predated Atlantis, which itself was quite advanced. Naacal tablets found in India tell some of the story," he said, as he illustrated Burma with the Image Reflector.

"The Garden of Eden and the biblical story of creation came from the teachings of this now submerged continent of Mu, and the ancient civilizations that followed drew their culture from this one common source. It was the Lagitard influence that allowed for the fall of man ----- not a woman named Eve."

Mu 4 and Mu 9 smiled at each other and gestured a "thumbs up."

"Before the arrival of the Lagitards, only love reined in the garden," said the Teacher.

The Mu(s) sat enraptured as their auras intensified. Sahab continued. "It was there, on this now submerged continent of Lemuria in the Pacific, that the Sun came to be known as the symbol of the deity and the seven-headed serpent was first recorded as a referent to the Creator and all Creation."

Sahab projected the serpent on the dimensional Image Reflector, displaying a coiled body extending upward into seven heads. Red and yellow colors were more prevalent in the tail or lower end of the snake, which gradually gave way to green, blue, purple and violet in each of the heads. A gasping sound of fear was heard from the group. "Do not fear dear students, the Serpent speaks of your Divine nature."

In parallel realities, Mu 9 reflected on her fascination with the Indian Holy Books, as Cindy walked to her bookshelf and selected a term paper she had written on the Upanishads. Why had she been so drawn to Indian Holy Books when she had been raised in the South on black-eyed peas and Gospel music? North Carolina was a long way from India, or was it?

Cindy had brought in the old term paper to stimulate her creativity on a project. She needed some ideas for a marketing piece for an Indian client. Her company was developing a piece of software for an Asian game of chance that was to be marketed on line. Cindy had taken a break from reading her manual. She thought,

110

Why am I holding this term paper? I must be losing it! She put it back on the self and sat down at her desk to continue reading.

Sahab continued. "An example of some of this has filtered down through the holy books of India, and is found in Vedanta through the seven mental planes.

It was there on Mu that we first realized that we came from the Creator, and that it is to the Creator that we return." Sahab's voice was deeply resonant and commanding as he talked about these truths.

"Yes, I remember this," said Mu 7 softly. Sahab continued.

"The basic foundation for the 'One God' Judeo-Christian and Islamic doctrines valued in the world today originated on the lost continent of Mu. She was indeed the Motherland of all the ancient civilizations from which all people came." Sahab paused for his own reflection. "This is your heritage."

"Tell us more about the Motherland," exclaimed Mu 12, enthralled.

"Well, something not commonly known is that the lotus flower was her floral symbol since it was believed to have been the very first flower to appear upon the Earth. The lotus continues to have great Spiritual significance to this day. Yes, dear Mu(s), we have done much coming and going since then, and we are involved in our work now to fulfill prophecy of *The Fulfillment* which was long ago proclaimed."

"What happened to our Motherland? Why did she sink?" asked Mu 3.

Using the Potential Projector to visually illustrate, Sahab continued, "It was a time of much tribulation in the Earth. All of it was the result of what the Lagitards brought with them ----- fear! Tribulation was the climax to the exponential growth of fear.

There were frequent and violent volcanic eruptions and many earthquakes, tidal waves, floods and natural disasters. It was a cleansing process for Mother Earth, a dying away to make room for a new beginning. It was similar to what is happening now on Earth. And there is more, much more to come. There will be Tribulation until 2012 but believe me, all of this is good."

The Mu(s) were experiencing a tingling in their energy fields that was exciting and anticipatory in ways they did not fully understand. Sahab continued with

111

layer upon layer of knowledge, building in a way that hardly gave them time for second thoughts.

"All of you, and the many you lead through the Dark Night of the Soul, are the ones who will form the new beginning, for the dying away and the new beginning must first take place within the self. Those who willingly place themselves on the amethyst alter of *Transformation* and *Enlightenment* are choosing to participate in the new beginning; indeed, this is the *New Beginning*.

Do not worry about the difficult times to come. That is what the teachings are for. That is why you are here now. What you learn here and practice on Earth will see you through to the other side of the moon, for you are to be the *Light of the World*, every single one of you!"

The Mu(s) were aglow with possibility. They had the adrenal glands of a body working overtime and their Spiritually charged gemstones were infusing their energies with increased electrical activity. It was as if they were high and speeding on gas made from ginko biloba and pure caffeine. They were thinking with great clarity, but wondering how and where they were to begin.

Sahab could see that they were overwhelmed. He recognized that they needed time to absorb the importance of the teaching underneath the teaching, to personally align and to tighten the nuts and bolts of understanding on all the loose parts of the wheel. He could see their determination not to get lost in the circular maze this time around. With great compassion, he sent them his message of peace and love.

"I think that we have had enough for this session. Follow these instructions now and we shall take a much needed break. Walk down the hill until you hear a songbird sing. Then walk to the right for twelve steps. On the left you will find a hot spring head that is emptying into a pool of water. I think it might be just the thing you need to relax and allow your thoughts to assimilate.

Water has a wonderfully peaceful effect on us in the material world. It is because the physical body is predominantly water that it is so familiar to us. That's why it's so easy to find Oneness with water. Yes, experiencing Oneness is always very relaxing and renewing. Allow your tensions to melt into the water. It will also help you to bond with Mother Earth. On an unconscious level, it is like returning to the womb.

When all of the tension has left your mind and body, you will be able to hear the sound of a single flute playing in the key of B flat. Let the music wrap itself around you, weaving a cocoon of healing. It will deepen your receptivity and resolve for the things that are to come. We shall be talking more about your assignments a little later. For now, be on your way and have a good rest. I shall be meeting you next in the Garden of Olives. Let yourself be led to this Garden by your own inner guidance. It will be very good practice for learning to trust it more."

Oh boy, thought Mu 6. *This is shaping up to be the Big Daddy of all trips! Wonder what my assignment is all about?* Mu 6 felt a nagging ache inside his stomach that said it all.

The other Mu(s) picked up on his thought. Their eyes widened as they wondered what the rest of their own trip would reveal. Sahab then bowed to them and they reciprocated through the use of the body he had divined for them. This conscious integration of both the spiritual and physical bodies, functioning as One, would certainly take some getting use to. *It's like dancing in armor*, thought Mu 10.

As they made their way toward the springhead, Sahab began to hum in the key of B flat as he battened down the hatches of Classroom #22. He was pleased with their progress and their willingness to step out on faith to find wisdom. It was all right there within their Divinity, and they were waking up to this reality. Learning to trust it as the Truth they shared with everyone, with all things and with The Source of All Good, would become a part of their consciousness to be realized on Earth.

113

CHAPTER TWELVE

The Work To Be Done

The Mu(s) were rejuvenating in the relaxing warmth of the hot, spring-fed, crystal blue waters. Each one seemed to be drawn to his own special place in the circular pool. They stretched their arms to the side and slowly dunked down, allowing the water to come up to their chins as they looked around at each other.

Mu 11 was the first to speak. "Looks like we have really done it. We've taken on body mass, now what?"

"Lord knows," lamented Mu 2. "It certainly does slow you down!"

"What do you mean?" said Mu 12. "You're already *there* now in a tub of lard and you're dreaming this. We all are. Supposedly, we're here to learn so we can help to facilitate the time of *The Fulfillment*."

"Oscar, Oscar, tell me more!" voiced the Mu 10 drama queen. She pushed off with her large, strong feet and hoisted her weight upward with dramatic arm gestures. Turning with grace, she moved like an accomplished, classically trained, synchronized swimmer. She reflected for a moment on the similarities between movement in water and movement in Spirit. Both had this wonderful sense of freedom once the initial impetus was made.

Mu 12 continued, "We're all here together. We must be some kind of a team."

"Just show me the money!" exclaimed Mu 8 as he slapped the water with his right hand and started rubbing his thumb and fingers together. With a glint in his eye and a broad smile, he looked around at everyone. They all enjoyed a good laugh as they continued to explore the watery medium with their divined physical bodies.

"All right, wise guys, settle down," said Mu 11. "Let's relax for a moment. You guys are going crazy with this divined physical thing. Let's act like we have at least a small vestige of a mind and start using it. Perhaps intuitional mind can put this thing together for us."

One by one, they closed their eyes and started concentrating on the relaxing sounds of the bubbling water. Their breathing became slower and slower. Sighs were heard at irregular intervals and simply ignored. Gradually, the muscles of their divined physical bodies reluctantly released the built up tensions created in Classroom #22.

Their feelings of anxiety gave way to an expanded clarity of mind as each one allowed his energy to melt into the Universal Whole of Perfect Peace. Their auras slowly reflected this change, as the ebbing of their colors of red and orange gave way to blue and violet.

Mentally they chanted, almost automatically, "One, One, One..." as they recaptured the experience of Oneness and perfect peace. Mu 6 then hiccuped for emphasis. They all giggled, but quickly found their way back home to that wonderful state of perfect Peace.

An interesting awareness was beginning to take place that inspired a real appreciation for the control each had over their own interior landscape. What a novel idea! They could control this physical vehicle in which their Spirit was temporarily riding. It was the heaviness of the physical body that had momentarily fooled them into believing that it was in charge. By contrast, their Spirit was light. They were getting in touch with these issues that were so easily confused.

While they were trying on this Sahab-created physical body, it crossed their minds that they had another one, on Earth now. They wondered: *Was this body male or female? What was it like? What were the lessons it was learning? Just as they seemed to have complete control over this vehicle, they probably had the same control over that one. They had just taken this divined body from over-stimulated to perfectly peaceful. Perhaps they had the same degree of control over the other body.* They wondered about this.

Mu 6 contemplated, *I thought that alcohol would bring me peace. Hummm...*

Mu 8 reflected, *Like creating wealth would bring me perfect peace.*

116

These thoughts came to them individually and at the same time flowed freely among them creating a group experience. It was interesting to behold. Each was benefiting and expanding in awareness from the individual thoughts and from the contemplation of the collective whole. It felt perfectly natural and they considered this to be a benefit rather than an intrusion.

After much consideration, Mu 9 thought, *The challenge on Earth then is to find our way to Peace and Oneness from within and not from things on the outside of us. The 'thorn in our side' is the impetus that manifests the opportunities for making the right choices. So, whatever we see as a problem is truly our salvation. Using intuitional mind allows us to be led by our Divinity. Hummm... I may be onto something...*

Great clarity of mind ensued as a pink aura surrounded the Mu(s). They continued relaxing. When their questions ceased, their consciousness seemed to progress from a state of thinking to one of being. Instead of thinking of themselves as One, they experienced the state of being One. It was beyond verbal description and completely owned by one's own sense of feeling. With it came a feeling of Love, purely felt and freely given. Gently, they began to hear the compelling sound of a single flute in the key of B flat minor. Mesmerized, they listened without awareness of time passing, as the presence of Love and Healing permeated the Whole.

When the music ended, Mu 7 slowly opened her eyes. As she looked at the other members of the group, she noticed their auras radiating boldly, far beyond their bodies. "We are absolutely beautiful," she said. "Open your eyes and look!"

They did so and they realized that it was difficult to tell where each one stopped and the others began. Their energies melted into each other like sunlight through a windowpane, and their vision of this spoke softly of their Oneness.

This is pure, unadulterated proof, reflected Mu 9.

The beauty of this awareness became the catalyst for tears of joy as they honored each other's holiness with thoughts of Peace and Love, born of their Divine recognition.

117

Mu 1, who had now come to be known as the Prince of Belgrade (with the divined body of a male) said, "It's time for us to find our way to the Garden of Olives. Let's close our eyes and see what comes."

"Yes, your Mu-ness" said the group as they bowed to him with tongues down-stretched, showing proper reverence for the eminence of his assumed authority. The entire group was euphoric and playful with him as they followed his instruction. More than willing to laugh at himself, Mu 1 smiled, closed his eyes and reflected, *This experience of Oneness has allowed me to become so much more of who I am. Hummm....*

Ideas that came to each of them were in absolute agreement. How could this be? Everyone received the same answers and identical directions. As individuals and as a group, they were absolutely certain that the path to Sahab lay to the Northeast. They opened their eyes, pointed in that direction and in unison, they said, "Let's go, team!"

Hoisting themselves from the freedom of liquid Spirit, they quickly scrambled off to the Northeast with the Prince of Belgrade leading the way. Mu 10 was right behind, walking backwards, being careful to hold up her kafkan with one hand so as not to step on it, while improvising movement and gesture and leading everyone in song: "Hi Ho, Hi Ho, off to Sahab we go...." The group had lightened up considerably; they were enjoying the peace and unadulterated joy that came with expanded awareness alive with the potent power of their intuition.

At the entrance to the Garden, Sahab had projected a divination of himself as an extremely seductive and sensuous woman. She had bleached blond hair and she was wearing a low cut, red dress with spaghetti straps. Her voluptuous, upper torso bespoke of silicone perfection. Chewing gum, she smiled seductively at Mu 5 as she slowly shifted her weight to the left. Mu 5 paused and cautiously gave her the onceover. *Big Red* motioned him closer with the gradual flexion of one index finger. Mu 5 smiled, saluted and said, "Hi, Teach! I see the Anthrax scare will not keep you from going out on Halloween, but it's a little too early to be in costume!" The rest of the Mu(s) smiled and cat-whistled. The divination then dematerialized and the Mu(s) continued into the Garden.

Making their entrance into The Garden of Olives, they found Sahab sitting on a large mound of granite. He was sitting cross-legged on the rock where he had been meditating for quite some time. There was an extremely large aura of green around him, tinged with blue, indigo, violet and gold which the Mu(s) noticed for the first time. They were intrigued with the vision of him, which they found soothing and complete.

The Garden was laid out in concentric circles. At its center was Sahab's round mound of granite. Then came a ring of wildflowers in yellow, pink and cornflower blue, followed by a meadow of mossy green grass and finally, by a circle of olive trees. The diameter of the entire Garden was only fifty-five feet. They had indeed found a needle in a haystack. Incredulously, they looked around at each other.

"This is unbelievable," said Mu 4. Mu 12 interrupted with, "How about *We* are unbelievable!"

Sahab opened his eyes, bowed to them and said, "You have done well! I am honored to be your teacher. Please sit."

Gratefully, the Mu(s) sat down. They were getting in touch with the fact that these divined physical bodies seemed to need a little more rest than they had realized; they were happy to get off their feet for awhile. Their labored breathing quickly returned to normal. The Mu(s) were thrilled to see their beloved teacher once again and their smiles conveyed their thoughts. Sahab smiled back at them.

"I am happy to see that you seem to have lost that over-blown intensity. Too often, it produces failure in the physical world. I am talking about the state where the body is so over-stimulated with adrenaline that it keeps the mind from functioning with clarity, peace and purpose," he said, as he pointed to his head. "We must work with the body AND the mind for them to function at their best. I encourage you to see the difference in this attitude and the belief that we are merely using the body and mind for the trip."

Mu 6 thought, *Not to mention the fact that I seem to be using mine up!*

"Never forget that fear inhibits function and can render you powerless. And,

119

here's something else for you to remember ----- the wonderful mental state that you experienced in the pool of water, *and fear*, cannot coexist in the same body at the same time. When one advances, the other must retreat. Think about it. What does this mean to you my students?"

Mu 5 raised his hand. He looked as though he was running for political office in his handsome and expensive, gray business suit. Sahab recognized him and he began to speak. "We can use the state of relaxation to overcome fear, can't we?" said Mu 5.

"Well said! In a very real way, overcoming the world is about overcoming fear of one kind or another. So, now you have a way to accomplish this, Hummm? Practice up on this one, for the trials and tribulations around *imagined fear* are what lead you to the Dark Night of the Soul.

Mu 7 jumped in, "What do you mean, imagined fear?" she asked, looking lean and spiffy in her warm-up suit and running shoes. "You mean it's not real?"

"No, no, no", said Sahab. "I thought we had already covered this and that you understood: *All of it* is only illusion. It just seems real! It's like going to a movie and, for a few moments, getting wrapped up in the plot. It seems real in the moment. Your adrenaline starts pumping but when the movie ends and you're walking out the door, you realize that it was only an illusion.

Make no mistake about it. The test is always this; can you hold onto the Truth when the valued perceptions of the World experience are crumbling around you? When your spouse leaves you for another, when you lose your job or your financial worth, when the most important person in your dream decides to wake up and leave the physical form: these are the things that can throw you off-kilter. When you lose a child, when you are wrongly accused or badly treated, when you lose an important competition that you worked for years to win, when your business fails: these are the things that throw you into *imagined fear* while you are in an incarnation.

It is *imagined fear* because it isn't real, even though it seems that way. It is like a movie playing and it will be over. The *thorn in your side* is what makes it seem so real. This is so you will take it seriously and overcome it. As long as you think it's real, it can stand between you and your Divinity. Once you recognize who you are, all fear becomes inconsequential."

The Mu(s) looked around at each other while slowly nodding. They seemed to be getting it now and Sahab was pleased. No matter how many times Sahab had explained this concept, it was always a challenge. He thought for a moment, *How quickly we learn and how easily we can forget.*

"When many of these things seem to be happening in close proximity or with escalation, you will know that you are Dark Nighting. The larger question here is simply this: when these things occur, do you forget that this is only a dream (more like a nightmare) or do you remember that you are Divine? That is its only purpose, you know, to allow you to remember who you are."

Sahab could see the Mu(s) studying these thoughts with the inner recesses of their minds, as they flashed through a multitude of remembered experiences. Their eyes looked upward slightly for a long moment and then directly at their teacher.

"This is what our experience in the pool of water was all about, wasn't it?" asked Mu 11.

"Yes, my child, it was indeed. And, what do you think it was that caused you to focus upon your Divinity which, by the way, was the very experience of Oneness that you shared?" asked Sahab, looking around at the group.

Mu 4 interjected, "Could it be the relaxation that we experienced? It seemed to neutralize our anxious state."

"Yes, my child, you were neutralizing fear, weren't you? This is the first thing that must be done. It is also why all of the Great Ones, the Master Spiritual Teachers throughout all ages, cultures and civilizations have always spoken of meditation and prayer. They are the esoteric methods to neutralize the fears we take on through the experience of adversity that comes with our Dark Night. The esoteric knowledge about this process is that it opens the gate to the realization of our own Divinity. We can only experience it through the vibration of Love, and we can only experience Love when we are without fear."

121

The Mu(s) were assimilating and integrating these thoughts as best they could. Sahab was happy to see that their auras naturally gravitated to a sea of Oneness and that they seemed to be quite aware of this. He smiled. "You are never alone. Isn't it wonderful?" They smiled at him in recognition of the dimensions of this truth.

"Be mindful that all of the feelings we have in a physical body that are not peaceful, loving and joyous are derived from fear. As such, they must be neutralized to allow us to pass through the gate of our Divinity. If you think about it, this is a belief that was shared by all mystics in the Earth's historical record. They are all quite solid in their ability to transcend fear. This is why I divined a body for you before I gave you that dose of reality in Classroom #22. It was to produce the physical experience of fear and anxiety within you, so as to provide you with the opportunity of a learning experience of finding your way through the gate.

Sometimes it's a tight squeeze through a narrow gate, but back there in the pool of water, I must say that all of you eased through it like professionals. Not everyone does. Taken to the far extreme, well, it can become like a *Bad Day of Day Trading in Atlanta.* You do remember hearing about the poor soul who shot his wife, children and many innocent bystanders because he had lost money in the stock market. Guess who he saw when he woke up?" The Mu(s) nodded.

Sahab quickly bobbed his head up and down while saying, "Yes, all of them, and now, he really has a mess on his hands! He wasted a wonderful opportunity to make it through his Dark Night. Make no mistake about it; this was all about fear. Had he simply found the way to his own Divinity, he could have neutralized the fear and found his way to Love. Now, he is back in Karma 101 on the Spiritual plane."

"Perish the thought!" said Mu 6.

The rest of the Mu(s) looked seriously at him and pointed their fingers at him warning him that he'd better be careful. Everyone roared.

Sahab rubbed the head of Mu 6 and said, "This child wonder put the first and the last # 1 on Karma 101, didn't you?"

"God yes! I was the egghead in the middle and I ain't going back again!"

"I am mighty glad to hear it," said Sahab.

Most of the Mu(s) were nodding but Mu 8 was also trembling and mopping his brow. He was allowing his thoughts to flow to the stock market and the whole idea of using the concept of money to make more. How well this Mu knew that money could be the source of much error, especially his own. Bunny and Lynn were ratcheting up the heat right now! John was determined to avoid the far extremes this time. He too remembered Karma 101 all too well. John had the potential of learning through the Mu 8 vibration because that is his predominant affinity.

Sahab continued, "Now, let's address, for a moment, the esoteric, fear-dissolving methods of meditation and prayer to understand how they can be helpful. Relaxation, or the setting aside of the physical body, is what allows one to be successful with either method. It is paramount. It is crucial. When you are in the physical body, you must learn to work with its physiology. You see, it is impossible to successfully meditate if the body is not relaxed, because all that one can then think about *is* the body. The whole idea is to stop thinking," he said, as he winked at Mu 9. She rolled her eyes and nodded as if to say, *Of course, what else*?

"The small portion of mental consciousness that is in a physical body can only think of one thing at a time. If you are thinking about the body's discomfort, well, forget finding the gate to your own Divinity, the body is not going to be denied! The only possible target of awareness is the discomfort of the body which, in itself, is a physical manifestation of fear. The same demands exist for both meditation and prayer," he said, as he stood on one leg, taking a Yoga stork position. He made a salutation to the sun while standing in perfect balance. The Mu(s) were quite impressed.

"You're losing me," said Mu 2. "I thought fear was mental and you are describing it as physical. I am not sure that I understand."

Sahab stood on both legs, came down from his rock and walked carefully through the flowers, being careful not to step on them. He paused for a few moments in thought before he continued. Turning to Mu 2, he began, "Fear begins in the mind as a misperception. When we accept it as real, it creates a physical manifestation of itself through our physiology, which then changes our physical body. This sometimes appears as discomfort or disease."

Mu 4 interrupted, "What about that other part, that stuff about only a *small portion* of our mental consciousness being in the body; where the heck's the rest of it?"

"Well, that's where the Seven-Headed Serpent comes in. Remember we were talking about it when we spoke about the Motherland of Mu. Here's the short version. You see, we are usually manifesting at seven different levels at the same time. Think of yourself as a group or as a team with the same goal. Each member is doing a job that needs to be done for the team to win, so to speak, although it is not a matter of competition. Perhaps, a better way to describe it would be as an evolving work of art. Some of these seven manifestations may be in physical form; some may be in other realms, but they are all going on at once."

The Mu(s) looked perplexed.

"I can see the short version is just beginning to peel the onion, but don't spend too much time worrying about this now. Just know that it's one reason why the serpent has seven heads. It is to represent that each manifestation always has its own connection to the Divine. Try not to get lost in the wilderness on this issue. You will understand more about these things as you desire to do so and as you are ready to receive the information.

Now, let's get back to the matters at hand. Relaxation, dear Mu(s), is the first step in making it through the gate to the experience of your own Divinity because the process of achieving it releases fear. *Easy does it moves you forward* and becomes then, both a tool for getting there and a gauge for your success, does it not?"

"Is this what the Flower Children found in the sixties?" asked Mu 2. This Mu wore western boots. There was sweetness and sensitivity about him that spoke of peace.

Sahab smiled and said, "They only found the first part of it. They never got beyond the *Easy Does It* part." He staggered, pretending to be high, and fell down into the lap of Mu 6 as everyone roared. He pulled himself upright, brushed himself off and continued.

"In the times since the Flower Children, we have forgotten the *Easy Does It* part and have instead paid more attention to various bastardizations of *Moving forward*, like FAST! Life became all about technology-speed, technology-speed and more technology-speed! *Easy Does It* somehow got deleted," he chuckled. "The time is ripe now for you to become instrumental in *putting Humpty Dumpty back together again.* One without the other will never get the job done in a Spiritual world. Never mind that it seems to be physical! That, dear students, is only a facade."

CHAPTER THIRTEEN

Jumping In

Jim was sitting at the breakfast nook having another cup of coffee and reading his Wall Street Journal. The book he had found earlier in his mailbox now rested on the table. He picked it up and looked at its cover. *Who left this? The Fulfillment sounds like it could be some Right-Wing, Christian Proslytizement. Maybe this is from the guy on the corner who leaves Christian literature on the doorstep. But Return of Mu? Doesn't seem to jive with Jesus Saves.*

Jim mentally heard a voice that claimed his full attention.

You have been so busy with the cash cow that you have forgotten your Spiritual disciplines. Can you remember the last time that you meditated?

Jim's eyes darted upward, then side to side to capture the information. *It was close to a year ago, the last time Alan and I went fishing at Altoona.* They had gone to church with Jim's mother and dad, then on to brunch. Jim remembered something his dad had said that jolted him. Afterward, as they were walking out to their cars, Dad said, "Son, we need to talk." Jim remembered experiencing an overwhelming feeling of fear. *What was on his mind? Was this going to be the conversation that he'd been dreading?*

"Sure Dad," Jim answered. "I'll call you this week." That Sunday morning before church was the last time Jim had meditated. He hadn't planned to stop. It was just something that seemed to happen naturally. Thinking about it took him back in time as he remembered he hadn't been able to call his dad on Monday. It wasn't that he didn't have time, even though Mondays generally were potboilers. He loved his dad but he had this sick feeling of dread regarding what the conversation was to be about. Jim had seemed to sense something different in the way his dad communicated and it resonated fear in him.

It was Wednesday morning when Jim finally called him. "Dad, can you meet me at Hotdog Heaven for lunch today?"

"Sounds like a good deal if you're buying," he chuckled.

"You're on! I know how you love that red dye #4. Can you make it at 1:00 P. M?"

"Sure, see you then."

Jim remembered being a basket case all morning, unable to concentrate on his work. And he remembered his dad's words before they even took their first bite. Sitting at a sidewalk table under a green and white striped awning, Dad looked straight at him and said, "Son, I've got prostate cancer, and we're not telling Momma yet. I have decided to have the radioactive seed implants. They will be calling me back with a scheduled date for the procedure today or tomorrow. Then, we'll deal with Mother."

Jim remembered sighing and starting to breathe again after what seemed like a *very* long time. "Oh Dad, I'm so sorry to hear that. What can I do for you?"

"You can keep Mom leveled out. You know how she can get. I'm depending on you to keep her in the middle of the road. You are the only moderating influence on her ten-decibel scale," he laughed.

"Dad, you don't seem to be too upset about this; I guess that's good."

"Son, you know how I've always felt. When your number's up, it's up! No use getting upset about anything you can't control. Maybe I should talk with your friend Tom though, about setting up some annuities. I've been thinking about doing that for awhile anyway, ever since he gave me the pitch at the Christmas party last year. He was certainly having a good time, remember?"

"Don't worry Dad, I'll handle Mom, and maybe you should talk to Tom. Here's his business card. That fool drinks too much, on occasion, but he does know what he's doing and he will treat you right. Give him a call."

The mental voice continued. ***You allowed fear to sever your lifeline to Spirit, didn't you?***

128

Jim closed his eyes, sat upright in his chair with both feet flat on the floor. He rested the back of his hands on his thighs, touching together his thumb and index finger of both hands. He then began to breathe deeply and slowly, recapturing a part of himself that he had lost.

Sahab continued the lessons in Spirit. "Meditation and prayer will help you to become successful because it brings you back to your Source. In essence, you find yourself using *Easy Does It* to create *Forward Motion* once fear has been neutralized."

Jim listened closely.

"Is one method better than the other?" asked Mu 7. "Is meditation more effective than prayer?"

"It is not a matter of one being better or worse," said Sahab. "They are both different aspects of communication with the Divine. Prayer is the act of speaking to the Divine and meditation, the act of listening to it. We could also say: one is more male and the other is more female, or that one is more analytical and the other more intuitive. The Yin and Yang are present everywhere, even in the Divine, although we have forgotten *Her* for a very long time. This too will soon be changing.

The certainty that does exist is that one method easily leads to the other whenever good communication takes place. This holds true for all relationships. Meditation sometimes more easily accomplishes relaxation, since slowing down the breath can make the difference in allowing the body to get there sooner. This always helps in quieting the mind; it's a matter of purposely using the physiology to help you achieve the goal."

"Are you saying, *If it feels good, do it?*" asked Mu 2.

"Yes, more or less. The method that will seem more natural to you often has to do with the culture of your physical world manifestation. The East is more comfortable with meditation, and the West more easily aligns with prayer. Neither is truly successful unless the practitioner can relax enough to set aside the physical body. Then one method will easily lead you to the other, and before you know it, you are both talking and listening to the Divine. Now, that's a novel idea, isn't it?" he said, as he rolled his eyes in the direction of Mu 9.

Cindy looked at her watch. It was 12:45 P.M. and the protein bar was long gone. She picked up her manual, left the building and walked a few blocks to the Varsity for a hamburger and some greasy onion rings. Whenever her head was buzzing, she felt a need to junk out. Today was certainly deserving! While this didn't happen often, today was something else! She thought about Tom and the fact that his lying was the worst part of the problem. *Why could he not take responsibility for his problem and quit lying about it!* Her finding one more hidden bottle was going to take the cake! She thought about leaving him sticky notes on each find.

As she chomped on her onion rings, Cindy continued thinking about her husband. No amount of analyzing his addiction had ever enabled her to change one hair on his head. God knows she had tried, and she was now at the fork in the road. It was time to fish or cut bait!

Cindy pictured Tom at home reading his manual and she wondered what that would bring. She would be finding out soon enough. She would soon have to confront him and let the chips fall where they may. She said a prayer for the two of them, then sipped her orange drink as she stared off in space.

Sahab continued, "If you are unable to relax with prayer, try meditation. The key to getting there quickly is slowing down your breathing. That's what worked for you in that pool of relaxing water, right?"

"That and closing our eyes," said Mu 3.

"Yes, both of those practices enabled you to set aside the physical body and the visual stimuli, while avoiding sleep, and that increased your mental clarity. It's called an Alpha level because of your brain waves. Then came the good part, aligning with each other in Oneness.

You might say that you have had some very good practice for trying days in Earth School. Tribulation has already begun, you know, and it will continue through the year 2012. Now," he said softly, as if he were half-whispering to the group, "if you add these numbers, you will find that they total to the number five, the numerical vibration that most indicates change. This manifestation of change will be magnificent when it is complete."

With this, Mu 5 stuck his thumbs under the arms of his dark gray business suit and looked around. Sahab smiled at him and divined himself into a female body resembling Bette Davis. She ascended a staircase with a cigarette in her hand. She stopped and turned, looked directly at Mu 5 and dramatically exclaimed, "Hold onto your seat; it's going to be a bumpy night!"

Jim straightened his back and exhaled deeply as he recognized himself as Mu 5.

The group laughed and Mu 5 said, "It looks like you have been hanging out in the screening room with Alcyona."

Sahab took a long drag on her cigarette and said, "You will have more fun if you learn to *have fun* with all of the illusions of the Earth experience." With that, he released the Diva-nation, took on his old form and continued.

Jim thought, *I can't wait until I'm out of here!* He looked at his watch. If he got the lead out, he could take care of business and make it to his attorney's office by 1:00 P.M. They would be going over both the terms of the offer and his response. There were a few points of negotiation to formulate. He left Alan a note on the fridge and bounded out the door.

"By 2012, profound change will have completed itself upon the earth," said Sahab. "These changes will usher in a thousand years of peace. It is all good. The things that shall die away are needed for the *New Beginning*. Do not mourn the loss and know that all of you are an important part of this process. That's why you are here in school now. It was optional that you attend, you know. You could be having some inconsequential fantasy somewhere else. You see, you have already dedicated your life to serving the Earth through this transition. You are just now waking up to it on this particular level of awareness. Mu 9, you seem to have question marks written across your face. What's up?"

"Will you elaborate just a little bit more on analytical and intuitional mind in this whole process. I want to make sure I understand the proper applications of each."

"Yes, yes, of course you do, for you are the student's student and that is good. It will drive you crazy at times, especially during the Dark Night because there will be so many things you won't be able to figure out. You are not supposed to be able to, but the willingness to continue trying is what's important. Einstein was cut from the cloth of the Mu 9 vibration. St. John the Divine gave the Spiritual process the name that we continue to use on Earth to describe the Dark Night of the Soul. Ah yes, the creation of the pearl in the oyster! You are in very good company, as you try to understand more. Just know that it will probably get worse before it gets better," he chuckled.

Mu 9 looked perplexed and Sahab patted her shoulder with understanding. Mu 9 softened with Sahab's gentle touch. It had the power to purify the dross from energy fields. She felt pounds of heaviness leave her.

"To go further with the explanation for Mu 9, while continuing with the pattern of our analogies, be mindful that when you speak to the Divine through prayer, its primary vehicle is analytical mind. When you listen to the Divine through meditation, its vehicle is intuitional mind. Now, who among you can say which is more important?" Sahab asked, as he looked around at the sea of eager faces.

Mu 9 was nodding her head in new awareness as she fixed her bun, making sure that every hair was in place. Sahab looked at Mu 9, as she began to speak, "I see what my problem has been. It looks like I've been making this gig a lot harder than it needs to be."

"Bingo! And here it seems as though we have stumbled upon yet another meaning for *Easy does it, Forward motion*, haven't we? Yes, much in the physical world is often easier for the Mu 9 vibration but, I can tell you, the Dark Night usually isn't one of them. In periods of adversity, it is often more difficult for Mu 9's to let go of analytical mind and to flow and trust their intuitive faculties. Mu 9's do not naturally trust intuition because they have the tendency to think that they are making things up. They can easily believe this because there is no visual proof, usually quite necessary for a Mu 9.

It is not just a problem for the Mu 9 vibration, but it can sometimes be a bigger problem for the 9's than for the other numbers," said Sahab, as he raised his eyebrows at Mu 9. She nodded her understanding as she pushed her steel rimed glasses back up on the bridge of her long, slender nose.

"Let's go back to the experience that all of you had in the pool of water while using intuitional mind. You were looking for an answer as to where you should meet me, weren't you? You were looking for directions. Note the profound thing that happened with the use of your intuitional mind. Every single one of you received the same answer. Wasn't that amazing? You acted on it and it proved to be correct.

It was no accident that you found a needle in the haystack. Intuitional mind can provide you with the answers you are seeking if you will have the confidence to seek its counsel and then the faith to act on what's given. It is always the answer you are seeking because the information is coming through your own Divine nature, that part of you that is One with the Creator."

Yes, intuitional mind is the answer, thought Mu 12.

"Now, all of this compounded itself and worked even better than usual because it was a group meditation. As each of you experienced Oneness, the power of the One grew exponentially in you and in everyone else throughout time and space who also experienced the One. To receive your answer from intuitional mind, you drew through many Divine natures, all at One with the Mother-Father Source and at One with you. That's why it was so powerful!"

Whistling and cheering, the Mu(s) raised up their heads, cupping their hands to both sides of their mouths. Sahab promptly divined the face of a different animal on each one. They looked around at each other, pointing and laughing. None seemed more *equal* in absurdity than the others and Sahab certainly enjoyed the moment.

Mu 9 had an over-sized elephant's head. Mu 6 had the head of a pig. Mu 5 had a buck's head with a full rack and Mu 11 had the head of a snake. He delighted in hissing at everyone.

Getting back to business, Sahab undid the divinations and continued on, "The answer you received was the answer you were seeking, and it came to you without difficulty. But, you would not have known it was the correct answer unless you had acted upon it. Is this not correct? So many miracles are missed because we fail to act on our inner guidance," he said, as he shook his head and raised his arms.

The Mu(s) nodded in agreement.

"And by the way, singing the song and dancing your way to the Northeast increased your confidence in your answer as the right course of action, didn't it? If you had doubted your answer, it would have taken you twice as long to get here. That's the way it works. Your path might have been zigzag instead of straight."

The Mu(s) nodded. They were getting the drift.

"It seems to me that intuitional mind is a whole lot more important than analytical mind," said Mu 3. Mu 9 promptly straightened her back, leaned in and listened closely.

Sahab smiled, "Let's say, for everything there is a time. There have been periods in many civilizations when a predominant use of analytical mind was exactly what was needed for the civilization to advance. There were Mu 9's everywhere, doing their thing with gusto. Generally speaking, applications of physical facts are almost always best handled through the use of analytical mind."

Mu 9 looked extremely pleased to hear this.

"This particular time of Tribulation, now through the year of 2012, serves as a bridge to what shall become known as the Age of Spirit. Intuitional mind shall clearly become more valued as a modus operandi. It is therefore more important now for us to learn to use our intuitive faculties consciously. Practice will enable us to become more functional in the new age and much more helpful to others. It isn't that one is any more important than the other. It is more about building confidence in our ability to use intuition as effectively as we use our analytical mind. Is this clear?"

For practice in her area of deficiency, Mu 9 began to hum softly in the key of B flat. She sat in the cross-legged Lotus position with her eyes closed, drumming the fingers of her right hand upon her right thigh. Sahab was catching this from the corner of his eye, daring not to look at her and *lose it* while thinking, *Talk about learning to walk and chew gum....* He chuckled and silently sent her a message of Peace and

134

Love before continuing.

The Mu(s) again slowly nodded their understanding. Mu 9 was on a roll now and she had stopped drumming her fingers.

"And so, this dissertation has brought us a little closer to our assignments and the vast amount of work to be done on Earth. Are you ready to continue?" asked Sahab.

In unison, the Mu(s) replied, "Let's go for it!"

"Stand up now, stretch and then join hands for a moment as we invoke the power of One."

The group spaced themselves out around the circle of wildflowers, standing just behind them. Sahab stepped up and stood atop his mound of granite and appeared as a giant lightning rod for the group.

"Spread out until each of you is equidistant around the circle, with your auras overlapping," he said.

Separating physically, they moved and spaced themselves while maintaining an awareness of their mingling auras. Once the adjustments were complete, they noticed that the circle of energy was an exact fit to the circular circumference just beyond the wildflowers.

Mu 2 exclaimed, "This worked out perfectly," to which Sahab replied, "It was no accident, dear Mu. There are no accidents or coincidences, in spite of the fact that it sometimes appears that way."

As the students looked around at each other, they saw rainbows arcing everywhere, complete with all colors, dancing around the circle. It filled them with wonder and excitement. As they looked up at Sahab, they saw two gigantic rainbows. Crossing each other through the top of Sahab's forehead, one stretched from North to South, the other from East to West. Everywhere they looked, there appeared to be the design of a circle or a circle within a circle.

Sahab continued, "The circle is the symbol of One. It was the first of all geometric designs. It represents the most important concept, not only in the Earth experience but in all realms at all times. Note that even the beginning letter of the word itself is a perfect circle. There is great power in the circle, for it represents and celebrates the power of One. When gazing at a circle, you will notice that you cannot find the place where it begins or ends. This is the reason it is employed in many rituals and symbols. Think for a moment about the many ways you know the circle to be employed."

Mu 7 spoke up, "The circle is often used in children's games."

"Yes," said Sahab, "It is such an important concept that children begin celebrating the power of One at the early ages, even when they don't consciously understand the significance of what they are doing."

Mu 7 continued, "Mother's breasts are circular. And her eyes are circular as they gaze at her children with Love."

Mu 4 jumped in, "Think of the wedding band and its significance. The two are now made One and the ring itself is a perfect circle." "Very good," said Sahab, "You will find the symbol and ritual of the circle apparent everywhere. It exists as a remembrance of the power of One. This is where all lessons and laws reconcile, reduce and come to rest. Many things of importance are expressed through the power of the circle. Think about it."

Mu 8 interjected, "Coins are round."

Mu 6 jumped in, "The shape of a bottle is certainly round, that is, for as long as one can see it!"

The Mu(s) chuckled and continued to mentally massage this whole idea of the power of One, until Sahab continued.

"The reason I am asking you to think about this is to make your assignments easier. It can often become a short cut to the learning process. For instance, let's say that you are involved in a problem or a situation that you cannot figure out or decide on the proper course of action.

The symbol of the power of One, will always cut through the details you have allowed to become quicksand for you. Sometimes this will work so quickly that you will think it's magic: like one moment you are wandering in the wilderness, and the next moment you have found your way home. You can always short-circuit the learning process through the power of One. It is another major reason to find Oneness everywhere."

The Mu(s) contemplated the many signs and wonders of the power of One in the Earth experience: the sun, the moon, the planet itself, satellites, a compass, wheels, and on and on this went as the Mu(s) mentally found Oneness everywhere.

Sahab continued, "It's the only thing we sometimes lose and it's the only thing we ever need to find... everywhere, with everyone and everything! Remember this, dear students, and your time will be used more efficiently. You'll arrive everywhere sooner. This is especially important in the time of *The Fulfillment*. There isn't a moment of time to waste getting into your costume, for the curtain has lifted."

With this, Sahab rolled his eyes upward and looked directly through the center of the rainbow-cross at the top of his head. A bolt of yellow light beamed down from above, directly into his forehead. It flashed into the top of the rainbow-cross and traveled in a circle in all four directions, then around and around the circle, energizing the group in an expanded awareness of the power of One. Alive with energy, the students contemplated, *I must remember this. I must remember!*

Sahab then said, "Open your right hand and look." As they did so, each found a small circular disk that was pearly white in color, with an inscription in purple. On one side of the disk and in the center was written the word "ONE". Slightly above the word was written, "Easy Does It" and below the word, "Forward Motion". On the other side of the disk was written, "Always With Love, Sahab." He looked at them sweetly and said, "Think of these things in memory of me."

The Mu(s) were touched. They looked at their gift with eyes wide in appreciation and surprise. They rubbed the disk between their fingers, as if to more fully "feel the message." It would become a point of focus for them, a reminder of the work that was to be done and the loving support that was always there for them. Now they had both ----- a mantra and a visual reminder of their mission to keep them focused on the goal of One.

Sahab came down from his granite pedestal and said, "Come join me," as he walked over to the grassy meadow. His class followed closely behind him, stepping carefully around the flowers, just as he had done. He gestured that the class members be seated. They took comfortable positions and looked up at him, still holding their disk and rubbing it. They could not seem to let go of it, not even to put it into their pocket for safe keeping. It had become both the symbol and the method of the work to be done.

Sahab said, "It is not necessary to hold on so tightly. If it were a little bird, you would have pinched its little temples together and what would Alcyona think of that?" The release they experienced through laughter caused them to become conscious of their tensions and to release them through deep breathing. "Remember also, that *Easy Does It* naturally gives you *Forward Motion* if you work through the power of One.

With that, Mu 6 began to flip his disk as if it were a common coin, catching it with minimal effort.

Mu 9 observed the action closely and replied in jest, "All that goes up, must come down," as everyone laughed.

Mu 8 flipped his coin up into the air and slightly over to the right, allowing Mu 7 to catch it for him, effortlessly, while he shrugged his shoulders, as if to say: *Easy Come, Easy Go.*

Sahab surveyed his class and said, "You're Smoking!"

Everyone enjoyed a good laugh. They put their good luck charm into their pockets while Sahab cleared his throat and continued.

"There's a message for you in the clouds," he said, as he gestured to the sky.

The students looked up.

Written in cloud formations, as if scripted by a skywriting plane, was the question, "Are you ready for your assignments?"

"Yes!" said the Mu(s) in unison. They lay back on the grass, thoroughly relaxed, with their hands under their heads. They looked upward at the question formed by the clouds, as if they were waiting for the answers to appear. Then, Sahab asked them to close their eyes, breathe deeply and slowly while focusing on their mantra. He began to set the stage for another adventure in Spirit.

CHAPTER FOURTEEN

The Assignments

Sahab divined a nighttime sky complete with a soft blanket of stars that sparkled like diamonds on black velvet. He paused to enjoy the beauty of it for a few moments before he began to speak.

"Open your eyes dear Mu(s), and focus on the stars." The Mu(s) were a little surprised that things had changed so quickly from day to night but promptly adjusted their eyes to more clearly behold the moment.

"In any direction you choose, draw a three-dimensional mental line from star to star and connect it to you, creating a unique design of your own choosing. When you finish, hold the shape of your design firmly in your remembrance." Sahab paused for a moment, giving them time to complete the task. The design levitated them upward slightly and then, an unexplained force seemed to pull them back down. "Do you feel its grounding effect on you?" he asked.

The Mu(s) whispered slowly with surprise, "Yes," each nodding in their own time, as they felt the power of their connection.

Each design was slightly different, one from the other, and each Mu cherished his own uniqueness. While Sahab could see the mental mosaic created by the twelve designs, each Mu could only see and relate to his own creation. They looked upon their work of art with a profound sense of aesthetic appreciation.

Sahab continued, "This particular design will support and assist you in the completion of your assignment. Since it is totally your own creation, it has everything you need. While it is an inordinately beautiful work of art, it may also help if you think of it as a toolbox with windows of opportunity. It is both beautiful and functional. In a very real sense, it is quite complete, as is the case with each one of you."

The Mu(s) gazed intently at the pattern of their design, scrutinizing every detail as they searched it for hidden meaning. While they were not entirely clear on their conclusions, they seemed to be very much aware of the evocative power of their design. As they continued to dwell with its presence, each one experienced a feeling of tranquillity and perfect peace.

"While it seems to you that you have created your design right now, you are actually remembering something that you created long ago, when you decided to volunteer for your present assignments."

Mu 5 interrupted, "You mean we already know what our assignments are? How could that be?"

Sahab walked closer to them and said, "There are so many levels of Truth, all correct in their own realm, but if you carried the awareness of all of it with you at all times, it would blow your circuits. You're electrical, you know. That's why it is necessary to forget some of the data from time to time, or to file it away when there is no immediate need for it in the present moment. To illustrate the point that you have already chosen your assignments, I am going to begin sharing information on these assignments and we'll see who feels ownership responsibilities."

The Mu(s) seemed somewhat amused by this and a little mystified but they were also interested to see where these ideas would take them. They sat up and leaned in to listen more intently, as Sahab continued.

"The assignments are broad categories where change is needed on Earth as we move through Tribulation to *The Fulfillment*. Your Dark Night is a part of this and you have chosen to experience it to allow for the deepening of your Spiritual nature as you complete your part of the assignment. As you do so, you assist the Earth with healing. You are also able to help others make it through their own Dark Night of the Soul. They can then join you in the reestablishment and expression of Divine balance on Earth."

"In other words, to implement on Earth our teachings here with you?" asked Mu 7.

"Yes, and while you are primarily concerned with your own assignment, I do not mean to imply that you are not involved with the other assignments. Whenever you are a part of the Earth's dream experience, you accept total responsibility for all of it. However, you have greater involvement, responsibility and even affinity for one of these areas. You will understand more when this unfolds."

As the Mu(s) looked at Sahab, they were impressed with his beauty and the golden light that shone around him. In spite of the fact that it was extremely dark on this particular night, they were able to see every detail of his presence quite clearly. Their eyes zoomed in on the sparkling wand he held in this right hand, as they fixated on the alternating bursts of light traveling from the center of his being, down his arm, the length of the wand, and outward into the dark night sky.

Sahab used his wand to outline a piece of the sky to resemble a screen to establish a point of focus. Images and ideas progressed much like a short filmstrip. There were children everywhere. Some were hungry and sick, others were being shot at school in Littleton, Colorado. Some of the Mu(s) recognized the Rocky Mountains to the West. Other children looked hopeless and bored, wandering the streets and wondering where their parents were. Some toiled for long hours in factories. Other children were being emotionally, physically, and sexually abused. These images were viewed against an ambiguous montage of priests and computer predators. Some children languished in a drug haze, while others ran away into the distance.

Mu 4 was moved to tears as she extended her arms to the sky and cried, "My babies, my babies, how can they do this to my babies!"

Sahab asked, "Is there any question whose assignment this is?"

Mu 4 nodded her head in understanding as her arms fell limply to her side. She struggled to regain her composure. In Atlanta, Georgia right now, there is a Mu 4 named Janie. There are many other Mu 4's throughout the world with real dedication to the plight of children.

Yes, I must do something to help the children of the world and I should start with my own, thought Janie, the mailroom supervisor who worked with John and Cindy. *What am I doing with Adam in day care? How did I come to abandon my role as a mother?* Janie had finished preparing the latest direct mail marketing piece for pick-up. She glanced at her desk and noticed a book that hadn't been there before. Standing in the middle of it was a round disk-like object.

Janie walked over to her desk to inspect this. As she drew closer, she could see the word *ONE* facing her. She thought about the meaning that it had for her. *There is only one window of time, one opportunity to be with Adam as he's growing up.*

She picked up the coin-like object and closed her left fist around it. She felt a tremendous surge of energy travel up her left arm. It took her by surprise and she quickly sat down at her desk. *What's going on here?* Her mind began to experience pronounced clarity and alertness.

Janie looked at the book and read the title, *The Fulfillment. Being with Adam in his formative years would be fulfillment for me,* she thought. *Do I really need to be here? After all, if we didn't have my income would we starve?* She heard an answer in her mind that whispered, No, my child, haven't your needs always been met?

Janie answered, *Yes, they have! All my income does is create a bigger Christmas and extra things. After the events of this morning, how important is that in the big scheme of things?*

She sat at her desk with the disk clenched in her left hand, her right hand resting, palm down, on the book. She closed her eyes.

Janie, you are a child of Mu. Read the manual and you will remember many things. Adam is also a child of Mu. He has extraordinary abilities that need your nurturing and guidance. He is pure-strain Mu, one of those known as a Crystal Child. Many of these children are incarnating now. Have you not already noticed some unusual things about him?

Janie remembered a time when he was in his crib and she observed him looking upward at a suspended mobile that he seemed to enjoy. As he focussed intently on it, the tiny airplane on the end began twirling unexplainably. She noticed that the window was closed and the paddle fan was not in motion.

That was one of your first indications that he was different. Yes, he was moving the airplane with his mind. And don't you continue to be amazed at how in-sync with you he is?

Janie remembered this morning. She planned to take Adam shopping for a new pair of shoes this afternoon after work. Adam was eating his cereal at the breakfast table when out of the blue, he stuck his leg out to the side so she could see it and he pointed to his left shoe. "I like them kind Mommy," he said.

"Adam, how about, *I like this kind*," she said, correcting his grammar. Yes, there were many instances when Adam seemed to know what she was thinking. Janie had always explained this to herself as coincidence.

Crystal children have special abilities and they need Mu guidance and nurturing while they are bonding with physical reality in their early years. They need a grounding for their Love vibration before they become too exposed to the Lagitard fear vibration in the world. It is one of the reasons why you volunteered to be his mother. Read your manual. It will help you to remember the things that are important.

Janie opened her eyes and looked again at the book and then, at the disk in her hand. She placed the book in her canvas carry-all, along with her lunch and her valuables. She flipped the coin once, caught it, put it in her pocket and answered her phone. "Mailroom, this is Janie."

In Spirit, the rest of the Mu(s) looked lovingly at Mu 4. They felt her dedication to the plight of children in need, and to Adam in particular.

Their attention was drawn back to the heavens and they saw images of the Earth in distress. Rain forests were slowly disappearing. Huge bulldozers toppled trees and vegetation, as housing developments and malls replaced them. Strip mining raped thousands and thousands of acres and the Earth was polluted with toxic waste, poisoning the water supply. The crystal blue waters turned to a bilious brown.

Mu 5 jumped to his feet, "How can they do this? How can they kill Mother Earth for monetary gain?" He sat down and slowly lay back with his hands behind his head, seriously contemplating his strategies by the light of the moon. He thought so intently on these things that the other Mu(s) were able to see and feel his visionary

143

thoughts. They saw him wandering through the Rain Forests in Costa Rica. His compatriots sent him their messages of peace, love and encouragement, clearly seeing the mission that this Mu embraced.

Mu 5s everywhere heightened their interest in environmental issues. This was certainly true of Jim. He had contributed substantially to nature conservation projects and many organizations that were dedicated to protecting Mother Earth. Some of his friends even called him "Mother Nature". He often encouraged others to contribute to the causes that were close to his heart. Of special significance to him were efforts to save the Rain Forests.

Visions in the heavens reclaimed everyone's attention. They were political and scientific, areas where change had far-reaching effects for everyone on the Earth. The first vision displayed a group of politicians in Washington where men and women were seated at a dark mahogany table. Several rounds of votes were taken. The results would be felt thousands of miles away and many in Afghanistan would perish. Votes continued to be cast, as several countries disappeared from the world map.

A congressman in New York and one in Washington, both of the Mu 1 vibration, were busy conversing on the telephone, enlisting each other's support for the many decisions that would have to be made. One was sitting on a park bench, talking on a cell phone and feeding the pigeons as they darted in and out. On a subliminal level, both politicians heard the sound of *One*. They could indeed make a difference!

The Mu(s) found it fascinating to pick up on so many levels of reality at the same time. It reinforced in them how closely connected everyone was. They picked up on Mu 1 vibrations in many other countries, trying to find their way *HOME. So much work to be done and so many assignments to complete*, they thought.

The Mu(s) attention was once again drawn to the midnight sky where a colorful vision began to emerge. A doctor was shown in a white lab coat. Letters on the back of his coat spelled out Genome Project. He sat at his computer massaging data. The vision slowly disappeared as another one emerged. A scientist raised a test tube of promise and viruses disappeared. Drug companies were seen in the background while dollar bills rained down on them like green snowflakes. Those who could afford to buy were allowed to live.

These areas clearly needed a moderating Mu vibration with great intelligence, one who was creative and comfortable with change. Mu(s) 1 and 5 seemed extremely empathetic to this vision. Many other Mu vibrations also existed in the scientific community throughout the world. They were hearing a wakeup call right now as a sheep named Dolly was seen grazing in the distance.

The rest of the Mu(s) beamed messages of support to the political and scientific communities. Speaking for the group, Mu 12 asked, "How may we help?"

"Voting is a good start," said Mu 1. "It will take all of us working together for the common good."

The heavens went dark for a moment, allowing the stars more contrast for their dazzling brilliance. The Mu(s) allowed their beauty to purge the darkness within them. They glowed with a crystal quality as the midnight sky again gave way to images.

In Africa, elephants were shot and their tusks were ravaged. In the American West, wolves were trapped and killed. In Gainesville, Georgia, the poultry capital of the world, chickens were pumped full of liquid poison until they expanded and exploded into chicken nuggets, to eventually be served through tiny windows.

On many farms throughout the land, calves were held prisoners in tiny cells for twelve weeks while they were fattened up for veal, then killed and sold for greenbacks. The colors and the images continued swirling. It was like sticking pins in a voodoo doll for the Mu(s) to see and consider these painful truths. Their empathy was escalating.

Like a deep and twisting knife wound to the gut, it hurt the sensitive Mu(s) to know that animals throughout the world were hunted down and killed so that their furs might be used for adornment. In the rural areas of Arkansas and West Virginia, dogs and cats were trapped and hauled off for medical experiments. Off the western coast of the North American continent, whales absolutely wailed, as they gave up all they had to a greedy world.

Mu 3 could hardly contain her grief. Large tears quickly turned to sobs. "Stop, stop, I cannot bare to watch another minute!" Mu 3 vibrations all around the world shared her sensitivity. At last, they were able to feel what each animal felt. For the first time, they recognized them as feeling, sentient beings and they wept in shame for the entire human race. Mu 3's classmates sent her Love and the power of One, as her green and gold aura extended seven feet beyond her body.

The Mu(s) took a deep breath trying to regroup and regain their composure, as Sahab looked to the heavens. A vision of an artist manifested. They saw the artist move through book, film, music, canvas and upon the stage and multiply. The Mu(s) saw many artists making compromises and struggling that they might share their visionary gifts with the world. Picasso went without food until the painting was finished. Isadora fainted from dehydration as Shakespeare poignantly captured the frailties of being human so that we might see and come to know ourselves. H.G. Wells prepared us for many things that would come to pass through science, in the twinkling of an eye. These mysterious things commanded the attention of every single Mu.

Mu 10 rose to her feet and, with tension in her body, she slowly stretched her arms upward and forward while taking three staccato steps toward the vision. Pausing and turning to face the group, she whispered, filled with emotion, "Is there even one single doubt that art mirrors life?"

"No, not one," answered the Mu(s) thoughtfully, as they slowly shook their heads.

Using gesture to amplify emotional impact, Mu 10 continued, "And the violence present in the arts today but speaks of the fear-spawned darkness within the heart and mind of all humankind, just aching to be healed, a liquidation of the Lagitard in us."

As the rest of the Mu(s) applauded her performance, she graciously took her bow. Mu 10 then walked back to her place and executed a crescendo-building Grahamesque tension-turn, gracefully lowering herself to the ground, like an overly dramatic coda made visible. Sahab appreciated the serious substance of her words, yet her overly dramatic performance caused him to smile at her display. *To laugh or not to laugh, that may be the question....* He managed to hold it together as he bowed to her graciously, knowing full well that creative artistic endeavors have always been life's leavening agents.

In Hawaii, a Mu 10 landscape painter named Gwen Ho was intent on capturing an artistic moment and making it real for us on canvas. The sounds of birds were heard flying overhead, applauding the transitional eloquence between the human and the Divine. Gwen was but one of many Mu 10s on Earth now to make beautiful sense of our illusions. Intent upon her work, she continued painting because she could do nothing else. It was such an integral part of who she was.

Sahab faced the Mu(s), glowing with radiance that commanded their full attention. "I ask you now to conjure thoughts from your memories of life. Think for a moment about the poor all over the Earth."

Quick to follow instructions, Mu 9 thought about the plight of those starving in Africa and dying of AIDS. The rest of the empathetic Mu(s) observed her thoughts and wept as they watched the bones, walking. Mu 7 recalled thoughts of life in Russia, where she saw people fighting in the streets over scraps of food, heroin and vodka. The sharing of this thought triggered a swallowing effect in Mu 6.

The homeless in America were huddled under bridges and overpasses with their shopping carts. This image was projected from the mind of Mu 7 and was profoundly felt by all the other Mu(s). The homeless shivered from the cold as their stomachs grumbled. There was no place on Earth where the poor were not found and their pain was experienced by every Mu. *Why,* they asked themselves, *do we throw away food and build shrines to our egos when many go hungry and the number of homeless grows exponentially?*

Mu 7 stood and slowly looked around at his classmates. He was simply dressed in a denim shirt, jeans and boots. He removed his Western hat and brushed his hair back. "Will you help me make a difference here? It will take all of us, everywhere."

"Yes, of course," said the Mu(s) in seriousness, as they instinctively placed their hands over their hearts. As they did so, the heart of Mu 7 began to glow with the soft white light of a sacred heart. The light was felt by thousands of Mu 7 vibrations throughout the planet Earth. They would now go forth and make a difference.

Heaven's screen turned green, as dollar signs in black began to progressively appear at random in the sky. They appeared to be shot through the air by machine guns in staccato four-four time. The sound and action commanded their complete attention. Once the screen was filled with dollar signs, the black melted against the green and began to fade.

The scene gave way to visions of war, seen in small vignettes and superimposed on a world map. The background for each war was the same, green with black dollar signs. How easily money became a catalyst for war. There never was a time or place when this was not so, even Holy wars. Yes, ethnic cleansing was too often material. Loss of land and monetary gain figured into the smallest of skirmishes. This would soon be changing as the world struggled toward Oneness and Divine Government. World trade and a global economy were the first prominent steps in this direction.

The observant Mu 9 couldn't help but reflect on how ironic it seemed that monetary issues could be the impetus in the world toward Oneness. *Go figure.*

Before she finished her thought, the vision gave way to a tobacco company's assembly lines. A worker, half hidden in the back, picked up a vial with XXX on it and added it to the mix. The vision then changed to the CEO in a meeting with his managers. "How can we intensify the craving?" asked the Anti-Buddha.

The vision changed again, displaying a hospital and several independent healthcare practices on its outskirts. A zoomed-in Accounts Payable department materialized before their eyes, where fraudulent entries became evident. The company was milking the government dry.

Mu 8 felt guilty and ashamed. He acknowledged his responsibility and said, "I have been a party to this kind of greed mixed with bad judgement, so I guess it's up to me to become a part of the solution."

The Mu(s) applauded his determination and gave him a strong thumbs-up. There was such energy in the air that the hair on his head stood straight up. It startled him as he laughed and slicked it down with both hands. The five-percent of Mu 8s around the world who controlled 95% of the money also had an energy surge wakeup call. A Mu 8 in Saudi Arabia felt an unexplained tick in his right eye as it blinked uncontrollably. One Mu 8 in San Francisco had a miscarriage at precisely the same moment that many other Mu 8s had wake-up calls after this morning of 9-11. The energy surges continued throughout the Mu 8 vibrations of the world and filtered down like sand in an hourglass to all the other Mu(s).

While the many images they had seen had been pretty realistic, the next round seemed more symbolic. Flashing in the sky were religious symbols, side by side. Clearly visible were the five-pointed star, the cross and the crescent moon. A small group lined up behind each symbol. One person seemed to be the spokesman for each religious group.

Each of them had two mouths situated side by side. Both mouths spoke at the same time. One mouth quoted biblical verses with perfect accuracy while the other mouth, depending on the particular religious group, spoke of different things, strange things indeed, filled with the Lagitard emotion of fear. Loudly they shrieked: "A Holy War is justified in the eyes of God!" "Ordination of women shall never come to be!" "Gays and lesbians are not a part of God's plan!"

From the back of each group there were mumbles, barely understandable. "Only the _____ race shall prevail." Every Mu thought they heard something different. Mu 10 thought she heard the word *white*. Mu 6 heard the word *sober* and Mu 8 was certain that he heard the word *rich*. Strangely enough, they all heard the same next line. "The rest are pigs who deserve to die!"

This was indeed a strange rendering. Sahab thought to himself, *And the sons of Sarah and Hagar are still at it!* The Mu(s) shook their heads in disbelief. *And this is Oneness? Hello!*

Mu 9 stepped forward, shaking her head and saying, "This one's got to be

149

mine!" She thought about the hypocrisy and prejudice perpetuated by so many religious groups in the name of God. She had always felt drawn to make a difference here.

Sahab smiled and gently said to her, "Try not to make the cure worse than the disease." She nodded thoughtfully, quite aware of *exactly* what he meant.

In unison, the rest of the Mu(s) said, "Go girl, go!" She pushed her glasses up, raised her eyebrows and smiled broadly.

The Mu(s) lay back down and released their tensions by breathing deeply. They stretched out with their hands under their heads, thinking about the many visions they had encountered when another image began swirling in many colors, moving counterclockwise. It was quickly beginning to have a hypnotic effect on them. The swirling colors slowly formed the substance of a woman, staggering down a dimly lit street at night. The intermingling of light with darkness cast a moving shadow on her coarse, grotesque face.

Across the street was an addict badly in need of a fix, trembling and sweating, as his eyes painfully searched for a solution. Before he knew it, Mu 6 had projected himself, like a missile, into the virtual reality of this vision. As he walked down the street, Sahab and the rest of the Mu(s) watched him with great empathy.

Mu 6 noticed that across the street, two stories up, a bored, unloved woman sat eating endlessly as she watched television. He paused for a moment to watch: popcorn and chocolates, she was going for them! He watched her go into what appeared to be the bathroom. While he focused on the shadow movement that accompanied the sound of regurgitation flushing, he gagged and quickly looked away.

Mu 6 continued walking. Two blocks down on the left side, five stories up, there was a man in ladies' French-cut leopard panties. He pushed the vacuum while a sadistic doll in black leather cracked the whip over his head. *Good grief!* He stared intently.

From the vision, Mu 6 turned to face the rest of the Mu(s) and exclaimed, "OK, OK, I know this one's mine, but am I supposed to be helping every damned addict on the face of this Earth?"

"Yes," said Sahab, "As soon as you help yourself. All forms of addiction are really the same, you know. All are born from a lack of self-love and a separation from one's own Divinity. Many expressions may be chosen but the healing is the same."

"OK, OK, it's a deal, just let me out of here," Mu 6 said. He jumped from the vision in the sky, rolling and tumbling to his place, thoroughly depleted by the whole ordeal. *Addicts look ridiculous when you're sober,* thought Mu 6. *Give me strength!*

The Mu(s) gathered around and gently comforted him as Mu 9 sneaked something into his shirt pocket, next to his heart. As she touched her hand to the outside of his pocket, she whispered, "This is for strength."

Mu 6 reached in his pocket and pulled it out to see what it was. He found a small and exquisitely carved rose quartz, baby Buddha. "It is beautiful," he said, allowing his delight to quickly release his tension. "I certainly need a good luck charm for this gig!" he said, as he looked at her and smiled. She winked back.

"If you rub its belly, it will help with the craving," Mu 9 dryly said, as the entire group shared a wonderful experience of laughter with them.

"Yeah," said Mu 8, "Especially when you're pushing the vacuum!" Mu 6 rolled his eyes in agony.

"All right, that's enough!" Sahab said. Costumed like the doll in Mu 6's vision, the Teacher stood before them in a black leather suit and cracked a whip over everyone's head. The group lost it completely! He gave them a few moments to compose themselves and he continued.

The group saw an image of a therapist counseling a couple who appeared to be heading for separation. There was much back and forth verbal embattlement in progress. Then the vision changed to a work environment where a supervisor was riding out a power trip on an employee. The vision melted and the liquid color and shape reconstituted itself to be a mother and child, sitting at the breakfast table quietly ignoring each other. The vision then quickly changed to a young boy outside, who doused a cat with gasoline and struck a match. The Mu(s) recoiled in horror. *What does this mean?* So many relationships, all troubled and sick, were indeed indicators of deeper distress. All of them cried out for healing.

Mu 2 was dressed causally in a brown tweed blazer, light brown slacks, a mauve silk blouse and trendy taupe leather shoes with comfortable one-inch heels. Without a doubt, she knew that she wanted to make a difference in the healing of relationships. She had already healed some of her own the hard way and she continued working on herself. She knew that here lay the key to Love expressed in the physical world, compounded and exponentially increased.

One manifestation of Mu 2 lived in Atlanta. She was the therapist for John's wife, Lynn. Her name was Dr. Andrea Rubin. The Mu 2 vibration was certainly needed and their mission of serving others by listening and catalyzing was for the purpose of saving time.

Mu 2 stuck her left arm upward as she used two fingers of her right hand to let go of a whistle. The rest of the Mu(s) jolted to attention and laughed, as she made a face, exaggerated a smile and claimed her assignment as a therapist. The healing of relationships would become her path to God and personal power. *Shazam!*

Mu 6 looked at her intently. *Mu 2 has just the right amount of objectivity, emotional detachment and a sense of humor. I hope she shows up in rehab.*

The sky visions then suddenly became a funnel of energy and disappeared with a loud sucking sound. Only the view of a dark night sky was visible, complete with twinkling stars. For a few moments, they again allowed themselves to become lost in the beauty of the dazzling diamonds that seemed to shine directly upon each one of them with great clarity and purpose. They listened and they heard a voice.

"A dark night is a dark night is a dark night." The Mu(s) began to scan the sky intently for the emanation of this communication and the deeper meanings of it. As they watched intently, the night sky accelerated into dawn, and then to the bold, bright light of a midday sun. As the round red circle of light ascended and slowly turned to glimmering gold, the Mu(s) watched, enraptured with the process. The voice was heard again, "After every Dark Night comes the Light. After every Dark Night comes the Light."

The Mu(s) quietly continued mouthing these words, concentrating intensely for the purpose of remembering them. This would be their silver thread among the gold, holding the fabric of their fragile lives together.

CHAPTER FIFTEEN

The Mission of All Things Good

Talk about another Dark Night ----- Evelyn had just terminated Ms. Bunny with her severance package sans credit cards. John would be paying for the condo until her lease ended on December 31st but her credit cards had been cancelled, effective immediately. Bunny was loose lipped and hopping mad! She was certainly glad she had written down Lynn's cell phone number from John's programmed cell phone directory. She knew exactly what she was going to do and it didn't take her long to place a call to Lynn. Bunny gave her an earful.

"Lynn, this is Bunny Baker. I've been having an affair with your husband John. I have a transmittable disease and I thought you'd like to know." Bunny quickly hung up and smiled. *This should even the score!*

It wasn't all that surprising, except for the part about the transmittable disease. *How could he? This is the last straw!* It was typical of John's reoccurring behavior. It was, however, the first time one of his bimbos had called her to rat on him. The part about the disease was unsettling to say the least. *What was it, AIDS, genital herpes or something in between? For God's sake, how could he?* It sent her straight to the telephone to call her therapist. "Andrea, can you work me in today? I'm in a major crisis!"

"You didn't have a family member or a good friend in the World Trade Center attack this morning, did you?" Andrea asked compassionately.

"No, no, it's nothing like that. It's my good-for-nothing husband!"

"Can you come in today at 3:00 P.M?"

"Yes, that'll work perfectly. It will give me time to throw some things together."

"See you then," Andrea said.

Sahab and the Mu(s) were still at it and the visions were continuing. They saw the Dark Night in many forms. There were people crashing and burning through many different situations. They all seemed to be losing something: children, fortunes, jobs, spouses, homes, businesses, crops, livestock. All were losing the things that made life seem secure; all were losing what they loved beyond all measure.

They cried out in anguish with pain so deep that it ignited the very bowels of the Earth in fire, which spilled forth as volcanoes and earthquakes. The Mu(s) recognized for the first time that their pain was not separated from Mother Earth. These massive eruptions of earth and fire created tribulation with wind and water, as hurricanes and sunamis were created and experienced. All of these things created devastation upon devastation and much unrest among the peoples of the Earth. The entire world responded to humanity's *Dark Night*.

Eventually, every single soul left standing would cry out to God; therein lay the key to understanding. The Mu(s), individually and collectively, recognized that The Dark Night of the Soul is not about losing things of importance. It is about finding the thing of greatest importance, one's own strength from within, that part of the self that is One with God.

Sahab nodded compassionately, as he observed the depth of their understanding. He wiped the tears from the corners of his eyes.

The Mu(s) continued quietly reflecting while intoning, "After every Dark Night comes the Light. After every Dark Night comes the Light..." They continued repeating the words over and over, in hopes that they would never forget this simple Truth.

They began slowly rocking together, thinking with One mind, while Sahab waited quietly and patiently for their readiness. Finally Mu 11 began humming and then leading them in song with his deep and soulful voice. They joined him in a song they all remembered well.

"Amazing Grace, how sweet the sound

That saved a wretch like me.

I once was lost but now I'm found

Was blind but now I see..."

They lost themselves in the depths of healing synergy created by the emotion of the words, the music, and their thoughtful evocations. This song poignantly spoke of passing through the Dark Night of the Soul on Earth. As they sang, each Mu celebrated his own passing through this process with anticipation and great joy, as the tears rolled down his cheeks.

Mu 11 stood up and continued singing the chorus by himself, just slightly flat. The other Mu(s) pretended not to notice the imperfection, as they looked up at him with great appreciation. They understood the significance of Mu 11's commitment to help those on Earth pass through the Dark Night of the Soul and create their exquisite pearls of great price. This Mu was to be a Human Guardian Angel for Dark Nighters. Mu 11 accepted his assignment with reverence and the Mu(s) sent him their messages of Peace and Love.

There were many Mu 11s, many potential Human Angels throughout the world who were awakening to their mission. They would come to be known as D. N. L.s, Dark Night Lighters.

The Mu 11s everywhere were deeply affected by this vision and this moment. They now understood their special role. They were to be the ones who uttered words of hope, spoken at just the right moment, to help others complete those actions with a shelf life that was long overdue. A reassuring hand upon a shoulder at exactly the right time, the provision of a roof overhead when one was needed or a kind word compassionately spoken, their words and deeds would be long remembered. Mu 11s everywhere took their assignments quite seriously today. These men and women were the Human Angels of dark days, charged with sharing Light and fulfillment.

It was also known, that the Mu 11 vibration had the potential of both the

Christ and the Anti-Christ. All vestiges of the Lagitard energy must be transmuted for the Mu 11 potential to be realized. Taking the fear out of change was what their mission was all about.

As Mu 11 continued humming perfect harmony of the higher thought potential, his aura extended to encompass all the other Mu(s) and Sahab. He continued with his ritual of dedication and transmutation for all those who ever did or ever would travel through the Dark Night, changing the face of centuries in that moment.

Mu 12 had been sitting on the grass in the Lotus position for quite some time. She was the most naturally intuitive of all of the members of this group. Mu 12 appeared to be extremely intelligent because she often came up with the correct answer, sometimes even before the question was asked. The truth of the matter was that she had average intelligence but an above average ability to trust her gut responses. This skill had been developed in many past lives where she had been a seer and a healer who had easily recognized her own Divinity. Mu 12 was one of those vibrations who always remembered from where her powers came. She never failed to give thanks to the Mother-Father Source of All Good and she was happy to be a conduit for The Source on Earth.

Sahab turned to Mu 12 and asked, "Tell us, dear student, what do you think your mission is?"

Mu 12 stood and said, "Look to the heavens." As they did so, another vision began. It depicted many famous people who had given much for many. There was Mahatma Ghandi freeing his people through non-violence and Mother Theresa helping the poor. There was Martin Luther King, Jr. in Washington, recalling a dream. The vision presented many others who worked with Love, in service to others to make a difference. There were doctors, environmentalists, human rights activists and many elevated minds with noble hearts.

The vision finished and Mu 12 began to address Sahab and the group. "My assignment is to help The Givers of the world by encouraging all of them to give more. I shall become the gentle inspiration for the giving of a gift, the gentle prodding should they forget, and the Angel on their shoulder should they think that there is not enough. I dedicate my life to giving and to helping others find the joy of giving more!" she said.

Using their minds and hearts to manifest and assemble a small bunch of wild flowers, the other Mu(s) levitated it over to her, with their Love. She smiled as she accepted their lovely gifts for all Mu 12 vibrations in the world, in this, their moment of activation. In this instant, all Mu 12s simultaneously felt an electrical surge in the middle of their foreheads.

"Well said and well done, Mu 12. Class, do you see what I meant about already knowing the work there is to be done?"

Mu 6 mumbled to himself, "I didn't realize that my part would be so broad."

Sahab repeated, "Mu 6, you say you didn't realize that your part would be so damned broad?" Laughter reigned while Mu 6 looked a tad wilted. He finally had to laugh at himself as he touched his hand to the pocket over his heart and joined the rest of the group in laughter. How the other Mu(s) loved playing with him.

Sahab looked at Mu 6 and smiled. "Remember that *Easy Does It, Moves You Forward*. Yes students, all of it is work that needs to be done because you are *The Fulfillment*! You make the journey that is already done. Together, you fulfill the prophecies of long ago and make way for Heaven on Earth.

Try not to make the mistake of thinking that you live in a physical world governed by physical laws while you are within the Earth's dream, even though it looks that way. The greater truth for you to chew and chew and swallow and digest is simply this. Regardless of appearances, we live in a Spiritual world governed by Spiritual law. Everything else that you see is pure illusion, which serves the common purpose of gently asking you the question: Have you gotten this yet?" Imploringly, Sahab extended his arms out to them.

"Why is this so difficult to see when we are part of the Earth experience?" asked Mu 9.

"It isn't difficult at all if you simply assume that the Earth is Spiritual instead of physical. When you understand this, you have rounded third base, and you're on the way home. Everything on the Earth will remind you of this Truth until you make the illusions real. Once the illusions become your reality, you can easily get lost in the circular maze. You can spin your wheels and go in the wrong direction; you can even fail to remember that you are looking for the Light. In doing so, you'll find darkness, that Lagitard remembrance born of fear. It's a game that you agreed to play until you figured this out."

The Mu(s) pondered these thoughts with great intensity as they pulled out their good luck charm and studied the side of it that had the large "ONE" inscribed in the center of the circle. They focused on the power of One and for the first time, they were able to see and experience a deeper understanding of Spirit in the world.

The goal of it all was to find Oneness, just as they were experiencing it now with each other, Sahab and their Creator. The way to achieve it stared back at them. "Easy Does It, Forward Motion," they whispered over and over again, as they looked at the letters at the top and bottom of their coin of the realm. "As above, so below," reinforced the Teacher.

Sahab then divined a large launching platform secured to the top of the large gold tuning fork from Racetrack Heaven. The platform's surface was covered with polished silver, so bright that it allowed reflection. Sahab beamed Light upon it, gradually increasing its intensity. "Think of this platform as your world, looking back at you," he said. "Fly on up here and prepare for the ride of your life!"

Each Mu(s) placed his good luck charm in his deepest pocket, being careful to divine a zipper on the outside of it for safekeeping before levitating up onto the platform. Mu 6 had additional concerns as he also divined some Velcro strips across the top of his left shirt pocket to protect his Baby Buddha.

"I'm going to need all the help that I can get," said Mu 6. Maybe this will be effective in short-circuiting small electrical appliances," he laughingly snorted, as he sealed the pocket and lifted upward. A tad behind the rest, he divined a broom mid-flight and flew in to join the rest amid gales of laughter.

"We are complete now. The class clown has arrived!" announced Mu 1.

Mu 6 bowed, accepted his applause, and with a slight of hand, he de-materialized the broom.

Sahab was watching this display with great enjoyment. As he looked at Mu 6, he smiled and said, "See how powerful you are? You could do the same thing with the bottle."

With that, Mu 6 slapped his right hand on his zippered pocket and then his left to his velcroed shirt pocket and broke out with a broad grin and said, "I'm definitely thinking about it." He bowed again to Sahab with arms outstretched.

In seriousness Sahab began, "It would be wise for you to remember that the *good luck charms*, as you call them, are not your power. Their purpose is simply to be a point of focus for your remembrance of the Truth, should you get lost. Your disk is to remind you that because all of life is a Spiritual experience, the mission must be Oneness, right? As it is above, it is so below, and one tool or method for achieving this on Earth is to remember that *Easy Going Moves You Forward*. Peace is a prerequisite to progress in the world. Peace within you is the process for the progress that you seek.

The disk itself has no power. It is but a reminder of the power within you, as you Co-create through your own Divinity with your Creator. As hard as it is sometimes for all of you to accept, you are Divine," he said, as he looked around at the group.

"Now, your Baby Buddha is quite another matter, Mu 6. You are special. If only you knew how special you are! It is proof for you that, through Compassion, a great one shows you *The Way*. You are on a special mission to end your craving and this is your role model and *The Way* to your Enlightenment. You are a Baby Buddha in the making," he said, as he compassionately looked at Mu 6.

Sahab flipped his coin of the Spiritual realm a few times. "The power is never in the object; it's always in your self," he said, as he caught the coin with perfect precision. "Remember that, all of you." Sahab looked around at the thoughtful sea of faces. They each placed a hand on their zippered pocket and patted it gently while nodding their understanding.

"A good use of this remembrance would be to picture the disk in the morning when you awaken and in the evening as you are dropping off to sleep. Whenever you are stuck during the day on any issue, take it out of your pocket and flip it up and catch it easily a few times to focus on the mission and the methods for achieving progress. Instead of struggling for solutions, let the right one find you. You can help the process along by slowing down your breathing as you are flipping your "round remembrance." If you mess up on the *Easy Going* part, there is a good likelihood you may find the wrong solution. Then, sooner or later, you will run into a brick wall in the circular maze and be forced into another direction. This is the way things work."

"It happens over and over again in relationships, doesn't it?" asked Mu 4.

"Yes, indeed!" said Sahab. "Relationships are perfect vehicles for getting lost in the circular maze. But then, we could say the same thing about all of the other assignments. This is why it would be helpful for all of you to use your disk to frequently and consciously align yourself with the power of One. If we felt Oneness with our children, would we neglect them?" asked Sahab.

"No," said Mu 4 sweetly, "we would love them!"

"And that love would create the power of One in the relationship, wouldn't it?" asked Sahab

The Mu(s) all nodded with understanding. It was all starting to *really* make sense.

Sahab continued, "The same is true for every other assignment. It is the power of One that will both create the healing and manifest the new order in the Age of Spirit. We could say that you are pioneers from the very heart of Spirit, and your coin of the Spiritual realm is your reminder of this. Don't give it more power than it deserves, but rather, use it to focus on your own power to transmute fear in the world and heal all things upon the Earth through loving kindness. And let me ask you this: Could loving kindness be any way other than *Easy Going*? Could it be anything other than Peace expressed?"

Mu 11 said, "Soft is *The Way* to action and reaction in the world. Soft defines *Easy Going*, doesn't it?"

"Yes," said Sahab, "be soft in the world in your thoughts and actions and you

162

will avoid the friction that slows you down. By doing so, you facilitate *your own Forward Motion*. This is your path to Light. Is it making sense?"

"Looks like I should avoid vacuum cleaning altogether ----- too much friction!" said Mu 6, as everyone enjoyed a good laugh with him.

Sahab then began to slowly dim the Light that shone on the platform, keeping just the slightest hint of glow on himself that they might see him in the dark night as their own reflection. They could not help but notice how beautiful and gentle he looked. As he began to speak, his voice seemed deeper and richer in tone, each word dressed more fully with emotion, yet so soft in its delivery.

"Children of Mu, we prepare now to learn the secret of how to be *Soft* in the world."

"Why is this so difficult to do?" asked Mu 6.

"Well," said Sahab thoughtfully, "it is time-related. If you place your future in the hands of your Creator, and if you release your negative thoughts on the past, your natural tendency is to be *Soft* in the world. The minute you take back these things, you start creating problems for yourselves."

This was definitely getting the Mu(s) attention for they now understood these thoughts dimensionally. They wondered though if they would be able to practice them consistently.

"Be very observant of your mental and physical responses. When you observe hardness or sharpness, simply affirm, 'I place my future in the hands of The Mother-Father Source and I release my past completely.' This is all that is needed to recapture your *Softness* in the world. Releasing the friction creates Peace and it becomes the impetus to your *Forward Motion*. Our next learning experience will allow you to have an even deeper understanding of this truth." His students were intrigued. They wondered what would be happening next.

Sahab then divined enough Light for twelve large circular coins of the Spiritual realm that became visible on the floor of the shiny silver platform. "Take your places, ladies and gentlemen," he said in his best carnival barker's voice. "Stand upon the *One* and prepare for take-off."

163

Back in the Buckhead section of Atlanta, Lynn was packing the absolute minimum. She could see that John was trying to reach her through the number display on her cell phone. She turned it off after the fifth missed call. She would deal with him later. A few nice outfits hanging, two large suitcases of clothes, her jewelry and cosmetics would be all that she needed. Lynn looked in her closet for her cosmetic case. She placed it on the bed and opened it. She noticed a book inside. *Sister must have put it there on my last visit. Strange I didn't see it when I unpacked before.* She stared at the book as she walked into the bathroom with her case.

CHAPTER SIXTEEN

Time, Endless Time

As the Mu(s) stood atop the *One* in the center of their circle, it felt as if they had stepped into a powerful energy field, locking down and amplifying their magnetic fields. Rainbow energy radiated throughout their auras as the divined hair on their heads stood on end. They felt euphoric and powerful. Light flickered and flashed around the platform, as Sahab divined a translucent bubble to contain the group. Energy flow then normalized. They could feel it happening as their hair relaxed.

"Whew," said Mu 4, as she primped and smiled. "I thought it was going to be a bad hair day."

Mu 6 was immediately behind her. He pointed his finger at her hair with intent and it flew in all directions, piling up like snakes. "Yes, Medusa," he said, as the group went wild. They were giddy with their increased power.

As the Captain of this ship, Sahab took his place in a large, purple, pilot's chair up front. He moved his right hand like a wand that created a set of controls in front of the chair. A set of gauges and knobs glistened in silver. There was one control in gold in the center of the board: the only one that seemed to have a name. Under the button was written the word, *Spiritmatic.*

From the floor up, there was complete visibility on all sides. There were three rows of circles, four circles in each, positioned for perfect visibility. The class noticed that under their teacher's chair was also a circle, with his chair perfectly centered on the "One." On the back of the chair, they could read the inscription of *Forward Motion* curving upward around it.

Sahab swung around to face them, as they stood firmly planted upon their circle of *One.* "Are you comfortable standing or would you prefer a chair?" he asked. "Either way, you will be perfectly safe."

165

As often was the case, Mu 1 began to speak for the group with assumed authority of the leader that he was. "We'd rather stand so we can see better," he said, as he looked at his classmates for their approval. Everyone nodded in agreement with him. Mu 1 was directly front and center, always in the lead. Looking handsome in his military uniform, complete with gold epaulets, Mu 1 was always eager to learn and experience life up front and personal. This was sometimes irritating to others.

Mu 6 looked at him and thought, *He's going to be a CEO of something so he can have a captive audience to drive nuts!* Using his creativity, Mu 6 de-materialized Mu 1's military cap and divined a large and unattractive hairpiece or "rug" as he called it. There it sat on Mu 1's bald head, unknown to the wearer but clearly seen by the rest. With the authority of a second lieutenant, Mu 6 said, "Big Wig has spoken!" as he saluted Mu 1.

As the group roared, Mu 1 looked around, trying to figure out what they were laughing about. He looked absolutely ridiculous in Mu 6's creation which only increased the gales of laughter, as they looked at far too much pitch-black against his fair complexion. It was every bit as bad as it could be.

"Sorry we're 'wigging out' on you," said Mu 5, as Mu 6 gently tipped Mu 1's rug to the left. The Mu(s) doubled over in belly laughs, as Mu 1 continued searching for the answer.

Sahab broke in, "All right *children* of the Mu, are we quite ready to proceed?" Mu 1 cleared his throat loudly and the rest of the Mu(s) donned a mask of seriousness and attentiveness.

Mu 6 looked at Mu 5 and winked. He raised his eyebrows and smiled back at him.

While Sahab readied the ship for departure, the Mu(s) looked upward. They focused on the stars and, almost instinctively, they began to re-create their own unique design, losing themselves in the power and beauty of this experience. Before they knew it, they were soaring in an absolutely silent sea of space. They had completely missed the take-off, so immersed they were in nonsense and now, in their star design

166

contemplation. They were moving, but it felt perfectly effortless, weightless and timeless as they glided onward like a well-oiled machine.

Sahab began to speak. "Class, we are traveling through a broad cylinder of Time known as the Present. See how smooth and easy it is to move through this realm? See how vibrant the colors appear against their background of white Light?"

"Yes," they whispered, as they looked around incredulously. "This is wonderful!"

"Off to the right and left, you can see the transparent membranes that connect us to the other dimensions. To the left is the Past dimension and to the right is the Future. Basically, they are nothing more than organizational domains for massaging data. Notice that the Past has a reddish cast to it and the Future has a bluish hue, while the Present is pure white Light."

The Mu(s) nodded. Yes, they were seeing it but beginning to wonder why.

" It is only here, in the Present, that we can create. Only here do we have the presence of all color vibrations, a necessity for creativity. The colors combine to create the white Light through which we are now traveling. It is out of this Light that we create both the Past and the Future."

"Really?" asked Mu 9.

"Yes, my child. Having the full complement of energy here, it is the only possible place where we can create. Whatever we create here changes both the Past and the Future. The Creator dwells here, in the realm of the Present, and it is only here that we can co-create. Notice that our travel here is effortless and our direction is forward," said Sahab.

"Easy Going Moves You Forward!" said Mu 12.

"Smooth sailing." responded Mu 4.

"Soft," whispered Mu 3.

"Exactly," said Sahab. "It can only happen in the Present. Off to the left in the red zone of the Past, there is great friction. The negative effects of anger and guilt are associated with it. Watch this," he said.

Sahab changed the direction of the craft to the left and easily pierced the

167

membrane into the red zone. The craft immediately experienced great drag and momentum slowed to a halt. Sahab revved the power core but no forward momentum seemed possible. "See what I mean?" he said. "The Past can halt our *Forward Motion.*"

The Mu(s) nodded and pointed with amazement, as they looked around, seeing many things they recognized.

"There's the Motherland!" said Mu 2. "She is so breathtakingly beautiful."

"Look at the plant growth and vegetation. It is lush and gorgeous," said Mu 1.

"Look over here," said Mu 5. "There's Hitler and the Death Camps of World War II. My God!" The Mu(s) looked and quickly turned away, appalled by the atrocities.

"Look behind," said Mu 3. "There's a dinosaur from the Paleolithic period. How powerful he looks!"

The Mu(s) looked around at the panorama of the Past, totally immersed in the many facets of the Earth's historical record. Sometimes they saw several versions of the same thing.

"How can this be so? It is like seeing double!" exclaimed Mu 5.

"Actions taken in the Present can change the Past as well as the Future. What happened here is that after one version of this was created, a different set of actions took place in the Present. This created a record of the later version and so forth," said Sahab.

Mu 9 spoke up, "Like there!' she pointed. "Look at all the different Bibles. There's the Torah, the Septuagint, St. Jerome's Vulgate, the Donquay, the Confraternity." Pushing her glasses back up on her nose, she continued. "Why, there's the Wycliffe Bible, the Tyndale, the King James and finally, the Revised Standard!"

"Yes," said Sahab, "A different set of actions in the Present created them all!"

The Mu(s) were alive with the possibilities that this presented. They immersed themselves in the Past, looking at many different versions of the same thing. They began to experience the Past from a uniquely different perspective, as various images floated by their craft. Different Mu(s) saw different things from the Past. They saw whatever they wanted to see in relation to their emotional charges, affinities and repulsions. Sahab allowed them time to dwell in this realm for a while.

"Had enough of this?" asked Sahab. "After a while, it seems rather lifeless and boring because there is no Spirit here. It's like a can of film from Alcyona's screening room. The Past is merely a record that documents a certain set of actions that took place in the Present. Let's go back to the Present now," he said, as he turned their craft to the right and shut down the power supply.

Miraculously or magnetically, they were not sure why, the craft was slowly pulled back into the Present, easily penetrating the membrane that led them away from the red zone and into the white Light of Present Time. At the moment of completed transcendence, all friction faded and all evidence of drag dissipated. The Mu(s) once again found they were moving forward effortlessly.

"Oh yes, this feels so much better," said Mu 10, as she took a deep breath and exhaled slowly. "We are absolutely flowing with our creativity!"

"How come it's red over there?" asked Mu 4.

"It's because of all the anger and resentment."

"Yes," said Mu 4, "We do seem to view the past mostly through negativity and regret, don't we?"

The Mu(s) nodded their agreement, as everyone flowed onward, thinking about these things.

"Hold onto your hats," said Sahab, as he veered the craft off to the right, piercing the blue membrane.

They had forged their way into Future Time. Once they were totally inside, the blue cast seemed to disappear. They saw many wonderful things that seemed to appear against a rose colored background. The craft experienced some drag moving into the Future. As it moved back toward the Light of the Present, the drag lessened noticeably. Sahab jockeyed the craft in various directions, allowing them to experience the differences in friction.

The Mu(s) saw many wonderful things. "Look over there," said Mu 5. The doctors appear to be vaccinating those children against cancer."

Mu 7 said, "Where are the poor people? I can't see them anywhere!"

"It's because of all the Givers. Look at *all the Givers*! There is so much joy being experienced by the many whom so willingly give. Wealth has been dispersed and while some have more, everyone has enough." Mu 12 was overwhelmed with happiness as she looked around at all the Givers. *How wonderful this is*, she thought. *I shall make a difference.*

"Stop! Stop Now!" said Mu 6. Sahab put on the brakes and the craft sat motionless, as Mu 6 pointed straight ahead. "There's another Mu 6," he said. "I don't understand why she's a woman." She was staggering badly and fell into a heap on the ground.

Mu 8 looked up at Sahab and asked, "How come she's a woman? I thought Mu 6 was male."

"See how quickly you get roped back into this gender thing? Right now, you are in a body I divined for you for the purpose of learning our lessons. You are not necessarily the same gender in the body that is sleeping now on Earth, although you might be. There are many of each Mu vibration living on Earth. In the many lives you have experienced, you have been both genders many, many times. Realize that there are many individuals, both male and female, of your particular Mu vibration who have challenges and assignments similar to yours. Most are a combination of more than one Mu."

"You mean: Here a Mu, there a Mu, everywhere a Mu Mu?" asked Mu 6.

Everyone laughed and Sahab said, "Yes, exactly! Most everyone on Earth is a Mu of one kind or another, except for the pure-strain Lagitards, but please try not to get stuck in gender as an issue of any great importance. You choose whatever you are for the blessing that it gives you to learn the lessons you are seeking. That's all there is to it. You are one slice of the pie."

"So, everyone is part of us," mused Mu 2, "and we are part of them, and that's how we are One?"

"There is just no substitute for great deductive reasoning. Give that gal a cigar!" said Sahab, as everyone roared.

They continued to drift in Future Time. "We are experiencing Future possibilities in the time of *The Fulfillment*. Some of them are wonderful, aren't they?" Sahab asked.

"What about that woman staggering? Does this mean that she isn't going to make it to sobriety?" asked Mu 6 mournfully.

"It's all up to her. It all depends on how and what she chooses to create in the Present," said the Teacher.

"Un-huh, I get it. Like it's up to me if I make it through rehab, right?" Mu 6 said, with that proverbial chip on his shoulder.

"It's up to you if you even need to *go* to rehab!"

Mu 6 put his right hand to his heart as he thought about these things. Focusing on his Baby Buddha, he felt strongly comforted and whole.

"Hold that thought. It's exactly what you need, Mu 6," said Sahab.

Mu 6's eyes glistened with emotion.

"All right group," said the Teacher, "Let's go back to what is absolutely real, the Present Time." He veered the craft to the left. It felt as if they were being quickly suctioned back into the Present and floating freely. As they pierced the membrane, they lost the rose tint of the background and the whole area looked blue again as they gazed at the Future from the Present.

"Why does it look blue now?" asked the analytical Mu 9 as she squinted through her glasses, trying to verify that it was indeed blue that she was seeing.

The Teacher replied, "It's because of the fear within you as you contemplate the Future. Without fear, it does not look blue. When you were in the middle of it, you lost your fear of the Future and that's why the blue disappeared. Remember the rose cast? All of you saw it. What do all of you see now?" he asked, as he pointed to the Future.

"Blue," they said, in unison, as they looked to the right. "It's all blue."

"See, you are not alone, Mu 9. There is a natural tendency for everyone to fear the Future. Most everyone seems to fear it to some greater or lesser degree. This fear makes the vision look blue. The bluer it becomes, the longer it takes for the future to arrive. Fear can absolutely paralyze us. It has the effect of freezing us in Time."

"Is this why Time sometimes seems to stand still?" asked Mu 2.

"Yes, especially when you are young; it is also why Time seems to pass by faster as you age in the Earth dream. Through maturation and learning come wisdom and the relinquishment of fear, because you more closely align with your true nature, your Spiritual nature. Does this make sense?"

"I think so," said Mu 2.

"Now, let's experience how some of this works," said Sahab. "See how effortlessly forward we are moving in the Present?"

Sahab placed the craft controls on Spiritmatic, as he revolved around in his chair to face them. Like beads on a wire, they glided smoothly forward in the warm white Light of Present Time. Looking outward, the Mu(s) noticed that the stars had turned into gold and they were twice as large, lighting up the heavens.

"All right class, give me your full attention."

Reluctantly, one by one, they pulled their focus away from the stars and fixed it on Sahab. Being totally mesmerized by their beauty, it took Mu 6 just a little longer than the rest.

"Welcome Home Everyone!" said Sahab. "We are all now fully here in the Present. This is the only *real* Time there is! Yes, I know there is this body of images to your left that we call the Past," he said, as he gestured in that direction. "And to your right is this other body of images we call the Future possibilities," as he pointed to the Future. "They are not *real* in the same way that the Present is real because the Creator is not there. The Mother-Father Source dwells only in the Present. It is, therefore, the only place where creativity is possible, and yes, the only place where you can function as the Co-Creator that you are!

These other realms can influence the Present only as you infuse them with emotion while contemplating them in the Present. So far, we have been dealing with Past and Future from an intellectual frame of reference. Let's see what happens when emotion is added. Look toward the red zone now and recall something from your past that you feel angry or guilty about." As they did so, the craft began to move erratically in angular and jagged movements, changing direction frequently, with randomly dissonant sounds. For safety purposes, the Mu(s) promptly divined a pole in the middle of the circle of One where they were standing and held on for dear life.

"This appears to be of the Past, but guess what? It's affecting you now, isn't it? And guess what? It's a Time-waster, isn't it? It's gobbling up your precious Time in the Present unproductively, isn't it? Look at what's happening to you." The Mu(s) were lurching this way and that. "I certainly wouldn't call this *Easy Going* and we have anything here but *Forward Motion*. There is also no experience of *Oneness*. There is only individualization and Separation as you contemplate this mess and you feel quite alone in the experience, don't you?"

"I feel woozy and I haven't even had a drink!" said Mu 6.

"Spend too much time here and you'll need one!" said Sahab, as they all laughed and nodded.

"When you give life to the Past through memory, and infuse it with emotions of anger, resentment or guilt, it always slows you down in the Present."

"I never thought about it that way," said Mu 6, as he looked at the group. They nodded their agreement.

"Now, let's see what obstacles the Future can present. Look toward the blue and infuse emotion into your greatest fear about the Future."

As they did so, the craft began spinning counterclockwise, holding a stationary position. The Mu(s) hung onto their safety pole with a death grip.

"Talk about spinning your wheels," said Sahab.

"I'm getting sick!" shouted Mu 11. "Let me off this damn thing! Thank God I'm wearing shorts and a T-shirt; I'm about to anoint them!"

"Stop focusing on the fear!" said Sahab. "Stop it now, all of you, and see what happens!"

They stopped dead in their tracks, pulling their focus from the blue to the white Light that was straight ahead. As they chose a different point of focus, the craft stopped spinning and leveled out. They began to move forward, smoothly. Gaining their composure, they began to breathe more slowly and deeply, releasing tension and feeling better.

"It all seemed real, didn't it?" asked Sahab.

"Oh my God yes, did it ever!" said Mu 11.

"The choice is ours, isn't it?" responded Mu 12, adjusting her turban and her robe. "We can lose the creative miracle of the Present by focusing on the Past with anger, resentment and guilt or by focusing on the Future in fear."

"Or," said Sahab, "you can choose to create out of Love in the place where you are now ----- the Present moment, the only *real* Time and place where you can create a better world. Remembering this is the key to the completion of your assignments in the time of *The Fulfillment*.

The Present is the only place that's *Real* because it is the only place where the Creator dwells. Therefore, it is the only place you can function as a Co-Creator. If you avoid the anger, resentment, and guilt from the Past, and avoid fear of the Future, Love is the only thing left to use to create the many wonderful things that are so needed now. Love and Oneness of Spirit can only be experienced in Present Time. Think about it. If you choose to dwell in the Present, you will surprise yourself with many miracles. Only in the Present can you walk hand-in-hand with your own Divinity."

The Mu(s) thought strongly on these things and the energy that was generated warmed up the cabin of their ship. The bubble enclosure began to fog up a bit. Sahab revolved around in his chair again to address them, "I think you're getting this."

"What about the bubble fogging up?" asked the ever observant Mu 9.

174

"I don't think we even need the bubble any more," said Sahab. "I don't think you need those safety poles either, do you? I think you are starting to trust more. You're trusting your conclusions. You are trusting your mind and heart. You are trusting your Divinity, but most of all, you are trusting your Creator, aren't you?"

Mu 6 was the first one to respond as he de-materialized his safety pole. Mu 9 followed suit. On and on it went with safety poles de-materializing one by one until they were One in their willingness to trust their Creator. When the last pole disappeared, Sahab said, "Trust in your Creator is the only thing that's needed for a feeling of safety in the world." He then allowed the bubble to de-materialize.

"I've got it! I've got it!" said Mu 6. The rest of the Mu(s) chimed in, identically repeating after him: "I've got it!" "Me too!" "Oh yeah!"

Little by little, Sahab then allowed pieces of the platform to de-materialize, leaving only the individual circles on which they stood. Like accomplished slalom skiers, they glided effortlessly on their coin of the Spiritual realm through the time zone of the Present. Looking like a group of well-trained Blue Angels, they flew with precision *Moving Forward* in the Present. They were flying free, in concert with the Creator. For the first time, they felt comfortable allowing the Captain to call the shots. Working together in concert, the group created something greater than any one of them could do alone, as they Co-Created with the medium of Love in the time zone known as the Present.

Sahab stood on a cloud in the distance, smiling in complete appreciation of their agility when the Angel Alcyona swooped in. Stopping on a dime as only she could do, she landed next to him.

"What do you think?" asked Sahab, looking at her sweetly.

Alcyona had tears of joy streaming down her face as she sputtered, "I'm so pleased with the children of Mu" and, as she looked at Sahab, she said, "And I'm such a softie. Forgive me for being so hormonal." Seeing the tears streaming down his cheeks, she quickly asked, "You too?" They laughed and gave each other a big hug.

"Try not to cry on my lavender pouf," she said. "It cannot withstand too much humidity." Arranging it as they separated, she smiled at him.

"What time is it?" asked Sahab, knowing full well there wasn't anyone better at knowing time than Alcyona. She could look in any direction and know instantly and correctly what time it was!

Playing psychic with great melodrama, she placed one wing upon her head and closed her eyes as if to receive the answer psychically. Then after a very long, conjuring pause, she opened her eyes and said, "Three birds to twelve! No, No…let's see… Ah yes, it's…it's…." She broke her posture and beckoned Sahab to come closer. Looking directly at him, she whispered, "Before the batteries run out on their training modules, we have just enough time for a movie." Sahab smiled and she stretched her wings energetically and winked at him.

"You're on!" he said, as he put his arm gently around her and they began moving toward the screening room. "Alcyona, which director are you interested in seeing today? How about Hitchcock?" he asked, knowing full well what her response would be.

A sly smile crossed her face as she thought for a moment about this director's brilliance and then, halfway in jest, she said, "Lord no! I've never gotten over that film he did about the birds! How about an oldie, you know, something light and joyous?"

Sahab knew exactly what she wanted and said, "Why not?" as he divined himself into formal attire and stretched out his hand to her. She snapped her fingers and immediately, she appeared in Ginger's finest white gown as the music began to play. Right hand in left, they became *One* as they danced The Continental on their way to the movies. "La da da da da, The Continental, La da da da …."

"Careful! Don't ruffle my feathers! You know how I hate it when you ruffle my feathers!" she sputtered, smiling at Sahab.

"Yes dear," he said, patronizingly. Singing and dancing, they laughed their way through Heaven!

CHAPTER SEVENTEEN

Change Happens!

The Time Zone of the Present had a crispness about it that made all things stand out clearly. The color of every object boldly contrasted against the background of brilliant white Light. It was like an acid trip devoid of ill effects. The medium of the Present was energized with pure, unadulterated creativity as new ideas and solutions cracked their way out of the egg quite naturally.

As the Mu(s) dwelled in the Present, it was utterly impossible to fail to recognize the existence of the Creator. There was a comfort that came from doing so. It was as if each Mu had plugged himself into an electrical socket of creativity. They recognized their own Divinity playing in perfect concert with their Creator.

Each Mu spontaneously understood that he was a conduit for the Creator's energy and that he was able to function as a creative extension of it. This was how Co-Creation took place. In the Creator's domain of the Present, they could take this energy, mold and shape it to create whatever they desired in the way of new inventions or things of substance in the Earth experience. There were no limits on their creativity or on the many things they could create in the Present. This was where all creation took place, where all intention found resolution in ways that were quite natural.

By contrast, the Past and Future dimensions were merely archives or repositories for past and possible results of actions taking place in Present Time. There was no before, during and after. It was all happening *Now*, as both past records and future possibilities were simultaneously recorded.

As actions took place in the Present, an instantaneous energy surge went to the right and left. The sharpness of the colors at both sides of the record keeping areas was somewhat muted by the predominance of either too much red or blue, depending on who was looking at it. Only in the Present were all colors in the color spectrum equally balanced to create the energized medium of pure white Light, the full pallet and the canvas needed for creativity. Trying to create without these things was indeed limiting.

The stark contrast created by the white background was also necessary for the Co-Creator to view and mold the creations. Of course, the Creator's energy was absolutely mandatory for giving form to new ideas. It was like scrambling eggs and observing the mixture go from a runny liquid to solid form, changing in color and in texture, creating something new.

While the Mu(s) were focused in the Present, they wanted to be nowhere else. They experienced complete satisfaction and total fulfillment. There was also a lack of time-awareness. As they soared through the white Light, they felt the blessing of profound knowledge and perfect peace.

The Mu(s) also felt perfectly safe, even though there was no protective bubble around them. Their feet felt magnetized to the round silver disk of "One" on which they traveled; they experienced great joy in their Co-Creatorship. They glided through the white Light of the Present with the awe and wonderment of a child on Christmas Eve.

Mu 6 was doing forward flips as he pressed the limits of his forward motion. The blue, green and mauve of his Hawaiian shirt tumbled with a fluorescent quality as the rest of the Mu(s) observed his color in motion. They delighted with him in his new found freedom.

Mu 12 was totally immersed in her intuitive thoughts. Here, she saw everything so clearly. She could read each action made in the Present, complete with its Past and Future possibilities. Centered in the Present, she was at her best in using her intuitive abilities to the fullest.

As she reflected on these things she heard a mental whisper say to her: *You have learned to dwell here more often than most, and this is how you have developed your gift of insight. Everyone has this gift. When they are unaware of its presence, they do not seek to use it, nor do they trust it when they find themselves spontaneously using it. They tend to discount it as their imagination. Teach them, my child, to use this*

gift that is the path to so many blessings.

Mu 12 instinctively knew that the Creator was speaking directly to her. She thought about how natural it was for her to be intuitive. It was a bicycle she didn't have to think about riding. If she could teach others to use and develop their gifts of intuition, she could make a real difference with The Givers on the Earth.

They would instinctively know where their gifts were needed. If they could only begin to see all of the Past and Future ramifications of giving, they would surely give to the fullest extent of their capability. At the moment, she could personally glimpse a minimizing of the muting of color in the red and blue membranes. If The Givers could only see that emptying the glass but allows a greater space for filling. Creative ideas for the purpose of helping The Givers continued flowing into her awareness.

Yes, the Mu(s) were flying free in the time zone of the Present. Their manner of progressing was easy going and their direction was forward. As long as they stayed focused in the Present, there was absolutely no drag whatsoever. They had tried this out several times to verify the proof of this reality, especially Mu 9, who had divined herself a set of horse blinders which she wore for training purposes.

This contraption is uncomfortable but it does keep me centered in the Present. If I don't look at the Past or the Future, it seems to help, she thought.

With her vision under control, there were only the emotions to deal with, and those were quite enough. She found that while she could not stop the negative emotions from coming into her awareness, she could allow them to pass through instead of lingering for a long unwelcome visit.

Mu 9 used several useful tools to accomplish this. Humming in the key of B flat was one of them. When she tired of hearing her own voice, she divined a set of earphones, which stretched across her head and attached to a cassette recorder that fastened to her belt with a metal clip. It operated on batteries and played musical compositions, all written in the key of B flat. Listening seemed to open a trap door behind her heart to allow the negative emotions to pass right through.

Moving to the left, the music seemed to slow down, as if the batteries were playing out. Moving to the right made the music sound as if it were on a fast forward track. Gliding forward, staying in the middle made the music absolutely "One" with her.

What a tremendous experience this is, thought Mu 9. Affirming to herself seemed to strengthen her learning process.

Cindy had arrived back at the salt mines after lunch. She went straight to her office and put her "Do Not Disturb – Email Only" sign on her door and closed it before anyone could grab her and slow her down. She had finished sixteen chapters of the manual so far. She found it fascinating, but there were deadlines to meet. *I'll get back to this later*, she thought, as she put it in her briefcase.

She hit her classical music CD six pack, as she called it, and put on her earphones. She found this to be the best way to enter the *ZONE* of creativity and keep the mundane everyday thoughts at bay. She had long ago learned to use this method to stay focused on the task at hand. Cindy had a deadline to meet on a project.

Another tool that both Cindy and Mu 9 used to stay focused on a task was the act of breathing. By purposely slowing it down and extending each part of both the inhalation and the exhalation to the fullest extent, Mu 9 was able to open another trap door in the back of her head, allowing the negative thoughts and emotions to pass on through. Once she had done so several times, she began to worry that this negativity might be finding someone else who was coming along behind her.

Wouldn't it be wonderful if I could lessen the impact of this on everyone else that experiences it? As Mu 9 continued her deep breathing while holding these thoughts of Compassion, she was able to decrease the velocity and intensity by a full ten percent. "Very interesting," she said, as she contemplated the importance of this finding.

She verified things by Divining and attaching a Velten Meter onto the chest of Mu 6 while keeping the remote to monitor his readings. She flew in front of him to see if she could measure a difference. Once she believed that she could make a difference, she found that she no longer seemed to require proof. "Very interesting!"

she said.

Mu 9 didn't even mind that she must look ridiculous to everyone, wearing the horse blinders and the earphones. She was simply thrilled that her methods seemed to be working for her and that she was clearly able to make a difference for others. She was able to stay solidly in the center of the time zone of the Present while allowing negative thoughts and emotions safe passage through her. By transmuting them through Compassion, she was able to lessen their impact on everyone else who would ever come along behind her.

If I never learn anything else, this is worth a million! she thought.

Mu 6 was flying along behind, playing the Velten like an accordion. He didn't know exactly what was going on. He did know that when he was in her down draft, he felt better. He felt stronger. He had more confidence in himself and that felt good!

This is one extraordinary experience, he thought, as he glided onward filled with Peace and Love.

Tom was still voraciously reading his manual in the yard with Pep. For a day that started out hung over, he was filled with energy he could not explain. He only had a few more chapters to go and he wanted to finish it today. On his last break to refill his coffee cup, he had looked through the yellow pages for in-patient rehab numbers and had written down three different names and telephone numbers. For unknown reasons, he seemed more willing to deal with his addictions today. He hadn't firmly committed himself to the Chinese torture treatment yet, but he was most of the way there. He thought about taking the manual with him and it helped him feel better about the process.

Mu 8 was having an interesting experience in the time zone of the Present. Being a natural number-cruncher, he had Divined a computer desk and laptop and was moving forward in an easy going fashion in the center of the energy field.

Crunching away on his financial data, he noticed that as he considered *Past* performance and *Future* projections, it ate the RAM and slowed things down. It was like going from a Pentium 4 on DSL to Morse Code on the Telegraph. The difference

181

in speed slowed him down, diminishing everything he was able to accomplish in the now. He could see the visual proof of this and yet, it went against everything he had learned while completing his MBA degree. How could his professors be wrong? *Am I missing something here?* He wondered.

In the Now on Earth, John was in his office working on a proposal for their Asian client. He emailed Cindy. "Don't forget me on the marketing promo for Infinity Plus. NEED TODAY! ASAP! Thanks! John." Cindy emailed back. "Under control and on it now!"

Thank God for her, John thought. *The numbers are starting to make sense. Once we integrate the marketing piece, this thing will be good to blast off. Then I can deal with Lynn. Wonder where she is? I've got a mess on my hands and no time to deal with it now.* John had already placed three calls to her cell phone and had gone to message every time.

Mu 8 had come to realize that considering Past performance and Future projections clearly seemed to slow things down in the Present, especially if he had even the slightest doubt about the idea or project.

Past performance and Future projections allowed for calculated decisions based on logic which seemed to slow down the progress made in the Present. The process of considering, both narrowed the center band of white Light and expanded the bands of red and blue to the right and left.

On the other hand, if he fully believed in his idea, Past performance and Future projections did not slow him down because he was not dependent upon them. *Belief is the thing that makes the difference!* he thought, as a light bulb went off in his head. *If you have that, it's all you need! And when you don't have it, you need to look at past performance and create future projections to achieve it!* Maybe this is the *how* and *why* of innovation in a nut shell. Entrepreneurs can ignore the Past and Future and work very focused in the Present because they have *Belief. All of the other stuff is irrelevant if you Believe in your idea and stay very focused on it in Present Time.*

Mu 8 picked up speed and whizzed by the rest of them. As a businessman, he began to calculate a *Belief Scale* by which he might judge the financial success of entrepreneurs. *Man, I am onto something!*

John too, was having some powerful new ideas and incorporating them into the proposal. He was busy integrating them when he noticed an email from Cindy.

"Here it is, in email attachment. Look it over and don't forget there's another piece to it in your lateral file; look in the Tunneyford folder. We used a piece of it for the marketing arm in that account, the lead-in portion. What I'm sending you tailors Tunnyeford to the new account. Look and see if you have what I'm referring to. Olga has it on disk and can pull it all together for you in a New York minute! Cindy."

John pulled open the drawer to his lateral file and began looking in the Ts: *Tailor, Trolland, Tunneyford* – He reached for the file. In it, he found a book. *The Fulfillment, Return of Mu, What the hell is this?* Right behind the book was the piece he was looking for. He placed the book on top of the credenza and quickly read through the Tunneyford marketing piece. He reviewed Cindy's email attachment. *OK, we're getting there!* "Olga, please come in."

He emailed Cindy, "I found Tunneyford and yes, it all looks good. Olga's on it. Thanks! By the way, did you put something extra in that file? There's a book there called *The Fulfillment, Return of Mu*. Can't figure this out. Do you know anything about it?" John

"Not a clue as to why it's there but I do know something about it. This is going to sound weird but a copy of it appeared on my car seat this morning and another copy appeared elsewhere for Tom. Take it home with you to read. We can talk about it at lunch on Thursday. You are not going to believe some of this! Definitely some hocus pocus going on – good stuff!" Cindy

"You have peaked my curiosity on this. Will take it home and yes, to lunch on Thursday. See you then and thanks for the great work on Infinity +." John

Mu 10 was definitely in her element, flying free in the *Present*. Her kafkan was flowing in the breeze. Catching it, a burst of wind took it upward over her head as wind currents carried it backward. There she was in her black leotard with her kafkan dancing. She moved forward effortlessly. To her it was like participating in a jazzercise class without gravity, and she was thoroughly enjoying the experience.

On Earth, Susann was in the wings, waiting to go on stage. She was in a New York touring production of *The Full Monty*. For a moment, there was an electrifying moment of clarity. She heard her cue, went on stage and gave the performance of her lifetime to a very small house.

One creative idea after another moved through her mind with rapid fire. It was only fear of the Future and pain from the Past that had previously slowed down the creative flow of ideas. Those stagnant fields to the right and left of Time had the power to dilute her performance in the Present, only if she allowed them to do so. Living in the Present was the place where she could powerfully create. Mu 10 continued improvising movement in the choreographic process for a new work she called, "Freedom."

Their training modules were beginning to slow down as the Mu(s) approached a large, circular, glass-covered dome that stretched across the entire Time Zone of the Present like a bridge.

Could this be the end of the ride? they thought. As if it were a perfectly planned event, the module safely delivered them to a platform in the center of the entryway. As the disk on which they had been riding stopped, each Mu stepped off. This continued until all the training modules were in a stack, piled up like chips on a blackjack table.

Mu 1 was the last to arrive. Standing atop the pile in his military uniform, he paused for a moment of oratory. "I stand here upon Mount Olympus to give thanks to our Creator. May we never forget these magical moments!" He slid down the pole placed to the side of the training modules with a loud Geronimo yell. Mu 1 joined the rest of the group amid their whistling and loud applause.

"Let's hear it for our fearless leader!" shouted Mu 6 as they all cheered.

The Mu(s) lounged in a circle at the center of the entryway to the circular glass-covered dome. Mu 2 was the first to speak. "How difficult we have made the Earth experience by choosing to dwell so much in the Past and Future! Why, we have absolutely wasted the opportunity of creating good in the Present. It is unbelievable that we have failed to see the opportunity that living in the Present offers."

During the trip, Mu 6 had thought about his dog, Pep, and manifested her Spirit in the dream. He brought her along for the rest of the ride. Mu 6 unhitched the pet holder and let his little dog down to stretch her legs. He had been carrying her in a backpack that he wore in front to restrain her against his chest for this ride through the Present.

Being able to see her somehow created in him a feeling of safety for her. He spoke to her as though she were a child, "We did get some very good ideas on the way, didn't we, Pep?" Pep looked at him lovingly and barked once, emphatically, as Mu 6 petted her and then held back her ears. "Look gang, doesn't she look like a baby seal?"

"Yes," said Mu 9, "if you've never seen one." Everyone laughed.

"The thing that happened for all of us," said Mu 11, "is that we experienced a moment of Enlightenment." He took his coin from his pocket, and held it up between his thumb and index finger for all to see. "We know *Oneness* only in the Present. It is only here where *Easy Going* can produce a *Forward Motion*. This is all there is to know. This is the Alpha and Omega."

Their visual attention was suddenly taken by a flock of birds flying over. Mu 11 paused for a moment and watched with the rest of them before he continued.

"We have experienced Enlightenment and we *are* able to live on Earth from that perspective. It will take us through the Dark Night quickly. Our eyes have seen the glory of the workings of The Source," he sang, as a Light shown all around him. The writing on his T-shirt began to flash like a neon sign upon his chest, "*Now*, I See Now!"

Mu 12 spoke up next. "I agree with you Mu 11, but I would like to add something. In the new age of Spirit, in the time of The Fulfillment, the tool that will most help us fulfill our goals and the prophecy of the ages is the use of our intuition.

Analytical mind only allows us to go so far. It is our intuitional mind that enables us to Co-Create," he said, as he looked at Mu 9. "This is because, to use it, we go directly to The Source. It requires integration rather than separation. If we learn to exercise it, trust it and act upon it, we just might have the answer, even before the question is asked." Mu 12 paused for a moment, as if she were contemplating the importance of what she said, and then continued.

"I have seen the way that all of you have sometimes looked at me," continued Mu 12, "as if I had extraordinary intelligence. I say to you that I am not as innately bright as most of you, but I trust, without reservation, my connection with The Source of All Good. The Creator speaks through the use of my intuition. It is the Source of all my knowledge and the path to my fulfillment. Remember this and find your own connection. You will amaze yourself."

Placing her hand on her turban, she said, "You have thought of this thing as an association with magic of one kind or the other. It is, rather, a symbol for me, of my use of intuition as a vertical path to Light." She extended her arm upward. "Sometimes we need symbols to remind us of the Truth," she said.

Mu 9 chimed, "OK guys, I hear you loud and strong and I'm getting there. It's just taking me longer because I've got all of this analytical mind baggage to trip over; however, I am willing to do whatever it takes to increase my reliance on intuitional mind."

Watching and listening from a balcony thrusting out from the glass-covered dome, Sahab and Alcyona watched carefully. "What do you think, Alcyona?" asked Sahab as he looked at her.

"Well," she said, "I think they are Divine!"

"They have certainly done well so far," he said. "Once they experience the *Forgiveness Chamber*, they should be good-to-go," said Sahab, as he leaned against the railing and thoughtfully looked at them. "Go ahead, lead them inside. I shall make the final preparations and meet you there." He turned and went inside the dome as Alcyona took flight from the balcony.

"Look!" said Mu 7. "There she is. There's Alcyona!" The rest of the Mu(s) were joyous as they looked to the sky to see their beloved Alcyona, showing off as she did a skywriting bit. She spelled out across the wide expanse of sky, *Bird Lady Back*!

Everyone cheered as she swooped in, stopping on a dime in front of Mu 6. She made her huge yellow eyes as wide as possible, looked directly at him and stretched her wings.

Sinking a bit, he said, "Uh-oh, I think I'm in trouble!"

She winked at him, fluffed her wings and tucked them in. Looking around at the group, she asked, "Seen any good movies lately?"

"Seen them? We've been starring in them," said Mu 10.

"I know, I know. I've been watching you!" Alcyona whispered. "I think you are all going to be up for an Academy Award! My darlings, I think all of you are going to be a smash!" she exclaimed, as she looked around at the group. Resting her gaze upon Mu 6, she said, "Sorry, poor choice of words," as she smiled at him. The group enjoyed a nice round of giggles.

She is so much fun, thought Mu 9.

"Go ahead, beat up on me," said Mu 6, as he Divined himself into a black sheep, running in circles around her, bleating.

Alcyona looked at the group and said, "I guess some things never change. Now, will my little black sheep take his place among the group?"

Mu 6 undid his divination, smiled broadly at her as he sat down next to Mu 9 and put his arm around her. She smiled at him and patted his shirt pocket as if to say, "Don't forget what you have here!" The Baby Buddha glowed with a golden light that emanated from the left side of his chest.

"OK group, Sahab is waiting for us inside. He has things to share with you that are most important to the success of your mission. Let's not keep him waiting." Alcyona turned and started toward the entry as the Mu(s) trailed along behind.

CHAPTER EIGHTEEN

Change Is Why You're Here

The Mu(s) followed Alcyona into the glass-covered dome, wondering what could possibly be coming next. The place looked strange and futuristic. Moving inside, they became immediately aware of the increased clarity of their thought processes. Everything they looked at or thought about was crystal clear.

The inside of the dome was one large circular space, forty-four feet in diameter. There were three different areas, which had the appearance of different set designs. Everything looked quite modern, almost space-like. *Were they in yet some other dimension? What was going on here?* The floor was blue marble and each of the three set designs was pure white.

One set design in the center area consisted of a slightly raked platform. At the top of it was a screen measuring eleven-foot square. Another area to the right housed a recessed circular pool of water, which slowly revolved in a clockwise direction. In a circular formation along the outside wall, steps with a low riser went down into the water. They remained stationary as the pool revolved. Large palm trees circled the pool like the rounded part of a new moon.

To the left of the center design area was a third domain. It was a strange looking round structure with twelve separate cubicles or compartments that looked like twelve tanning beds, standing on ends. From above, massive lights focused downward on the beds. There were seven lights, each a different color, ranging from red to violet. All of the lights fed into a larger central mixer; through twelve separate feeders, they focused on a particular compartment below.

Through the middle of the glass-covered dome, which enclosed all three areas as one continuous space, a top center area of the space inside the lights permitted a view of the heavens. This was also true of the other two areas.

Sahab bowed to his students and to Alcyona and said, "It is good to be with you again." Alcyona stretched her wings in salutation as the students bowed their heads.

Excitedly, Mu 10 looked around. "Are we going to perform?" she asked, hoping that she might be able to present her latest choreography.

"In a manner of speaking, yes," said Sahab. "You are now in the Assimilation Area. It will ground you in the Truths you have remembered."

"I'm ready for a swim!" said Mu 6 as he pointed toward the circular pool. "All of that living in the Present took its toll on me."

"Yes, I saw you playing your accordion," said Sahab. "That must have really tired you out! Come over here and find a pillow." He motioned them to the center platform with the screen. There were twelve lavendar pillows arranged in rows of four on the dark blue marble floor in front of the platform.

Each student chose a pillow and sat down on it, taking a Lotus position and giving their full attention to their Teacher. Sahab sat down on the front edge of the platform. "This is where it all comes together for you," he said, as he gestured to the three areas. "This is how change happens."

Alcyona was busy checking the other two areas. She seemed to be testing the water temperature of the pool. Then she moved to the other side and appeared to be adjusting the feeders that shined Light onto the twelve cubicles. Satisfied that all was fine, she moved to the back of the group and perched unobtrusively on a large, round sphere of pure blue marble supported by a white Grecian pedestal.

With her wings outstretched, she could have been a commercial for overnight delivery. Once she tucked in her wings, she appeared to be part of the aesthetics of the sculpture. Alcyona watched the students with great interest as Sahab continued.

"Let us begin by practicing your mantra to re-orient you to your mission. You all have the same goal, you know, to realize Oneness with everyone and everything."

The Mu(s) closed their eyes and began chanting, "One, One, One...." It became the deepest of all meditations for each of them as they lost track of time and found perfect peace. Once alert, they noticed that the general lighting had dimmed. A revolving three-dimensional sphere of the planet Earth projected onto the screen. The colors of blue, green and brown were the most prominent. The image then swirled and recreated itself into the representation of a genderless form of a human body. It looked like a puzzle, with many different interlocking sections.

"Think of the Earth as one body of which you are a part. While you are a part of the Earth dream, you are using the space of one small piece of the puzzle. You can use the dream to work in concert with the rest of the body or you can work against it. Let me demonstrate by placing Mu 8 in that part of the puzzle that is the right kneecap." Mu 8 was diminished in size and instantly transported.

"If he chooses to work with the rest of the body in Oneness, harmony can prevail. But he can also work against the body in Separation. Suppose he decides to shoot at the left knee? It could be a *Boom, Boom, Boom*, like in New York and Washington." Mu 8 took aim and shot at the left kneecap, shattering it to bits. The left leg crumpled and the body fell to the ground. "See what happens when we choose Separation?"

"We injure a part of ourselves," said Mu 9.

"Yes, exactly!" said Sahab.

"It's like cancer, isn't it?" asked Mu 5, "When the cancer doesn't realize it's a part of the body and destroys the very environment that gives it life."

"Yes, exactly! This is why finding Oneness in the Earth experience is not elective, it is mandatory for life to continue in harmony. We've been taking potshots at ourselves for centuries now. Osama is bringing this to a head now so that we can see it for what it is. Terrorism is a disease of the mind, gone berserk. It is not coincidental that his name begins with an "O". It could just as easily stand for Oneness instead of Separation. His power could just as easily be used for good. Instead of guns, his resources could be used to feed the poor."

Sahab then directed all the individual pieces of the puzzle to go haywire and attack other parts of itself as the Mu(s) watched the dissonance and winced in pain.

Sahab then abruptly halted the hostility and said, "Everyone knows better, Palestine and Israel, Pakistan and India. P and I, power and intimidation, on and on it goes! The problem is that they simply do not always remember everything they know. At a cellular level this Truth is encoded in every living thing, but here's what happens. Caught up in the illusion of having separate bodies, they forget that they are all part of the one body," he said, as he pointed to the large puzzle on the screen.

The image began to swirl as the human form gave way and re-materialized again as planet Earth. "You are to bring wisdom to the process of living. And, let me ask you, what do you think will be the biggest help to you in living from a perspective of Oneness?" he asked, as he looked around the group.

Mu 6 responded, "Living in the Present."

Sahab continued, "That's right! The old P & I warriors are choosing to live in the past. Forget history. Forget getting even! By the way, I did notice that Mu 9 seemed to be doing the most experimentation with the Present. Tell me, Mu 9, what happened when you were free of intention while you were in the Present?" asked Sahab.

"There was a clear and steady drift to the left," she said.

"That's right," said Sahab. "It takes work to stay in the Present. That's exactly what was happening when she was intent on hearing the music at its clearest and best. When she intentionally stayed in the center of the Present, she achieved perfect Oneness with the music. Intention, class, intention, clear intention is what is needed to remain in the Present. Without it, you will usually experience that slow and steady drift to the left, to the Red Zone of the Past. It is the biggest problem that most people have."

Mu 2 jumped in, "But what about the future? At times, I seemed to drift to the right. I didn't pass through the blue membrane but I felt the pull in that direction."

"This is the second biggest problem most people have ----- fear of the Future. Focusing on these fears makes you drift to the right. You have your assignment as a therapist, Mu 2, because you have understanding and empathy for both anger and resentments of the Past and fear of the Future. At a gut level, you understand it. A

192

good therapist must be prepared to recognize this and deal with these areas of potential sabotage."

It was now 2:50 P.M. and Lynn had arrived at Andrea's office in Decatur. Lynn sat down on the couch in the waiting area and sighed. Her eyes darted around the room and came to rest on a book that was resting on the cocktail table right in front of her. *The Fulfillment, Return of Mu...This is the same book I found in my cosmetic bag. This is weird.* As she was reaching for it, Andrea opened the door to the waiting room and smiled at her.

"Come in, Lynn and tell me what's going on with you."

"Hi Andrea, can you tell me about this book?" Lynn asked, as she pointed at it.

"Which book?"

"The one in the middle there, *The Fulfillment.*"

Andrea picked it up and looked at the cover for a moment before she answered. "I wonder who left this for me? Someone must have left me a gift," she said as she opened the cover. On the first page was a dedication, 'To Mu 2 with Love'. "Interesting, I don't know who left it here, but I guess I'll have to read it now. It has peaked my curiosity." She scanned the first few pages of the front matter. "Yes, this does look like something that I want to read."

"Andrea, I found a copy of this book earlier today at the bottom of my cosmetic case and I am not sure how it got there. What do you think is going on here?"

"I don't know. Did it have an inscription?"

"Beats me, I didn't look."

"A little mystery is fun, isn't it? It looks like there might be something here for both of us. There are no coincidences, you know!" Andrea started walking into the office with Lynn following along behind.

"Yes Andrea, and wait until you hear about what's going on with me! Thanks for working me in on short notice.   I'm maxing out and I really need some confirmation that I'm sane."

Lynn flopped down in the overstuffed chair and let the wind out of her sails. "As you know, John has never been the faithful husband. Today, his latest Bimbo called me and blew the whistle on him. You could hear the white-hot passive aggressiveness in her voice. His secretary, Evelyn, probably gave her walking papers. He doesn't even have the balls to tell them in person! She was probably trying to get even."

"What did she say?"

"That she had been having an affair with him, that she had a communicable disease and thought I ought to know."

"Yes, go on. And how did you feel?" asked Andrea.

"Try stunned and ballistic! The last straw was the part about the disease! I've had it with him! I don't understand why one wife is not enough! Lord knows how many women he has kept! I know about five of them but that's probably just the tip of the iceberg. Evelyn, on the other hand, could probably write an x-rated novel that would make Peyton Place look tame! I'm leaving him today: I guess I just need to hear I am not crazy."

"Why do you think you haven't left before now?"

"The usual things ----- the children and the good memories. It wasn't all bad you know. Like a fool, I thought he'd come to his senses! He can talk a good game. How many times have I heard, 'This will never happen again?'"

Andrea handed Lynn a tissue and she dried her tears. "It's good to release your pain," Andrea said compassionately. "So, what's the plan?"

"The amazing thing to me is that I'm not afraid! Andrea, I can't understand it. Always before, I was so afraid to even picture life without him ----like what would I do and where would I go? My career has been that of a model wife with a resume of volunteer activities, not work experience. Guess what? Today I don't give a shit about my memories of the past and I have absolutely no fear about the future! In some ways, it astounds me! Maybe the tragic events of today, in the world at large and in my own world, have made me wake up! This is all I know! I'm on my way to

Santa Fe. Figuring things out from there will work just fine for me! I guess I just needed a reality check from someone who knows me. Have I lost my mind, Andrea?"

"No Lynn, you may have found it. Looks like you've gone a long way in releasing those things that were holding you back from living healthily in the present. And how does it feel to you?" asked Andrea.

"It feels right. I can't say it feels good. I'm still hurting, but I know it's the thing to do. And the amazing thing about it is I'm clear, I'm so clear. I'm not conflicted at all about what I am doing. I've never felt this clear before. I'm leaving today! My car is packed right now! When I leave you, I am driving across country. I'm going to stop and see my sister in Gulfport, Mississippi and spend some time with her, catching up, and enjoying a day at the spa. A massage, a facial and a reflexology session sound good to me and we may go pull a few handles in the casino. And then, it's on to Santa Fe."

"What about the disease? Don't you think that you should check on that?"

"Yes, I intend to while I'm in Gulfport. My gut feeling is that there is nothing to it. I am not living in fear but I will have a check-up and be thoroughly tested."

"Well, that sounds like a plan," said Andrea. "It looks as though you have made some important decisions for yourself and you are on the way to taking action. I want to affirm for you now that you are perfectly sane!"

"Can we have some sessions by telephone if I need them?"

"Of course and when you get settled, let me know where you are and how you are doing. You have all the strength you need Lynn. You are just starting to use it in a way that supports your needs. Congratulations! Shazam!"

In Spirit, Sahab continued with his explanation. "The other two areas, or set designs, as Mu 10 calls them, are for neutralizing the negative vibrations of your Past and your fears about the Future. You might say that Alcyona and I are going to help you to level your playing fields."

Alcyona then stretched her wings, as if she were posing for a picture, and stood on one leg in perfect balance with her yellow eyes crossed.

Sahab continued, "Now, stand up and stretch for a moment. We are going to get involved in some experiential work on your two nemeses in the Earth experience. We shall begin with the Future. Let's move over to the circular pool," Sahab said, as he led the way to the right.

Standing at the steps, the Mu(s) watched the water slowly moving clockwise while Sahab continued his explanation. "In a moment, I shall ask you to step down into the pool and call to mind your worst fear about the Future. As you hold the thought within these healing waters, your fear will be neutralized. You will feel a slight tingling while this process is taking place.

Once the worst fear has been neutralized other smaller Future fears will begin to surface in your mind but they too will leave you. Go ahead now, walk down slowly. Get your bearings with the movement of the water and then close your eyes and call to mind your greatest fear about the Future. What are you afraid will happen? What are you afraid will not happen? It's really all the same. Call these monsters to the forefront of your mind."

Mu 6 wondered: *Will I ever be free of my addictions? Am I able to conquer myself? It's so difficult! What if I fail? Will I ever get this monkey off my back?*

The Mu(s) melted into the exercise. The water movement continued to increase. Cindy, as Mu 9, began to think: *Will Tom ever conquer his addictions? If he doesn't, what will my life be like without him? Is there something I can do to help him that I haven't tried yet? God, if only I could stop analyzing this! It's driving me nuts!*

Mu 9 began to settle into the experience. The rest of her classmates made progress too, as they worked with their strongest fears first, then on to the lesser ones. Golden flecks shot upward like popcorn popping. Watching the gold flecks evaporate, Sahab turned to Alcyona and smiled. When they ceased to emanate from the water, he knew that the process was complete.

"OK," he said, "open your eyes. How do you feel?" he asked.

"Great, absolutely great," said Mu 1, swimming about as his epaulets fanned

196

outward in the water like a Stingray with many tails. "Without fear, I know that I can lead more effectively!"

Sahab nodded in agreement. Far away in a cave in Afghanistan, another #1 vibration struggled with these concepts.

"What about you, Mu 9, how's it going?"

She was doing a backstroke. Apparently in her own world, she didn't hear him as she continued stroking around the pool. Sahab noticed that her bun had been loosened and her hair was floating freely. He smiled at her and she winked back at him.

Back in mid-town Atlanta, Cindy had wrapped up her days work and was out the door to beat the rush hour traffic home. She usually left after the rush hour but today was different. So much had happened! She had met her deadline and she wanted to hurry home to Tom, hug him and hold him close. There was so much to talk about ----- the dreams, the crazy happenings in the world, the teachings in the manual. *I wonder if he has finished reading it yet? We're going to talk about his drinking! For the first time, I have no fear about him succeeding this time, no fear at all!* Cindy sent Tom her special message of Peace and Love as she veered right from I 85 onto 400.

It wasn't long before she was approaching the glass Buckhead business complex that straddled 400, creating a tunnel underneath for passing through. *It could be Atlantis rising*, she thought, as she drove underneath the glass buildings. Before she knew it, she was at the tollbooth, tossing in her two quarters and thinking, *Easy Does It Moves Me Forward.*

"Come on out now class," said Sahab. "Let's work on the hardest one of all." He gestured them to come toward him.

"I feel wonderful!" exclaimed Mu 2. She seemed to float up the steps.

"Me too", said Mu 7. "I feel light as a feather."

"It's amazing how much fear of the Future can weigh you down, isn't it?" said Sahab.

Mu 6 chimed in, "Yep, that's probably why there are so many fat girls in the world, too much fear about what other people think!"

Mu 2 frowned at him as she gave herself the once over. She not only felt lighter, she looked to be thinner.

"And the really interesting thing is that while we hold these fears, we are unaware of how heavy they can be," expressed Mu 9.

"The interesting thing for me is that my intuition seems to be working even more powerfully," said Mu 12.

"That's interesting," said Mu 9. "I hope that doesn't mean I am going to become even more analytical!"

"All of you were affected in a positive way," said Sahab. "For instance, fear of not getting the correct results is crucial to the functioning of your intuition. Without such fear, there is nothing to stand in its way," said the Teacher. The Mu(s) were incredulous at what a difference this process of neutralizing fear had made in the way they were looking, feeling and functioning. The process had certainly lightened their load.

CHAPTER NINETEEN

The "F" Chamber

Lynn was on her way to her automobile thinking about John and the life of disappointments she had lived with him. Thank God she now had the strength to move on with her life. She was firm in her resolve. There was no doubt, only regret for not having the strength to do it sooner. *I wonder if I will ever be able to forgive him? Better yet, will I ever be able to forgive myself?*

Tom was thinking about the many times he had let Cindy down. *It's a wonder she's been able to hang in there with me! I don't deserve to be forgiven until I get this monkey off my back. God help me; I've got to make it this time! I love you, Cindy! Thanks for not giving up. Please don't give up on me!*

There wasn't a Mu, Mulag or Lagitard alive that did not, at least secretly, have some issue of importance to forgive. Doing it was the hard part! Scattered throughout the world, it was the Mu(s) who seemed to have more issues with self-forgiveness. This was because a part of their consciousness had never forgotten the greatness of their heritage. While many of them recognized forgiveness of self as a short-cut to the reclamation of their Divine inheritance, doing it was quite another matter.

The Mulags continually resisted forgiving others. "Why should I do them a favor?" was often asked. "Who's wrong here anyway?" Focusing blame on the other person was the reason why the process was so difficult for them. While it wasn't impossible for them to forgive, the Mulags resisted and made it ten times more difficult than it needed to be. As long as they maintained the separation between themselves and the person or issue at hand, it caused them to go around in circles, which escalated their anger and resentment. This behavior firmly anchored them in the past.

Once they began to unify their focus on resolving an issue, they could step off the wheel of the Past and move to the Present. It was necessary that they frame the picture in the Present so that they could then step into the picture frame and become one with the person or the situation. If they only looked at the picture and maintained their separation, nothing good happened. When they became a part of the picture, watch out world! How to accomplish this was what they needed to figure out.

The Lagitards had the most difficult struggle because they misperceived the entire picture. For instance, if the Mu(s), Mulags and Lagitards ever experienced the same event, their individual account of it would be quite different. It had more to do with the wiring of their brains than anything. The Mu(s) had a tendency to blame themselves and the Mulags would always blame the other person. On the other hand, the Lagitards were something else!

The Lagitards would not only blame the others involved but somehow justify a violent correction. They would give ownership of this correction to God who then became synonymous with the leadership of their group. This usually resulted in doing the wrong thing for the wrong reason. The Lagitards perception was their reality. The problem was that their reality was based on their own misperception.

Throughout centuries, this had been their modus operandi. It was necessary that they do this because it was the only way to make their wars Holy. It made forgiveness impossible without defeat. Many were killed in the process. All of it was framed in the past and nothing would change until they moved into the picture frame and became one with the other side. It was the only way to move things into the present and Co-create a different future.

The Lagitards would first have to face the fact that their perception might not be reality. Until doing so, it would be a difficult task for them to approach the subject of forgiveness. However, it would not be impossible. Experiencing enough Love could change the wiring of their brains. This Love could be silently projected toward them without their conscious knowledge that the gift was being sent.

Sahab addressed his little group of eager minds. "Let's put some effort into neutralizing the Past," he said, as he began to walk toward the cluster of twelve chambers. He motioned for the Mu(s) to follow him. He then gestured for them to be seated on a long bench facing the chambers. They looked like a football team before the Super Bowl, full of enthusiasm and Spirit.

"So, what's up, Coach? You gonna put us into those ovens and zap our Past?" asked Mu 6.

"As usual you're half right," said Sahab. "I'm going to put each of you into a chamber but YOU are the one who must zap your Past. YOU are the only one who can!" Sahab glanced at the different members of the class to see if they had questions before he continued.

"I think you all understand that the Past is merely an emotionally charged record of something that took place in the Present. Your Past becomes your biggest problem while you are in the Earth dream because it takes your focus away from Co-Creating good in the Present. It's like this ----- we have X amount of time in the dream to create and we can use that time any way we choose. However, while we are dwelling in the Past we cannot create in the Present.

We must constantly work to release the Past. We are not trying to deny it ever happened. That's impossible! So many folks miss the boat on that when they try to forgive. What we're trying to do is to defuse the negative emotional charge that the Past has on us in the Present ----- so we can think about it differently. We can't think differently about it until we change the emotional charge. Until we accomplish this, it's the part that keeps us stuck. Do you understand?"

"Kinda, but how exactly do we do that?" asked Mu 5.

"Intention mixed with creativity can allow us to see it differently," said Sahab. "What we're trying to do is change its emotional impact on us. Now, *how* we get the job done is totally up to us and to our use of creativity in the Present."

"Is it like creating a work of art?" asked Mu 10.

"Yes, it is indeed!" said Sahab. "With both applications you take ideas and you give them form in such a way as to create something new. The process and the new form bring healing. The artist may very well be creating out of the pain of the Past, but the new form this pain is given, forever changes its emotional impact on the artist."

"I think I understand what you are saying!" said Mu 10. " I have such an inexplicable satisfaction after completing each new piece of choreography. It is like a new part of me has been born! Is that what you mean?"

Before Sahab could respond, Mu 11 began. "So, we are going to get into one of those ovens and create a work of art?" asked Mu 11, as the rest of the Mu(s) laughed.

Alcyona stretched her wings, bobbled her head from side to side to make a visual statement and, with her eyes crossed, gently said, "Coo Coo, Coo Coo, Coo Coo." Sahab smiled at her while the group went wild.

"Let's put it this way," said Sahab. "You are going to get into one of the chambers and Co-Create. Through the process, you will find what works for you, what it is that allows you to view the Past differently, that is, devoid of negative emotional impact. The Earth dream has given this process the very unfortunate name of *Forgiveness*."

"Oh that!" said Mu 7, disillusioned, as grunts and groans were heard from the other Mu(s).

Sahab smiled, "See how unfortunate a label can be? You were excited while we were talking about it until I used the unfortunate Earth label to describe it. Doesn't that tell you something? Doesn't that say to you that you have quite another idea about what Forgiveness is?"

"Yeah," said Mu 7, "Like impossible!"

"That's because you are trying to pretend it never happened. That's what's impossible. If it is a part of the record, it's there. It happened! You are not going to change that. It's like the Bible; all you can do is to come up with a different version, a different way of looking at the same thing. Then *that* becomes part of the record and changes the Future possibilities for you. See?" Sahab surveyed the group and continued, "You are not trying to wipe it out; you are trying to change the way you look at it. That's all forgiveness is. Maybe you should call it give-up-ness," he chuckled. "There is always a different way of looking at things."

202

Mu 9 began, "Religion has caused us a lot of problems with this one, hasn't it? Like: wipe it out, impossible to do, feel guilt, try again, fail, more guilt and so forth!"

"You're an independent thinker, Mu 9. Be creative. If it isn't working, find another way that works. Don't get stuck in blame; it's unproductive. Get invested in solutions. The process I am talking about will free you from your crippling negative emotions of the Past."

"OK, already!" said Mu 9. "I'm ready to give it a go."

"Good!" said Sahab. "And what about the rest of you geniuses?" They sprung to their feet and began bowing profusely again, with tongues down-stretched, first toward Sahab, then toward Mu 9, repeating the process over and over again.

"OK you guys, give me a break!" said Mu 9, as she pushed her glasses up and brushed her hair to each side of her face. She was not quite used to her "Lady Godiva" look and there was something about the thinking process that moved her glasses down her nose. She looked so different to the rest of the Mu(s) with her hair down.

The Mu(s) had a good laugh and Sahab continued, "*Children*, I emphasize, *Children* of Mu, we are going to learn to use one of your most important tools for making progress in the Earth dream." He nodded to Alcyona and she swooped down from her perch to his side. "Alcyona will take you to your compartment in the Forgiveness Chamber. Wait for her to direct you, for she will take you to the one that will best facilitate your healing." Unknown to the Mu(s), there were green crystals embedded in each chamber with a unique significance for each of them.

"You see, the cells are all tuned a little differently to catalyze with your personal growth profile. Alcyona will be strapping you in because your alignment in the chamber will change. This part has to do with safety. There are OSHA regulations everywhere," he chuckled.

Alcyona handed each one a set of goggles. "Put these on, my darlings." One by one, she led them to their assigned chamber and strapped them in. They could feel a slight tingling as energy moved through their meridians when their buckle snapped.

"Are we ready, team?" asked Sahab.

"Yeah, Coach!" they cheered and waved. They could have been at Six Flags about to begin a toss-your-cookies ride.

As the lights above them came on, Sahab said, "Now close your eyes for the process is a purely mental one, which can only take place in the Present through creativity coupled with great intention." They closed their eyes with anticipation.

"You must believe that it is in your power to change the way you view a situation and you must desire to change the way you see the record of the Past. Call forth your most troubling Past memory and affirm these ideas in relation to it." Sahab paused to give them time for their reflections.

As he walked around the Forgiveness Chamber, he empathized with the emotions they were experiencing and sent them his message of Love and Compassion. Sahab continued as if he were speaking for them, "I believe I have the power to change the way I see this and I desire with all my heart to change the way I see this record of my Past." He paused again briefly, allowing them a few moments of silence and continued. "Now, use your creativity in the Present to evolve for yourself the way that works for you to view this difficult situation differently."

At various speeds, the individual compartments began to rotate vertically while Alcyona controlled the overhead intensity of the lights. Mu 6's compartment began to flip at dive-bomber speed as Alcyona increased the intensity of Light upon him. This enabled him to have all of the Light that he was willing to receive. His eyes widened and his jaw clenched as he revolved in the chamber.

Mu 9 looked quite comfortable with her goggles restricting the movement of her glasses and holding her hair in place. While all of them could clearly hear Sahab, the electrical energy moving through them established an altered state of consciousness.

Alcyona was above them on a catwalk that circled the lights. Most of the intense diagnostic work for her had been completed and she could now allow her mind some down time. "Da da da da, The Continental..." she hummed to herself while remembering.

Before she knew it, she was dancing on the catwalk totally immersed in her memories. She played Ginger's part. Then she danced Fred's part. Getting just a little carried away, she stumbled in close proximity to the Light over Mu 6, kicking it up to flood light intensity. His vertical axis changed to horizontal as he began revolving at propeller speed gritting his teeth. Slowly Mu 6 began to plane out. His expression relaxed into a smile as he continued revolving ever so slowly, the epitome of *Easy Going* and *Forward Motion*.

Alcyona smiled at Sahab as if all of this had been planned as he gave her a look of "Let's get serious!" Mu 6, on the other hand, was grinning; he appeared to be happy as a clam as he continued revolving. There was freedom in his smile that looked absolutely joyous.

Alcyona smiled as she presented Mu 6 with her wings, she said to Sahab, "There are no coincidences," to which he rolled his eyes and smiled.

Tom had just finished the last chapter of his manual and dialed a telephone number. "Yes, hello, this is Tom Gorman. May I speak to an in-take counselor?"

The Mu(s) were quite ingenious in the way they used their creativity to defuse the Past. Mu 7, who had been abused as a child began to picture her parents as little children lost in the woods, as she sent them a message of Peace. They had long since passed over. One had died of an overdose and the other had committed suicide. It was not possible to send them Love in this moment or to forget the beatings, but she found that she could send them the possibility of Peace.

This lessened the negative, emotional impact of her memories of them. Love would have to come later, much later! But the important thing is that she was making the connection that it was within her ability to change the way she allowed her Past to affect her now. Her creativity with intention in the Present was the medium through which she could create change that was beneficial to her. The motion of her compartment leveled out and began to imitate Mu 6's.

Janie thought about a secret fear that she had had for a long time. She had never shared it with anyone, not even Ron. She feared that something could snap in her and that she could mistreat Adam in the same ways that she had been mistreated.

Sometimes dreams about this would awaken her in a panic. Ron thought she was just having a nightmare.

After each dream, she would find herself being especially patient with Adam. Perhaps she had been afraid not to have him in day care, for at least some of the time, just to give herself a break. There was a tiny part of her that was a little fearful of what she might do under stress. Janie had empathy for the woman who had drowned her five children. She didn't condone it, but she did understand how something like that could happen. So did every mother, even the ones who harshly judged the poor soul. The clouds were starting to lift for Janie and it felt good.

One by one, the Mu(s) found their way to Peace by creating different ways to view their past that were acceptable to them. This wasn't easy but it slowly defused their negative emotional reactions. While the memory of the event was still there, they were able to *feel differently* about it.

So this is what forgiveness is all about! thought Mu 10. *It finally makes sense to me. I can dig it! It is pure creativity with intention that defuses a stick of dynamite! All right!* Mu 10 had worked on forgiving her father for not being present in her life. He died when she was very young. She grew up in a family as the youngest, the only girl with four brothers. She had majored in English but was always interested in the performing arts, especially dance. Mu 10 worked on her issues with the father that she could barely remember. What a revelation it was to her that she could choreograph forgiveness!

As each Mu found a more positive way to view his personal disharmony, the movement of their compartments changed to the horizontal axis in rotation and joined Mu 6 and 7. Before they knew it, they were revolving effortlessly with forward motion. Sahab waited patiently for all of them to make it through the eye of the needle before he continued.

"Creativity with intention in the Present is what Forgiveness is all about. It is the only way to change the emotional impact of your memories and open up your Future possibilities. It's not so much about changing the record, but more about creating another way to see it. And now, Children of the Mu, it's time for you to return to your Earth dream and to start functioning more completely as the Co-Creator that you are. I send you forth to change *Your* world. This is why you are here!"

The rotational axis changed again from horizontal to vertical, preparing for their trip back into the Earth illusion. The glass dome opened and Alcyona flipped the switch for their release. The Mu(s) soared through the opening into the dark night sky through the illusions of Time and Space to their dream positions on Earth.

Alcyona had swooped down to Sahab's side and together they watched their fledglings take flight.

"There lies the hope of the world," said Sahab. Alcyona was in tears as she watched them soar and contemplated the vastness of this possibility.

"Yes," she said, "they are going to *LOVE* their way to freedom, aren't they?"

"Yes, dear Alcyona, because *that* is the way to *The Fulfillment*. The new age of Spirit is on its way! The Children of Mu shall Co-Create *Heaven* on Earth."

"Blessings, Blessings to them all," expressed the feathered one.

Pensively, the Teachers watched the vast expanse of sky. The residue from twelve streaks of Light fanned outward across the horizon like lines on a power grid. The circle would complete itself through the Power of One, aligning Mu(s) of every number far and wide to exponentially grow into Critical Mass.

Each one would now work on personal healing to complete his assignments. They would begin to recognize each other by their actions in the world, as life fulfilled itself in this *New Age of Spirit on Earth*. The countdown for Tribulation had indeed begun and it would initiate a turbulent time of cleansing. There would be many journeys through the Dark Night of the Soul, many changes, and every single one of them would bless this special time on Earth, the time when all hearts learn to beat as One.

CHAPTER TWENTY

Return of Mu

FIVE, FIVE, FIVE, the number of change was now upon us. As the Earth prepared to enter her fifth dimension, change would be happening faster than ever before. Many lies would come to light, to the liar and to the lie-e. CEOs of large corporations would lead the way. Number 1s would indeed start the ball rolling for personal healing through many dark nights.

Changes that were long overdue would now move forward with ease. It would first begin with individuals, making changes that were needed on personal and professional levels. On a global level, there would also be economic, environmental, scientific, political and Spiritual changes. The world would now seek *Oneness* because it was mandatory.

Change would be quite easy for some and more difficult for others. Everyone who had long ago agreed to accompany Earth into her fifth dimension would now accomplish the tasks that would allow them to succeed with their Divine Plan. The rest would simply facilitate the plan. This was the agreement and it was all happening now!

The war on fear was just one part of the process as Jihad and all of the believers of "This is better than that" found compassion, acceptance and a reverence for all life. It would precipitate a thousand years of Peace. The foundation for it all would be in place by the end of 2012, as the lesser dimensions gave way to the many changes demanded by the fifth.

Inherent in this process, would be the activation of green crystal energy. It would create a time of unparalleled prosperity. Gone would be the predominance of red and blue. No longer would the majority of time be spent dwelling in the past or future. No longer would the emotions of anger, resentment, guilt and fear claim the day. Green crystal energy would fuel the white light of NOW ----- creativity and Co-

Creation. Prosperity would be the fruit of the tree.

The Mu(s) would wake up everywhere, in every country around the globe and they would teach through by example. When the majority of examples were good ones, the world would change for the better and not one moment before. Once personal healing had taken place through action, each one would become a catalyst for others on the path. The game of Dominoes had just begun its trip around the world!

John went home that evening to an empty house ----- expensive, elegant and empty. There was a note from Lynn waiting for him on the kitchen counter. His hand trembled a bit as he picked up the envelope and looked at his name. He recognized Lynn's handwriting. *Not good,* he thought. *Think I'll fix a scotch before I face the music.*

He picked up the envelope and took it with him to the bedroom. He changed into comfortable clothes. John stuck the letter into his shirt pocket, went to the wet bar and poured himself a Chevas Regal. *How quiet the house seemed.* John's son, the reluctant adult, was in the Bahamas spending his Trust money and Lynn was gone. He went to his den and sat down in his favorite chair, pulled the letter out of his pocket and stared at the front of the envelope.

He knew exactly what was inside, not the details but the real substance of it. He certainly wasn't looking forward to verifying the truth of the matter. He took a few sips of scotch and looked out the window as a bird caught his eye. It was black with a small red spot on its wings and it called out loudly as if something was wrong. John stared at it for a few moments thinking, *Lynn would probably know his name.* He took another sip and looked back at the envelope. Tears were forming in the corners of his eyes that he could not hold back. They rolled down his cheeks.

In Alpharetta, Tom heard the garage door opener begin. *Good! There's Angel Girl, and earlier than usual too!* He met her at the door with a kiss. "It's about time you got here!"

"Oh, you missed me, huh? What's cooking?" she asked.

"You mean food or food for thought?" he asked.

"Either or both," she said, as she put down her briefcase and started toward the bedroom. "Come talk to me while I change. I junked out at the Varsity for lunch today. It was delicious but these clothes have been fighting the bloat all afternoon."

"Ok," he said, trailing along behind "But I don't know that I can hold my train of thought looking at a voluptuous woman!"

"Well, try!" He sat down on the bed and leaned back on the chair pillow while she changed into shorts and a T-shirt, chatting away.

"Can you believe what happened today?" she said. "Did you see it on TV? I could hardly believe that what I was seeing was real! You know, it made me stop and think about all the things we tend to take for granted...like each other. There are a lot of people out there who lost their significant other and, as Mailroom Janie said, 'A lot of children lost a parent today.'" Cindy sat down on the bed and put her arms around him. "I'm so grateful that you're here, in one piece, for me to come home to."

"Me too, Angel Girl, I'm grateful for you too," he said, as he kissed her forehead. By this time, blind Pep had stumbled through the dog door and found her way to Momma.

"Hi there, Sweetness," Cindy said, as she reached down and scooped her up and held her like a baby, gently rocking her. "How's my little Angel doing today?" Pep lovingly looked up at her with cloudy eyes and bad breath. "The Vet says you're looking through a snow storm, stinky girl. Imagine that! Wish we could do something about it. Let's see, according to the Vet, you are now 92! My, my, how time flies!" She kissed the top of her head and put her down, rubbing her haunches a bit.

"She's going to sleep good tonight! She's been keeping me company in the yard all day while I read my manual."

"Let me see it!" she said. She needed to verify that the manuals were alike.

"Here it is," Tom said, as he reached for his manual on the nightstand. "Is this what yours looks like?" he asked.

"Yes, let me get mine. It's in my briefcase. Bring your book with you and I'll meet you on the patio." She pulled out her copy and looked at it. "I think I'll pour

211

myself a glass of wine before going out. Want one? I know you are drinking again."

"No thanks, I've got a cup of coffee here. I'll nuke it and join you outside."

Cindy walked out to the patio thinking, *What's happening? Is this my Tom or is someone else impersonating him?* She placed her manual on the table, sipped her wine and surveyed her rose bushes for black spots while she waited for Tom to catch up. *Miss Tropicana is really thriving.* Cindy sat down, looking again at the front of her manual.

Tom joined her at the table and they began to compare his manual to hers. They seemed to be exactly alike. "Far out!" he said.

"What do you think is going on here Tom?"

"Well, first I thought that you left this for me to read and I thought it had something to do with getting back on the wagon. I must admit, it irritated me."

"I wonder why!"

"I know Angel; I've slipped again. But I can tell you this, reading the manual helped me meet an aspect of myself today that I have never met before." He paused for a moment, cocked his head in her direction and said, "You know, Doll, I'm not totally convinced that you didn't plant the book with recovery in mind. Tell me the truth now."

"I promise you Tom, I didn't. Are you sure that you didn't plant mine on my car seat?" she asked. "That's where I found it this morning."

"Are you kidding? Me plant it? In the shape I was in?"

"Tom, Spirit had a hand in this. Remember this morning, we were talking about our dreams? All of this is tied together somehow. And here's another weird thing: John found a copy of this in his lateral file this afternoon!"

"Whoa! Really? Well, wait til you hear this! Jim found a copy of it in his mailbox this morning and asked me if I had left it there for him! There's something going on here, all right. I don't know what but I do know this -----whatever it is, it's good! I've made some important decisions today. This Mu 6 is going into rehab. I've already called and I'm booked for tomorrow morning. Can you drop me off?"

"My God, Yes! This is wonderful, Tom." She jumped up and ran over and wrapped her arms around him. "I've been so worried about you and I love you so!" Tears were streaming down her cheeks as they held each other close.

"There, there, Angel Girl, it will all be fine; it will be just fine," he said as he patted her back. "I've got some things to do tonight. I've got to pack a bag and I've got to finalize my paperwork on the applications I took last night and get those in the mail. There are some bucks there that I can use to pay the bill for this vacation. This is the last time, Babe. I know I'll make it this time. I can't tell you how I know. I just do."

"Do you know how wonderful you are?" Cindy asked, "And how much I love you?"

"Yep, on both accounts! I know I told you I would take care of dinner but if you can order Chinese carry out, I'll start handling my paperwork. It will take me about thirty minutes. We can eat while we watch the news. There's going to be plenty of it tonight! I'll pack my bag later. Can you handle that?"

"Certainly, and I'll even help you pack. Tom, I'm so proud of you! I'm thrilled and I'm so grateful! You just don't know. My prayers have been answered. After today, I may need hospitalization! I love you, I love you Tom!"

"And I love you. Life just wouldn't be the same without my Angel Girl."

Tom went to his study thinking *Easy Does It Moves Me Forward.* Cindy called in the order and went back out in the courtyard to talk to her plants and to check the birdfeeder. She stopped at the crepe myrtle and spoke to Clarice. "Can you believe it? Mother, he is doing it! Something about this time is different. I believe that he will make it now. For the first time, instead of hoping and praying that he makes it, I truly *believe* that he will!" A subtle breeze blew through Clarice's branches which Cindy acknowledged as agreement.

Lynn had been driving for a few hours and was tiring of the silence. She turned on the radio. 'On the road again, Just can't wait to get on the road again...' *How appropriate*, she thought. Now if she could make herself sing along with him, she just might change her mood.

Even though she didn't really feel like it, she made herself belt out a few lines as she made her way toward Gulfport. She then went on to all the songs she knew. She ended with "I'm Alabammy bound, There'll be no heebie jeebies hanging round..." Singing always had a way of lifting her spirits. She had a beautiful voice and she had long ago learned that music could usually heal a bad mood.

Lynn was heading South on I 65. She called Sister on her cell phone to relay her coordinates. "Hi Sis, I just passed the turnoff for Greenville and I'm almost hoarse from singing." She started up "On the road again, Just can't wait to get on the road again." This gave Sister a good laugh.

"Good grief, you'd better take your temperature: you're not well! You're not on drugs, are you?" she asked, laughing. "I'm just glad you're not singing, "Poor John is dead, Poor John is dead...," she sang, deeper than her voice could go. They both laughed a good one. "Do you think you'll make it here tonight?"

"Maybe, I'll see how tired I am when I get to Mobile. If I'm too sleepy, I'll find a motel and see you first thing in the morning. Schedule a spa visit for us in the afternoon, you know, massage and the works. I need some healing, badly! Anytime in the afternoon will do. If I don't plan to arrive tonight, I'll call you from the motel. Looking forward to seeing you. We have lots to talk about. I'll save the gory details until I get there."

"You mean like what's her name this time?" asked Sister. Sister's real name was Cathy but as far back as Lynn could remember she had always called her Sister, sometimes Twisted Sister.

"No, that much I can tell you now. Her name is Bunny. Isn't that charming?"

"So he's into animals now," Sister laughed. "Honey, I'm glad you're out of there! I can't wait to see you! We've got a lot of catching up to do. Hope you're planning to stay for awhile."

"We'll see. I do want to talk with Willard about some legal stuff and the divorce." Willard was their cousin who was an attorney in Biloxi.

"Sounds like you're really serious this time!"

"I am, Honey, I am! I plan to spend several days with you. By the way, did you put a book in my cosmetic case the last time I was there?"

"No dumplin, I didn't."

Big changes were already beginning to dot the landscape, and not only in Buckhead and Alpharetta, Georgia. Changes were happening everywhere, as the vicariously experienced dreams rolled on! In Paris, France, Peter received a manual anonymously mailed from Atlanta, Georgia. In Puerto Rico, Ana Maria's manual appeared in Spanish, mailed to her from a cousin in New York. It was like a mystery unfolding. *Que es Mu?* Ana questioned, as she studied the cover.

A month after September 11th, Cindy was picking up Tom to take him home. He looked radiantly healthy. "It's been a tremendous month, Angel Girl! It's so good to see you!"

Tom had read his manual many times and had even started his own informal support group. He had negotiated with one of his counselors to get copies for each member of the group. The Fulfillment had already helped many Mu 6s who would now go on to help a few more of them that were caught on the wheel.

Each time Cindy had gone in for family therapy, she was more and more amazed at his progress. It seemed that the more she read her own manual, the more clarity and freedom she could see in him. Her analytical mind enjoyed pondering this connection which she could only confirm intuitively.

Later that week, Tom met Jim for lunch in Decatur at their favorite Mexican restaurant. "Hola Jim, como esta usted?" he asked, as he gave him a big hug.

"Muy bien! Muy bien, gracias! Congratulations Tom, you look great! How're you feeling?"

"Couldn't be better! And how about you?"

"Closed on the cash cow yesterday and I'll be leaving in a week. I found a good deal on a boat repo in Lauderdale and I'll be steering her on down to Costa Rica."

"No kidding! Wish I could join you. We could fish along the way! Is Alan going with you?"

"Yes, and you won't believe what has happened?"

"What do mean?" asked Tom.

"Well, you know the story; here I am forty-two years old and you know I've always been in the closet around Dad. Mom has known for years but I've never been able to be honest with him about who I am. Not that he shouldn't know by now! Alan and I have been living together for twelve years."

"So, you told him?" Jim nodded. "Congratulations, my friend! And how did it go?"

"Tom, it couldn't have gone better. Surprised the heck out of me! Here I have lived in fear for forty-two years, afraid to tell him because I thought I'd lose him. Do you know what he said?"

"What, what?" Tom asked excitedly.

"He said, 'Son, I love you and I want you to know that there is nothing that you could ever do or be that would ever make me stop loving you! I don't understand why you would make things so hard on yourself but it doesn't change the way I feel about you. You're my son.'"

"And what did you say?" asked Tom.

"Well, first I lost it. I cried like a baby and then I said, 'Dad, this was never a choice. Do you think that anyone would ever choose so difficult a path? No, Dad, this is who I am! No one ever chooses to be gay'.

Dad looked me straight in the eye and listened to me carefully. Tom, he was really trying to understand. I should have given the old man more credit sooner. I guess my fear was too overpowering.

I said, 'You know, Dad, the biggest favor I ever granted myself was to accept who I am. I was able to stop using drugs. Then Alan came along and I was able to commit to the relationship and to make a life with him. It was then that I was ready to start my business and to focus on the things that were important to me. Accepting myself allowed me to free up my mental and emotional energy for productive use in the world. My only regret, Dad, is not telling you sooner! These kind of secrets aren't good to keep from those you love.' He hugged me and we both cried. It was the most emotional and liberating day in my life!" Tears came to Jim's eyes as he remembered the experience.

"I'm proud of you, Buddy! You pushed through that fear, didn't you? And it turned out just fine, didn't it? Cindy and I have been telling you for years that you're the only one this really makes a difference to, well, maybe you and the religious right," he laughed. "I know that I couldn't love you any more if you were my own brother. What am I saying? You are my brother! And I'm glad that you are out of the closet where it matters!"

"Fear, Jim, is what life's all about, and being able to overcome it in one way or another. That's what I was doing in rehab, overcoming my personal fears. No doubt about it, my fears are different from yours. I don't go in for platform shoes," he said, as he swished his feet at the table in a mock ballet movement while Jim rolled his eyes. "But it's certainly not a problem for me if you do!" They both had a good laugh.

This was their private joke that referred to a time long ago when they were roommates at Tech and were at a party. To hear Tom tell the story, "This 'sissy guy' wearing platform shoes, started making eyes at Jim." Tom knew then about Jim's sexual orientation. They had discussed it. It never really mattered to Tom and it never affected their friendship. Tom's classic remark was: "I'm straight and I guess that means you're bent. What else is new?"

Somehow Tom thought that playfully teasing Jim about it would somehow convey the thought that he was cool with things. Because the atmosphere had always been open and accepting, it helped to strengthen their bond. Empathy, understanding and compassion developed between them. It was a wonderful friendship that would last forever.

It worked both ways. Jim was tremendously supportive of Tom over the years, as he struggled with his sobriety issues. How many times had he hidden Tom's car keys and driven him home? They were hard to count. Cindy often told Tom, "You don't deserve a brother like Jim!" She too had grown to be good friends with Jim. He had gotten her through many a dark night with Tom.

And Jim never failed to "tell it like it was" when Tom got sober and became

217

a remorseful puppy. Jim made sure that Tom remembered his embarrassments. He recounted everything that he had observed. He knew that Tom had blackouts and often remembered nothing. He never failed to remind him of his face falling in a plate of spaghetti or whatever it was that had happened. Jim felt that if he were made to face the reality of his behavior, sooner or later, this would be the wakeup call that worked. They were indeed an interesting support system for each other as they went through years of struggling with a different set of fears.

"So, what does life feel like to you right now?" Tom asked.

"Oh, try *Easy Going, Forward Motion,*" said Jim, smiling.

"And which Mu are you, my friend?" asked Tom.

"Well, I think I'm a Mu 5 with a mix of Mu 1 and 10."

"That sounds about right to me," said Tom. "Now, as for myself, I am pure strain Mu 6!" They laughed heartily.

Tom looked at his watch. "I've gotta run. Have an insurance appointment across town at 2:00 P.M. Now don't forget, Cindy and I want you and Alan to come over for dinner before you leave. What about Saturday night?"

"Plan on it," said Jim. "I've got the check. Go!"

Tom gave his humorous rendition of walking out on platform shoes while waving good-bye.

A couple of months had passed since Janie had taken her son out of daycare. She was standing at her kitchen window rinsing dishes, loading the dishwasher and watching Adam playing in the backyard. Stevie, from next door, was visiting and they were playing on the jungle-jim. She saw Stevie fall and cut his knee. She could see it bleeding and heard his crying. She ran outside to help. When she reached him, Adam had placed his hand over the wound and was softly humming a melody in a minor key. Stevie lay on the ground perfectly relaxed.

"Let me see, Adam!"

"It's OK Mommy, it's OK." Adam lifted his hand. Janie could see that the knee looked perfect. There was no wound at all and the only visible blood was on Stevie's hands. Janie was in shock. The boys jumped up and started playing again.

Janie watched them for awhile, thinking about what she had just experienced and then went back into the house.

Looking at the boys again from the kitchen window Janie thought, *How wonderful it is to be able to be with Adam.* Indeed, he was a special child in so many ways, and now she knew that he was also a healer! *Where will this adventure of motherhood be leading me?*

Janie and Ron had earlier discussed their finances and decided that her income was really not that important. After giving her two-week notice, John, her employer, presented a wonderful arrangement whereby she could work from home for four hours per day on special projects.

Janie was absolutely thrilled about this arrangement. She was able to stay at home with Adam and she was actually coming out better financially, having eliminated the cost of day care and commuting. *Talk about having your cake and eating it too! Life's about deciding what you want, taking action and then allowing God to work out the details!* This Mu was clearly onto something!

There were Mu(s) waking up everywhere with a willingness to take full responsibility for everything they saw in the world. Seeing prejudice, they worked on the prejudice within themselves. Effort was expended on the inner vision of things rather than on the outer circumstances; this alone was enough to create change.

Jim was finally at peace with himself in Costa Rica. He and his Dad caught up on years of separation by emailing often and talking frequently on the phone. Dad's health was on the mend and stable. The charter fishing business was going great, so great that he and Alan were able to take care of their expenses and still contribute 55% of their earnings to *Save the Rainforest* projects. They had gone from 10 to 55% in just two years. It was unbelievable. The more they gave away, the more they made. In another year, they figured that they would be giving away 90% of their earned income with plenty to spare. Life was good!

People everywhere were becoming more generous and compassionate and because of it, they were able to see more generosity and compassion in the world. The majority had also become less rigid in their thinking and more open to others who thought or looked differently. They sought to understand rather than to judge. Creativity was valued more than ever before, and the use of intuition flourished. This allowed the heart and mind great freedom for authentic communication.

Mu power was growing and it was evidenced by the Light increasing. The drama of Life began to resemble a friendly neighborhood at night, with lights going on, house by house, randomly, until every home was filled with Light. Respect for Mother Earth was evidenced by the way the flowers in each yard leaned in toward the dwelling, mesmerized by the Light within and drawn in its direction through mutual love and caring. Love flourished and exponentially grew.

John was on a pilgrimage to find and cleanse himself in the mountains of Tibet, where he studied with a Spiritual Master. Cindy had agreed to hold down the fort in John's absence. She was enjoying the challenge. She was totally at peace now with Clarice, which totally liberated her energy. She had learned to use her analytical and intuitional minds equally and found that this increased her effectiveness tenfold.

Cindy was on the phone to a new client. They put her on hold, and instead of the usual elevator music, she heard: "La, da, da, da, da, The Continental…" *Is this on the line or in my head?* she questioned. *Who cares!* The sound of it evoked a special feeling of peace and joy within her.

Tom was also in control now. He had been promoted to Vice President of an annuities firm. He worked diligently with his regional managers. It was amazing to him how much time he had, now that he wasn't drinking. He continued with his Mu 6 support groups and found tremendous satisfaction in helping them to short circuit small electrical appliances, come to terms with their fears and find their way to Love.

The masculine and feminine energies were balanced at last within each beautiful being and with that an amazing thing happened. Violence and abuse decreased. Terrorism, even Holy Wars, diminished and disappeared entirely by the end of Tribulation.

The Lagitards, who could not heal, departed and helped to cleanse the world of landmines! There was simply nothing to prove at either end of the continuum! There were no prescribed roles imposed on either gender that could be perceived as limiting. Men and women were generally happier with each other.

Wage standards were no longer genderized which became apparent by the disappearance of glass ceilings. Windows of opportunity opened to everyone according to their capabilities. CEOs became more sensitive to gender issues and all forms of prejudice in general. When they noticed one aspect of the work force as predominantly male or female, they began to ask why and make necessary corrections as needed. The thing that had drastically changed was that they were now able to see the prejudice that they had unknowingly perpetuated in the past. Seeing *now* was all that was necessary. Clear vision and congruent action became the impetus for change with every child of Mu.

Cindy became an exceptional CEO. She made it her business to employ the Golden Rule, and harmony reigned. Her employees were more creative and more productive and it was clearly seen on the bottom line. While Cindy was enjoying the experience, she was looking forward to John's return. She had plans to start her own marketing company. She also thought that someday, there just might be a book or two in her about the *Return of Mu* from her remembrance.

Yes, everyone seemed more comfortable with who they were and what they were accomplishing. They felt more valued, loved and appreciated. Without self-consciousness they hummed in the elevator, on occasion, as they made the trip to the fifth floor. "La, da, da, da, The Continental, da, da, da...." This warmed Alcyona's heart and she watched with great interest.

The original students shared their dreams with many others on the path who were ready to embrace their own wholeness, end separation and exalt the power of inclusion and balance on Earth. "One, One, One" was heard often, sometimes in the waking state, sometimes in a dream. Very soon after it was heard, a manual appeared, just as magically as it had for Cindy and the others.

When they reviewed their manual, it catalyzed for them a remembrance of all the dreams they had forgotten. They began to *believe* again in dreams and to materialize them, as the body of Mu increased. In truth, it was every bit as Mu 6 had said, "Here a Mu, there a Mu, everywhere a Mu Mu."

The Mu(s) Co-Created with focus and and clear intention. Technology was used for purposes of Good. Through Co-Creatorship, their experience in the world became joyous, productive and prosperous. The green crystals of prosperity were now activated. The year of 2012 would arrive and a thousand years of peace would begin. Tribulation would softly end with the sound of one-note singing.

The manuals continued to magically disperse around the world. They continued to be found on a pillow, in a desk drawer and in the most creative of places. Sometimes the doorbell rang and a manual was resting on the doormat! The Truth of One continued to speak to everyone so that they might never forget the sacred truths that were now remembered.

As often as not, the manual recipients did not know from where their manual came or from whom. Discovering it was often a delightful surprise, like finding a diamond in the rough or an exquisite pearl in an oyster. The jewel was intended to be their own. Once they began to read the manual, it was difficult to put down until the process of osmosis was complete. Then their real work began, as did their mentoring of others, whose manuals also surprisingly appeared. The chain remained unbroken.

Some had conscious memory of these dreams and some simply accepted them on faith because of what the dreams resonated in them. None of the details really mattered. The important thing was that Love flourished, exponentially grew and blessed the world, as form found *Fulfillment*, and prosperity and abundance increased.

By 2012, the Creator's ABA musical form had swept across the face of time. It started with a single sound of one heart yearning for its full potential of love expressed and one mind reaching new heights in unimagined creativity. All souls were now at peace with The Source of All Good for all people. The Creator's plan had found completion. All things were utterly transformed from one note into a symphony with a new arrangement for the sound of One on Earth.

As Above, So Below.

About the Author...

Sandra Elizabeth Gustafson holds the Bachelor of Science, Master of Fine Arts and Doctor of Education degrees from the University of North Carolina at Greensboro. Dr. Gustafson has taught with distinction at the college level. She was selected as an "Outstanding Educator of America" and is a member of the "World Who's Who of Women in Education."

Dr. Sandra E. Gustafson has managed senior retirement and assisted living facilities and is a specialist in the field of long term care insurance. She is self-employed as the *Guardian Angel* of Angel Insurance and she lives in Georgia. Dr. Gustafson conducts a seminar called: *Long Term Care / Planning for the Future* for business, professional, church and civic groups and is recognized as an expert in this specialized field. To learn more about Sandra as a long term care insurance specialist you may go to her web site at **www.Angelins.com**.

Sandra strives to live as a Spiritual being in the business and professional worlds. It is important to her to be a blessing in the lives of others through her work in the world.

The author is a life-long student of human potential and Spirituality from a non-denominational perspective. She believes there are no limits on The Source of All Good in the world and that all views of God are correct that strive to become the Golden Rule in action. She further believes there is no prejudice in God and therefore, all forms of prejudice on Earth are un-Godly in their practice.

Sandra feels that the meaning of this time on Earth, for each of us, is to heal the emotional pain and the limitations we have placed on ourselves. We can then remove the barriers that separate us from each other and experience *Oneness of Spirit* right here, right now on Earth.

The author is available as a speaker. She is willing to conduct seminars on the ideas expressed in *The Fulfillment* as fundraisers for worthy causes that help others and lovingly support the concept of Oneness on Earth. Thank you for sharing this book and our web site with your friends, loved ones, all of the difficult characters in your life's drama and everyone you seek to bless.

www.thefulfillment.us

If you wish to use the information presented in this book as a tool for personal growth, go to our web site for instructions. Click the **About The Fulfillment** page and the CHANGE link at the bottom of the page.